TILL I BLEED NO MORE

ALEXANDER ELLIS

Published by Alexander Ellis

Copyright © 2023. All rights reserved.

ISBN: 978-0-6457641-0-9 (paperback)

First edition, 2023

For book orders and enquiries,
contact: mavlock17@gmail.com

A catalogue record for this
book is available from the
National Library of Australia

Contents

Past Transgressions

It all happened so quickly… the end of an age that I thought would last forever, but it didn't.

"We need to check for survivors Casper, survivors or corpses, either way we must search for them."

The voice belonged to a boy named Fletch, a young redhead that I hardly know.

"We need to find our provisions first, once there unearthed we can worry about the others."

"But Casper! The men, they'll need us," urged Fletch.

"I outrank you still, so provisions first, then we'll look for the men."

I'm on the southern beach of an island, and anyone that had survived the last encounter would wash up here. Past transgressions have left us stranded and alone, while the woman who'd killed us sails away in a pitiless fashion. It's the year 1728, piracy is dead, and everything has gone to hell. My clothes are soaked, my body is tired, and my face is burning, in more ways than one. Salt from the water had seeped into the burns on my face, causing agony beyond imagining. I had no idea what it looked like, but I imagine they'd be no fixing it. There would be no respite from the scars of defeat, the woman who'd killed us had made sure of that. The sand beneath me is dry and shallow, and the air is humid, all though at least there's a breeze. Seagulls and herons flew above us, and they cried in the background while Fletch and I gathered ourselves.

I approached Fletch and leant him my help, but he knelt into the sand afterwards, and I joined him. A large wooden crate lay behind us, and it was the raft that had brought us to this island. Fletch rose moments later and I helped him, then we headed further inland to find our supplies. A months' worth of goods had been stockpiled on this island three months prior, and these goods resided inside two chests, two brown chests which contained our entire livelihoods. Our captain wished against it, but if we had listened, then we would've had nothing. We walked until we approached a peculiar patch of grass, then we started digging. Fletch dug sluggishly so I took over for him, and a while later I uncovered them, two brown chests just as I remembered them. I passed the first one to Fletch after lugging it out of the ground, then I repeated the process for the second one. Fletch opened his chest immediately while I returned the area to normal, then I opened mine.

Inside there was food, water, and rope, as well as some cloth. But there was also wooden planks, and a single whetstone. Fletch's was very similar, the only difference being gun powder and shot instead of a whetstone.

We organised our goods then headed out to look for survivors, all though I assumed that there wouldn't be any. We were familiar with the island but our fatigue would slow us down, so scouting for men could take hours, though I hoped that wasn't the case. A long while later Fletch and I counted seven bodies that had washed ashore, three of them managed some brief words, but after that, we were alone. We took the bodies from the shore and put them to rest, but once they were buried our fatigue became too great.

"There's a cove nearby, we should investigate it and perhaps stay there for tonight."

"Can you take first watch?" asked Fletch.

"I can, though I'll need to get us a fire while I do."

Fletch and I headed towards the cove, and upon arriving its greyish exterior seemed to be eroding. Instead of grey it would soon be white, but it didn't matter as long as it stood and housed us for the night. Fletch went inside and laid down, while I went out to gather sticks for our fire. The shallows teemed with pale crabs, and entering them required caution, all though they seemed to keep their distance. I wanted to stay close to the cove, but the surrounding area lacked tinder nearby. Large rocks occupied the cove's surroundings, but grass and tree's weren't far from its position. At the beach there were three tree's that almost touched its sands, and next to those trees resided grass, grass that barely popped out of the sand.

I settled for whatever I could find nearby, then I left and carefully moved around Fletch when I returned. I got to work on the fire and kept hand drilling until my hands turned red, it took an eternity to get a spark, but finally, I got the fire to rise.

With the fire's presence night followed shortly after, and I was craving rest, so I woke up Fletch. Sleep did not come easily even though we'd switched places, but when my eyes finally drooped Fletch left the cove without warning. Fletch woke me however long after, but my body was like a log even though Fletch assured me that I'd slept for hours.

"So what do we do tomorrow Casper? How do we survive this? How do we do this without a crew?"

"We are the crew now Fletch, everyone else is gone so all we can do is survive and stay together, if we do that for long enough, then we'll be ok."

"Yeah maybe, but for how long? The war is over, they've won."

"They've won for now, but once we return… things can change."

"You can't go after her! She just defeated us and the rest of the pirate world, you'd be mad."

"I'm not mad, I'm just angry."

"If we return to civilization we have to think about a new life Casper, we can't afford not to, our captain should've been proof of that," urged Fletch.

"Well I'm not my captain!! And I know it's a long shot, but I want my chance at her: I've lost too much not to try and take one, you should too."

Fletch sighed instead of replying, but I'm sure he wanted revenge as well: he was just trying not to admit it.

"I've had my fill of pirate hunters, and if you want to go after her then you'll be doing it alone, and if you do it alone then she'll kill you; you're lucky she hasn't already."

I shook my head at him but he didn't care, Fletch's freckled face reeked of a man who was finished with life. He's only eighteen years old and yet he seemed more jaded than I am, and I'm only twenty three, yet I feel much older. Fletch's brown eyes pierced into my own.

"How did she find us? And how come no one knew anything about her? Do you think the captain knew?" asked Fletch.

"I don't know, I just know that I have her to thank for my charred face, and less than ideal fate."

Fletch smirked after my comment, and he seemed amused by my new appearance, but it was far from it.

"We should try and scour the wreckage tomorrow, it's a long swim but with rest I think we could make it."

"We need to hunt first, and we'll have to save our rations for the night: we won't make it otherwise."

"We're good at hunting ships not animals, how are we gonna do that?" asked Fletch.

"I don't know but we're gonna have to learn fast, we'll learn more about what's out there tomorrow, then we'll make our decision after that."

"Do you think she'll come back? Do you think anyone will come back after what's happened? Maybe we should take our chances with the sea."

"No... I'm confident that if we survive long enough then someone will find us, the only question is, what will we do once that happens?"

Fletch shrugged his shoulders as a response, and I tried picturing what that day would look like on the inside.

CHAPTER 1

New Arrivals

A month passed and it was now February 2nd, dawn was upon us and Fletch and I had awoken early to tend to the graves. The remnants of our crew were in these graves, the remnants of our comrades, even though our captain was not among them. We were never able to recover his remains, so all but him were buried here. Had there been more of us the chain of command would've fallen to me, Casper Nait, the naval man who'd turned pirate. I was once a naval instructor for Kingston before turning to piracy; and Fletch had a hard time believing that until I proved it to him through example. I said some final words then left, and I hoped that Fletch had our breakfast ready by now. The graves were just piles of stone, along with names that had been carved into the sand alongside them; unfortunately it was the best that we could do; and we had to be wise with our materials, so to our great shame we stripped them of their possessions. Clothes and belongings were valuable, so we had them leave this world in the same way as they'd entered it.

I walked back towards the small thicket of trees and bushes, and Fletch joined me while I walked. Upon return Fletch showed me his haul of four crabs, and afterwards we spent several minutes preparing them. We sat in silence while we cooked and ate the crabs, and Fletch broke the silence after eating.

"I've spotted something on the horizon, I think it's getting closer but it's hard to tell."

"Do you think it's a ship? Maybe we'll finally get a visitor."

"I don't know, but should we prepare anyway?" asked Fletch.

After our ships demise our spyglasses were lost at sea, so any look out beyond the shallows was difficult to report on. The island didn't have any look out points, despite its distinct landscape of grass, sand, stone and water.

"We'll prepare, you take first watch on its position then we'll switch over after a while."

"Agreed, but what are you gonna do for the time being?" asked Fletch.

"I'll try and get you some more water for the watch ahead, after that I'll work something out."

Fletch nodded: then left the camp with haste.

I filled up my coconut siphon and brought some more water for Fletch, and when enough time had passed Fletch returned to me and I handed it to him. I followed him towards his discovery, and Fletch pointed to a spot on the horizon which I had to squint at in order to see what he wanted me to see. There was a glimpse of something on the horizon, but I couldn't distinguish it any more than he could.

"A tall Englishman like you can't spot something on the horizon, what gives Casper?" joked Fletch.

I ignored his remark but Fletch smiled to himself afterwards.

"I'll take over now you red devil, go and bugger something else."

"Maybe I will," said Fletch.

He jogged off after, leaving me to look on at the horizon in wonder. A few days after our incident we managed to recover barrels which served as our water catchers, but after a month they were pretty low, and there were days where'd we have to go without regular hydration. Fortunately they'd been scarce, but it was always a concern that resided within me. While I took my watch I thought back to the day the Revenant was attacked, and by some miracle our ship had survived two hunter attacks before that. We were in no shape to fight off a third, and there were only nine of us left when the third hunter found us. We established a reputation after sinking the first two hunters, and our ships namesake was truly earned after we did: since it refused to roll over and die.

We fought off two brigs until the colonials got serious, then they sent a frigate after us, and somehow it came from nowhere. It was terrifying, and we have no idea whether it found us through betrayal, or through luck. Intentional or not it didn't matter once it arrived, its firepower was unyielding, and the damage was catastrophic. We never had a chance to fight back, but with cannons or crew it wouldn't have mattered, either way the barrage was too much for us to handle. I remembered laying in the water afterwards with my consciousness fading in and out, then I received a glimpse of the woman who had destroyed us all.

A middle-aged brunette with rectangular glasses and a smoky grey coat, an English woman had done this, an English woman had defeated us. According to dying survivors she was the one who had killed off the other pirates at large, but no one knew who she was, not even our captain it seemed. I remember thinking that she was like a ghost, one who'd been sent here to haunt us until its task was complete. While I tried escaping from the wreckage she saw me, and I assume she watched while I desperately tried to find something that was floatable. She eyed me emotionlessly, then turned her head towards the floating bodies nearby.

'The war is over pirate, be grateful that you lived through it.'

She assessed the wreckage and when she was finished I thought that she'd kill me... but she didn't, in fact, she acted like I wasn't even there. She sailed away afterwards and Fletch never got to look at her like I did, but my description seemed to enlighten him.

A presence suddenly interrupted me and Fletch approached from nearby, I'd failed to keep watch, and because of that my watch had turned into a sighting.

"We should get down to the beach, I've made some preparations in case there hostile," said Fletch.

"That's good, but no shots though, we might need that for later."

"Ok, but without ammunition I won't be that helpful."

"Use the slingshot if you want but rely on your bayonet, you're not half bad with it."

"I guess we'll find out won't we?"

While departing my eyes turned towards the sighting, and a schooner with grey sails came into view. It was very unusual but I suspected it was nothing to worry about, it was probably just a trick to try and hide its true identity.

Fletch and I arrived at the beach and the schooner suddenly came to a stop, which meant that a landing party was likely on its way. I took cover behind a log while Fletch moved towards the trees, and I was hoping that he could get some use out of his recently built slingshot. I thought back to last week when he was building and practicing with it, sometimes on me!! But only on rare occasions. I'd kept telling him not to use his pistols, so he got fed up and decided to make an alternative. Back in the day Fletch was something of a ranged specialist, always preferring firepower to cold hard steel. Being here I've tried to change that, encouraging him to fight with his bayonet more often: but his doubts usually trip him up. I'm glad that he was able to acquire the weapon from a redcoat though, since many of our comrades have died from that infernal contraption.

All though the schooner had stopped I couldn't identify its figurehead, and even though the ship was clearer now, I still didn't know anything about it. I kept low and observed the schooner from behind cover, then a longboat started moving towards us. I unsheathed my dagger and held it up so that Fletch could see it, this signal indicated that landlubbers were approaching, and when I brought it down Fletch would prepare his attack. Several minutes passed and the boat drew near, and I brought my dagger down and hoped that Fletch had his slingshot at the ready. I prayed that the new arrivals were oblivious to our signals, and the boat arrived and eased itself onto the shore. Fletch claimed that he'd practiced with the slingshot for at least three to five days, but now it was time to see if there was any truth to that sentiment. I'd only seen him practice with his bayonet, and that's only because I frequently requested it. Training against it was invaluable to me, since I'd need it if I survived this place.

The arrivals dragged their boat further up the sand after reaching shore, and I prepared myself for what was to come while they did. I peeked from behind the log and became baffled by what was there, it started off as surprise, but then quickly turned into confusion. Women… what Fletch and I had prepared for, was women, women dressed as seamen.

CHAPTER 2

A Divide in Decorum

They moved towards us until Fletch fired his first shot at them, and his large stone hurled towards a woman and struck her down instantly. The women stopped walking afterwards, and one of their comrades tended to their injured ally. One of them then stepped forward.

"Reveal yourselves! We are not here for trouble, in fact it's quite the opposite," said the woman.

Fletch and I remained quiet, and a deathly silence followed as a result. I observed the group more closely and the woman who'd spoke was a ponytailed Englishwoman, a young brunette with large blue eyes and a bright blue bandana around her head. She carried a sword unlike the rest of her crew, whereas the others carried other unusual weapons.

"We are the crew of the Serpent, and we seek only shelter from the colonials who have expelled us," she continued.

We hail from Kingston, but now we are banished from its shores."

I contemplated her words, then moved to take another look at the group. While I did an axe was suddenly thrown towards me at high speed, and it swiftly ingrained itself into the log five inches away from me. I was a little stunned afterwards, and now I had no choice but to reveal myself. I stood up and gazed at the group more clearly, and my appearance frightened them, so I took my time.

"My friend and I have been stranded here for the past month, and we are the remnants of a pirate ship once known as the Revenant: so we're also enemies of England."

The women gasped after my revelation, and they whispered amongst themselves in the meantime.

"How are you alive? Piracy was declared dead weeks ago in Kingston, Governor Lee Manson himself gave the speech," said the young woman.

"I can't explain that, but we are who we say we are."

Fletch emerged from hiding and appeared confused by what was happening, all though his appearance seemed to help convince the women of my claims. A serpent crewman moved to retrieve their axe, but Fletch fired another stone at the woman, and she limped back empty handed.

"Fletch! What are you doing? There was no need for that."

"She had no permission to move, I want to know more before we drop our guard," countered Fletch.

The young woman eyed Fletch and I dirtily, then I went and retrieved the axe myself. I handed it back but Fletch remained unfazed by his actions, and he moved towards me afterwards.

"My name is Avery, and I am the nominated captain of the Serpent, this here is Bellamy, my quartermaster", said the woman.

A blonde radiant woman approached us, and she had faint blue eyes and milky white skin; like Avery her hair was in a ponytail, all though it was prettier, far prettier. Fletch and I were quite smitten with her, and my eyes couldn't help but stare.

"If all is well between us I'd like to get my crew settled for the noon, may we do that?" asked Avery.

I turned to Fletch and he expressed no displeasure, under some basic unspoken rules I guess.

"Keep your camp away from ours and your crew under control, if you do that I'm sure things will be fine."

"Great."

Avery turned to Bellamy who smiled and nodded at me while leaving, all though Fletch received a blank gaze from her, which was understandable I suppose. Stern looks were thrown my way from the Serpents crew, then they left to settle themselves on the island. One particular woman was very displeased with us, a tanned blonde who was treating her friend's facial wound. She glared at me then turned away out of contempt, and she was unusually young, more like a girl instead of a woman. While they went back to fetch there supplies Fletch and I left the area, deciding it was best to leave them for the time being. We walked back and a rush of footsteps suddenly approached us.

"Wait! Don't leave," shouted a woman's voice.

I stopped near a thicket of trees and bushes, and it was Avery's voice that had called out to me.

"May I walk with you? Sailor to sailor if you would?" asked Avery.

Fletch and I were surprised, but I obliged and Fletch left until it was just the two of us. She breathed and composed herself, and I guess she needed to since I'm sure she's travelled far today.

"Shall we?" asked Avery

I nodded, and we began our walk.

I didn't know what to say at first, and Avery didn't know how to begin, an awkward silence developed between us, all though Avery appeared to be brooding.

"It's been a long time since we've encountered another pirate, the colonials kept preaching about their demise, and yet here you are; two young men surviving the odds."

"We're not pirates anymore miss, we have no ship, no crew, no captain, that line of work is gone now."

"Maybe so, but I'm aware of the Revenants history, so don't think that you can lie to me about it," warned Avery.

"Wouldn't dream of it miss, so don't worry."

"How did you survive? The attack, the marooning, it's a story that someone should know."

"I survived and then I was spared, that's all you need to know."

"Spared? By who? The commodore?"

"I guess that's what she is now, so yes... by the commodore."

"How very odd."

"She left me here to die, there's nothing odd about that, she was just sure that I'd perish and be done with it."

'But you didn't, you denied her that, and yet you still seem certain that you'll die here."

I turned to Avery to reply, and I stumbled on it, and that cost me my cue to keep talking.

"If you've survived this long then you must have a plan for leaving here?"

"We had a raft at some point, but without a way to navigate the sea I was too scared to leave. Fletch wanted to take the chance, but I convinced him there was no point."

"We'd last longer here than we would out there," I added.

"So the last of the pirate republic will die here, I'm sure society will take great comfort in that."

We walked until we exited the green thicket of nature, then we arrived on the eastern side of the island. The shallows and the seagulls came into view, and the feisty birds patrolled the sands nearby.

"What would you do if you could leave this place? What would you be?" asked Avery.

"Is that an offer? I'd remain the same; I can't walk away from piracy, not without trying to reclaim it first…not without avenging its losses, and mine."

Avery fell quiet after my response, and she diverted her gaze towards the horizon while she brooded.

"My crew was formed due to an insurrection in Kingston, myself, Bellamy and Kaleen created it because we were tired of colonial injustice, along with piracy. We revolted against them, but only so that we could move on and start anew. If you commit to this path then you'll lose everything, and whatever's left of your life will be gone."

"I know… but I've given too much to let it go, so if you're offering to take me away from here, then this is what will happen."

Avery fell silent again, and her eyes showed that she wanted to leave.

"I better get back to my crew, but thanks for the walk and talk."

I nodded and thanked her also, then I walked back after contemplating our discussion.

I wasn't sure if I believed her insurgent story or not, but she believed my pirate one so I suppose I should. For a so called rebel there seemed to be much fear and anxiety within her, she kept gazing away from me at times, but with my appearance I'm sure that was normal.

Several minutes passed and I returned to the shoreline that Avery and I had met on; only to find that no one was here, only the longboat that had been left on the sand. I betted on Fletch still being here, but I guess he took my walk and talk as a chance to do something more practical. I continued walking until one of Avery's crewmen came into view, and they sat alone next to a shrub. It was a dark skinned girl with black hair and brown eyes, and she drew into the sand with a stick or a branch. I quietly observed her and she appeared to be unarmed, then while I moved closer a commotion suddenly came from my camp. The young girl heard it and looked at me, then she turned away out of sorrow.

I didn't have time to try and figure out what was going on, so I raced towards the thicket of trees, then brushed past the bushes while trying to avoid getting cut by them. The young girl called out to me, but I couldn't distinguish her words while I ran. A few minutes passed and a yelling sound lured me towards the origin of the commotion, and I ran towards it. I arrived several moments later, then spent a few more trying to stomach what was in front of me. Two of Avery's crewman assaulted Fletch, and Avery and Bellamy just watched them. I moved towards them and Bellamy instantly turned to me with a nervous expression, Avery turned as well, and I unsheathed my dagger and pointed it at her. I wanted to do more, but the fight was still going, and Fletch had just been knocked down, and his groans told me all I needed to know.

I turned away and the two culprits beat Fletch with large sticks, and they offered him no quarter, no reprieve from there merciless assaults. I glanced back at Avery in disgust, then confronted the two women who were beating Fletch.

They saw me approach and there gaze immediately diverted to Avery, then they turned it back towards me. The blonde tanned woman was among them, the one who'd nursed her friend after Fletch's attack, suddenly this all made sense, but it had to end.

"If you hurt him again you'll have to fight me as well."

I drew my cutlass to validate my threat, then they moved to double team me, but I remained still and they quickly backed off. I cautiously approached after and Fletch was groaning and crying from his injuries.

"All right everyone let's go, what's done is done so let's leave the pirate's be," said Avery.

Everyone left the area afterwards until only Fletch and I remained.

"I know this looks bad, but he attacked us and the crew demanded a response, I couldn't sway them from retaliation," said Avery.

"If your there captain then your word should be absolute!! It will take weeks for Fletch to recover, and this is far worse than what he did to them."

Avery's reply was disrupted by the presence of a lingering crewman, and suddenly the maroon girl reappeared close by.

"Zaria? What are you still doing here? I told everyone to leave."

"I'm sorry, but I wanted to see if everything was ok; I overheard what you had planned and I couldn't ignore it, it was too difficult," said the nervous girl.

Zaria came closer and her features became clearer, for a maroon she was cute, and I could see why she wanted to be away from this. Fletch started slipping away in my arms, and he would lose consciousness soon due to his wounds. There were cuts and marks all over his arms and chest, and I placed my hand on his back and he instantly yelped in pain.

"It's over now, whatever grievance that has been dealt is behind us, and starting tomorrow we can begin repairing this rocky beginning that we've had," said Avery.

"I want you to leave and keep your crew away from us, and if they don't then I'll retaliate in kind."

Avery nodded then quickly left, but Zaria still remained, and I didn't have the strength to dismiss her.

"I'm really sorry about your friend, if there's any way I can help him please tell me."

I turned to her with a mix of rage and sorrow, and I sensed that the slightest misstep from her would set me off into one of those two directions; but Zaria waited for me, and when I was calm, I quietly looked at her. I struggled to formulate words, so in the end I just settled with these.

"Will you help me?"

That was all I could manage.

CHAPTER 3

Control or Collapse

After the unpleasant events of the morning I spent most of the afternoon watching Fletch. I had nothing to heal him with, so all I could do was cover his wounds and hope for the best. Fletch was still unconsciousness so at least he'd feel nothing while I tended to him, and Zaria still lingered in the camp, all though I was reluctant to talk to her. The evening was approaching and all I wanted to do was meditate, to take my mind off things, but with Fletch's condition I wasn't sure if I could. Zaria noticed that I wanted to leave and be alone, and she sat next to Fletch and watched him.

"You should take some time to be alone, Fletch will still be here once you return."

"I can't leave him here, if he dies then I'll quickly follow in his stead."

"He won't, I promise he'll be fine with me."

"Forget it, I'll just do it somewhere over here."

"Do what exactly?"

"Meditate, it's been a great help while I've been stuck here."

I moved ten steps away from the camp, then sat down and prepared for my meditation. I was close enough so that if anything happened I could reach Fletch in time, but since Zaria was unarmed I trusted her enough for now. I usually had a specific spot where I liked to meditate, a spot where the moon was clearly visible, and where the canopy of trees was perfect. There were two oval shaped stones which were positioned behind and in front of me, along with a winding sand path which led to the secondary reef this island possessed. I still had the sandy grass patches, but I wished I was there currently. I placed my sword out of reach, and kept my dagger in my lap, then I prepared for my activity. Several minutes passed and my attention finally gave out, and a few moments passed while I sat there, contemplating the images that I'd just seen.

When I first started this it was to deal with my growing stress and concerns, but it soon evolved beyond that, and instead it became a way for me to relive my past memories. These memories were growing fainter the longer that I stayed here, but I was holding onto them as long as I continued with this. The commodore's ship appeared in my mind, firing upon us and causing panic all over our vessel. I remember trying to find captain Maroo amidst all the chaos, only to learn that his leg had been broken in the attack. His life was forfeit then, yet still he spoke to me, in order to give me hope for what lied ahead.

"You must find my maps Casper, you and any survivors must find them and keep them safe; there our only hope now," said Captain Maroo.

"Is this what your plan was captain? You should've told us this earlier."

"I know, but I wanted them kept safe in case our enemies ever found them."

Cannon fire continued peppering the hull of our ship, and I quickly took cover as one hurtled towards me nearby.

"You have to leave me behind boy! Whoever's left will look to you now, you're in command as of now."

"I can't do this without you captain! You're our leader, and you're also mine."

"Not anymore son, and if you don't leave then you'll die, so go to my cabin and find them, find them before it's too late."

The image ended, but there was still more to play out afterwards. During that moment I understood what failure was like, but there was more to it than that. In order to rise everyone had to fall, but for me it wasn't like that, for me it was the fight that motivated me... not the outcome. The fight to determine my own fate or my own fall; that is what I needed to reclaim. A chance to cross the finish line, before I inevitably hit the wall that awaits me if I do. Pirates don't get happy endings, and most of us don't deserve one, but we deserve a moment in the sun, before the shade comes along and smothers it. I got up and left and while I did footsteps quickly approached, then something sharp suddenly grazed the side of my cheek. I held my dagger at the ready and wiped the blood off my face; then a shadow suddenly leapt up, and it kicked me right in the nose.

I stumbled back a few paces and tried squinting my eyes to locate my shadowy attackers. It was hard to see straight but eventually two women came into view, and both of them were armed with a various assortment of knives. They were tall and they each had long hair, all though one of them was tanned, and I surmised that these were the women who had attacked

Fletch earlier. The tanned woman attacked and I lunged for my sword, and she slashed at me while I reached for it. The knife cut into my shoulder and I tried containing the pain; then both of them suddenly charged at me, and I swung my sword at the tanned woman first. She avoided the slash and easily outmanoeuvred me, then her friend thrusted towards me, and I caught her blade in my daggers cross guard.

I pushed away from the blade lock and swept her legs, and she fell momentarily. While she was down her tanned friend swung wildly at me, and even though she was quick, she was reckless, which would cost her. She swung once, then twice, then a third time and she opened herself up after. I thrusted my sword into the side of her rib, but my aim was off, and instead of just grazing her, I accidentally penetrated and sliced off a small slab of her skin. She screamed terribly, and even for me it was sickening, this woman looked no older than Fletch, and yet I'd just stabbed her. Her friend attacked me in a burst of rage, swinging just as wildly and recklessly as her friend. I could've done the same again, but I didn't want to misjudge the attack like last time. I intercepted her next swing and quickly grappled and overpowered her, and she resisted after.

Unable to pull away the girl kneed me heavily in the crutch, forcing me to use all of my willpower to hold on, then I retaliated with a knee of my own. The blow copped her right in the belly, and she fell to the ground winded. A few moments passed and both of us recuperated from our bout, and her friends struggling movements distracted us from one another. Cries and sobs echoed now that the clash of blades was over, and I almost felt bad, but they brought this on themselves. It was getting dark and we couldn't keep this up for much longer, so I had to defuse the situation.

"Your friend needs help so whatever this is you have to call it off, and I'm willing to help her if you'll walk away and keep quiet about what happened here."

"Why should we trust you? You're a pirate and we were supposed to kill you, then we could take this island for ourselves."

"Well you've failed, and now she's bleeding out and possibly dying. Let me take her back to my camp, then she can rest there for the night and we'll see how she is tomorrow."

Uncertainty spread across the girls face, then her friend's cries prompted her into agreeing.

"Before we do anything I have to ask, did Avery or Bellamy send you? Did they have anything to do with this?"

"No they didn't, this was our idea and nobody else knows about it."

"So you all sailed here together yet you have your own plans? That's very dangerous."

"We can talk about this later if you want, just help her please."

There was a quaver in her voice while she spoke, and I remained quiet to see if she had anything else to say. She said nothing and I helped carry her friend, then I turned around and Zaria was nearby. She'd made a fire for us at some point, and she remained quiet while she saw the woman's friend being carried towards it. Zaria and the woman exchanged subtle gazes, but I wasn't sure what they were derived of. I placed the woman's friend by the fire, then Zaria approached me and led me away from the woman.

"Your friend is awake, he called for you shortly after you left."

I nodded my thanks and moved straight towards him.

"Hey what are you doing!? My friend is injured and you're just leaving her to die," shouted the girl.

"He needs to talk with his friend Leri! The friend you and Daze attacked, let him have his moment with him," said Zaria angrily.

Leri cursed and mumbled unpleasantly, and I turned to Zaria with gratitude and she nodded to me with a slight smile.

Fletch sighed in relief upon seeing me, but he was struggling to hold himself together.

"You're going to be all right Fletch, you'll survive: you have to."

"I should've been more careful Casp, I'm sorry for putting you through this."

"No, this isn't your fault, it's theirs: and I will deal with it, I promise."

"That maroon girl, she might be the only decent prospect of the bunch, how long has she been here?"

"A while it seems, I haven't really got to know her."

"She's nice, that's all I know, and she's unarmed, so she's different to the rest of them."

"You trying to set me up with her are you?"

Fletch laughed and it quickly became too painful for him, so he was forced to stop and smile instead.

"There's something you should know Fletch, the women that attacked you are here, and I'll be treating one of them tonight."

Fletch sighed and turned his gaze from me, clearly showing his displeasure with my words.

"You were always too nice for your own good Casper, always had that naval man mentality of trying to improve everyone around you."

"If I don't then there could be further trouble for us, I have to help her in that regard."

"Well obviously I can't stop you, so go ahead, do what you must," said Fletch bitterly.

I lowered my gaze after he'd spoke, and Fletch turned away from me uncomfortably, remaining quiet except for a few grunts of pain. I moved back towards Zaria and Leri, then I began preparing for Daze's treatment. I lifted her shirt up and assessed the wound, and the patch of skin that I'd penetrated had begun to scab, and I dampened the cloth and started washing it. Moist blood still remained near the wound, and I started there then moved on towards the scab. Leri cupped her friend's mouth during the process, and she tried helping her friend manage the pain in the meantime. A few minutes later I finished cleaning the wound, then I bandaged her up afterwards.

"It's all done, now you need to leave and come back tomorrow, you can check on her then."

"I'm not leaving her here with you, what if you hurt her while I'm away?"

'Unless you want to carry her back alone then you're gonna have to take that chance, but you're going to leave now, otherwise I'll make you leave."

Leri's expression quickly filled with spite, but I was growing tired and my lack of empathy was starting to show.

"Come back tomorrow and make sure your alone, but for now, leave us be."

Leri sighed angrily, but she did as I asked and ran off without another word. Zaria moved along as well, but I reached out for her to stay a little longer.

"I think we should talk more tomorrow, and give each other some time to get to know one another. Fletch seems to like you, so I feel like I owe you that much."

"I'd like that, it's a bit lonely with the Serpents crew sometimes; I'm not really with them by the way."

"I guess that'll be a story for tomorrow then."

"Only if you'd like to hear it."

She left with a wave, and I gently waved at her back.

CHAPTER 4

A Tale of Caution

A loud groan awoke me from my sleep, and I turned to see Leri trying to help Daze get to her feet. It was early morning and after I awoke Leri stopped trying to help Daze.

"Can you help me get her back? If we work together then we could get her to the ship before anyone notices."

"I helped patch her up but I have no interest in doing anything else for her, besides she needs to stay here, if you move her then you'll only make things worse."

Leri's reply was suddenly interrupted by Daze, who whispered something into her friend's ear. Leri looked displeased with her friend's words, but she respected them and let them be. Fletch suddenly groaned and I moved to check on him, and I quietly hoped that he was ok. He awoke and I helped him sit upright, then he saw the two girls in our camp.

"Are they staying or leaving?" He asked.

"Daze has to stay, but Leri can leave unless she wants to help me with something?"

Both girls looked surprised, but Leri was uninterested in my proposal.

"I'll come back later to check on Daze, since I'm sure I'll have other tasks that Avery will want me to do."

She said goodbye to Daze afterwards, then shot off without another word. Fletch's eyes remained fixed on Daze after, still treating her as a threat even though she was just as injured as he was. Daze remained still while she sat next to the campfires ashes, and she kept looking at Fletch and I, but said nothing while doing so.

"If you have something to say then say it, what's on your mind?" asked Fletch.

"Why did you bring me here? You could've killed me and Leri and yet you didn't, for someone claiming to be a pirate that seems odd."

"That's a question that I'd like answered as well, why did you spare the women that tried to kill you and I?" asked Fletch

"Because I don't want a blood feud on this island, I'll save that for when I leave it, if I leave it."

"So you're a coward? You're too afraid to fight while you're here."

"It's not fear its smarts, and if it weren't for that then you wouldn't be here right now."

"True, but you showed mercy to an enemy, what kind of pirate does that?"

"The kind that hasn't always been a pirate, and the kind that's not used to fighting women who think that they can play alongside the men."

"Ouch," added Fletch.

Daze looked away in guilt, probably because she knew that I was right, she was out of her depth here. Zaria approached the camp afterwards and waited just outside.

"I'm gonna take a walk with Zaria, and I expect the two of you to play nice, don't disappoint me."

Daze nodded in understanding, and Fletch begrudgingly did the same. I beckoned Zaria to come walk with me, then we left the camp moments later. Several minutes passed and eventually I spoke up.

"So how does a maroon girl end up with a gang of Kingston insurgents? Unless you're not actually a maroon."

"I'm not, I used to work in my family's shop selling clothes and other accessories, until we closed down due to a robbery."

"I'm sorry to hear that, what happened?"

"Bandits happened, at least that's the theory, after that I turned to piracy to try and help my family; but I failed to steal from them, and I was press ganged into their service for a time."

"You were a pirate!? That's astonishing."

"Not by choice, eventually when I'd had enough I tried to leave, but the crew held me against my will, and if it weren't for my friend then I'd still be with them."

"Who was the captain? Anyone I would know?"

Zaria didn't answer, and she seemed uncomfortable with the question.

"Never mind, I'm sorry I asked."

"My friend died because of them that's all you need to know, but nevertheless I never believed in the lies that England and Spain had spun about piracy, I know that some of you are decent men; and I've seen a few examples of it in the past."

"So you joined Avery's insurrection as a result, to get away from that life? Or maybe it was something else."

"It was just to get away, to get away from colonials, pirates, and Kingston, to start again elsewhere."

"I see."

My seeds of suspicion started growing, and there seemed to be a lot of discourse amongst this crew.

"But why are you here Casper?" asked Zaria.

"I'm here because of colonial rule."

Zaria giggled slightly in response, then she repeated her question.

She knew that I was hiding something, and there'd be no lying to her, even though I wanted to.

"I'm here because I bet my life on this island, and because I foresaw an end of an age that I wanted to be prepared for. Fletch foresaw it as well so he helped me, and we brought a months' worth of goods here, and left everything else to fate."

"You foresaw it but you became convinced that it would come to pass? Why? Piracy existed before, and someone brought it back, so why did you prepare for its demise instead of trying to fight it?"

"Because I lost faith in it, and I lost faith in my captain, because for as long as I could remember he was piracy; captain Maroo was the man who'd brought it back, and yet he's also the one who let it die all over again."

"How so?"

"Because he changed, I didn't know him for very long but after spending a year with him he changed, and in 1727 he became someone else, someone secretive and unknowable."

We continued walking until the grass and bushes ahead silenced me, then I started paying closer attention to our environment. I scanned the area until a large stick shelter came into view, and I assumed that it belonged to another castaway like myself. I took a deep breath and composed myself, then

I turned to Zaria. Fletch and I had come here in the past, but only a few times since the risk usually wasn't worth the reward; soon Zaria would learn the same thing.

"Up ahead is a stick shelter that once belonged to a stranger here, we think they arrived a few days before us, but we never got a chance to find out for sure."

"What do you mean? What happened?"

"I'm about to show you, and it will be quite the tale of caution for you to tell once you get back."

I sighed momentarily and took a deep breath, then there was movement nearby, and it was too quick to distinguish.

"You take the lead and I'll watch your back."

Zaria grew nervous, but she obeyed and took the lead.

"Is there something in there?" She asked.

"I certainly hope not."

I quietly drew my cutlass and Zaria still heard it, and this made her even more anxious. While we moved closer towards the shelter a foul smell quickly entered our vicinity, and it smelled like death, all though Zaria didn't question it. She continued walking all though she struggled to control her gag reflex, and I signalled for her to head towards the shelter. Upon arrival Zaria suddenly froze in terror, and I walked over to where she was, and just as I expected… it was still there. She turned to me slowly with a mix of dread and disgust, and I couldn't blame her, since it was unpleasant to look at.

A boa constrictor lay next to her, with green, brown and black patterned skin. The creature was massive, and it had a nasty look of menace about it.

"Why!? Why have you led me here Casper!? Are you trying to get me killed?"

27

"I did this for your benefit, to warn you that you have more than pirates to worry about while you're here, not that you have anything to fear from me."

"You could've just told me!"

"I wanted to show you this before any of your crew found out, because like I said before, I was offering you a tale of caution."

Zaria's eyes screwed up angrily, and her mouth looked like it wanted to speak but couldn't, and instead it just moved from side to side, or up and down. There was movement nearby afterwards, and suddenly the snake awoke. I examined its size while it spent a moment or two unravelling itself, and my heart gasped once it was finished. Zaria bolted as soon as the snake moved itself into an upright position, and my best guess was that this monster was at least three or four metres long.

I ran towards Zaria before the snake could react to me, and Zaria grabbed me as soon as I reached her, then we both rushed out of there with our hearts pounding wildly. Several minutes passed while we ran, and we noticed that the snake wasn't pursuing so we stopped. Zaria fell eerily quiet, and I wasn't sure if I liked that, and we both caught our breath in the meantime. A loud cry suddenly emanated from nearby, and it appeared to originate from where we'd just come from. Begrudgingly we ran back to whence we came, and upon return something even worse awaited us.

The snake had constricted itself onto Leri, and she was helpless as the snake tightened itself around her leg. The boa had also sunk its jaws into her thigh, causing her enormous pain and agony. It seemed that Leri's taller frame had not discouraged the animal, since I figured that the snake would be more interested in going for someone smaller like Zaria. I rushed over to where Leri was, and she struggled terribly and I quickly unsheathed my sword. I slashed the animal lightly and it released Leri from its grasp, then the snake hissed at me, and brought its body up to meet my neck.

"Kill it Casper! Kill it now while you still can," yelled Zaria.

Leri yelled the same thing, but I didn't want to kill the angry reptile unless I had to. The snake sized me up like it was preparing for a strike, and I waved my sword at it to try and dissuade it from doing so. Zaria grabbed one of Leri's knives and threw it at the animal, but it just struck the creature on its head, leaving it unharmed and further agitated. Refusing to be deterred the snake suddenly lunged at me, and I quickly retaliated by slashing its neck. A line of blood splashed across the ground after I'd struck it, and the snake's body flopped to the ground afterwards with a thud.

The erratic women calmed down after it was dead, but Leri moaned and whimpered straight after. Zaria assessed her wounds delicately, and the bite seemed to be the worst of it, all though I'm sure they'd be bruising in the coming days.

"I'm sure your crew will have heard your screams, so they'll be on their way as we speak."

"Does that mean that you're leaving?" asked Zaria.

"Yes it does."

Leri moaned what I assumed was a thank you, and I left them alone to consult with one another.

When I was far enough away I spied on them from a distance, then I tried thinking about what I would do next. I'm sure this would be kept quiet just like Daze's incident, but they'd have to admit to the snake bite, all though my involvement they could conceal for the time being. Daze would have to stay at the camp for at least another night before she could be moved, so that would give me some more time with her; and it would give Fletch some more time to work out his grievances with her... and vice versa. I have to find a way to keep the peace between our crews, if Fletch and I are to have any chance of leaving this place, then I had to deter any further bloodshed that could happen between us. Fletch was far from recovered, so for the rest of the week I'd have to do most of the activities alone; but I would also have to work on trying to bridge our two crews into one.

I wasn't sure if that was possible with Avery and Bellamy in command, but I had to try, since our very lives depended on it. After all this could be all that's left for me, this could be all that life was willing to provide anymore, a crew of women who held the key's to our lives or deaths. It sounded like an old wise tale, one that would've been preached to me repeatedly by crustaceous old men. Or maybe it was just another cautionary tale, one that only the balance knew for certain.

CHAPTER 5

A Common Goal

I returned to the camp and Daze was missing, and Fletch lay injured once more. He gave me brief directions while he lay on the ground, then he fell unconscious. It seemed that she had attacked him, though her wounds were serious so I had doubts about that story. Nevertheless I had to find her, to make sure that she wasn't bleeding out next to some tree. I couldn't afford to have her crewmates find her before I did, otherwise they'd get the wrong idea. A while passed and I walked until nearby footsteps forced me to stop, and after hearing them I tried pinpointing where they were coming from; but I couldn't. I continued walking and blood droplets appeared on the ground, but there was no trail that I could follow, however I paused to absorb the surrounding scenery.

Minutes later the footsteps started again, and this time there culprit revealed themselves. Bellamy arrived wielding a grappling hook and a small axe, how cute.

"I'm looking for Daze and Leri, they didn't return last night," said Bellamy.

"I haven't seen them."

Bellamy frowned, and more footsteps quickly approached us, until Avery came into view.

She was armed with her rapier, and she kept it ready for whatever was to come.

"Daze told us what happened, and we're here to put an end to it," said Avery.

"I'm afraid I don't understand, put an end to what?"

Both women paused, then readied themselves for an attack. Avery drew her rapier while Bellamy started spinning her grappling hook.

"Whoa, hang on, hang on, I think there's been a miscommunication here."

"I think it's rather simple actually, Daze and Leri encountered you last night; so you attacked and kidnapped them in retaliation. The next morning you hold them captive, but Daze manages to escape so that she can warn us," said Bellamy.

"And now we've come to get Leri," added Avery.

"She's lying, she and Leri attacked me! You can ask Leri that once Zaria has helped her recover."

"You liar! Daze saw her, you were gonna use her as bait," scathed Bellamy.

"I'll take you to the camp then, and prove to you that you're wrong; there's been enough fighting between us, and I don't want anymore."

Both women were suspicious, and they talked amongst themselves then agreed to follow me back to camp. They kept their weapons fixed on me while we walked, and there was an eerie silence while we travelled towards our destination. Several minutes later we arrived, and upon arrival the women wasted no time in searching the area. They looked for signs of restraint or captives, and when they found nothing they turned their attention back to me.

"You could've hidden her, Daze might not have seen it but she could be close by," said Avery.

She pointed her sword towards me and inched it closer and closer until I became agitated.

"She's lying Avery; your crew is divided and when you sailed here you might've had a common goal, but now you don't, because you've clearly lost them."

Avery tried maintaining her composure, and Bellamy eyed me with a grievous look, but I didn't care, since this was for their own good.

"Both of these girls attacked me and Fletch, and they went against your commands because you're not feared or respected by anyone; pirates are feared and respected, not runaway lasses who think that they can prove something to colonials and pirates alike."

Avery slashed at me in retaliation, and I drew my dagger and parried her blow away with its cross guard.

"I'm impressed that you've made it this far, but you're not ready for what's ahead, none of you are."

"Stop talking! We just want Leri back so that we can leave, because unlike you we have a crew to look after; where as you only look after yourself," said Bellamy.

"That's not true! But as you can see Leri isn't here, and if I was lying then why would I be so calm?"

Avery held my gaze momentarily, then lowered her sword and sheathed it.

"You're not actually believing him are you? We should take him in, let the crew decide his fate."

"I wouldn't threaten me if I were you, you may have the numbers but I have the experience."

Silence followed afterwards, and a few moments later Avery backed down.

"What happened with Leri? Is she ok?" asked Avery.

"She was attacked by a snake but she'll be ok, all though you'll have more than pirates to worry about while you're here."

"You could've told us that sooner," said Bellamy.

I smirked at her in response, and she became even more infuriated afterwards.

"If you return to your ship or camp then I'm sure she'll be safely returned by now, and I need to check on Fletch, so I'll be leaving."

Both women remained cautious, and while I turned to leave Avery lingered, then she reached out for me to stay. Bellamy left without warning, leaving us alone once more.

"We'll be departing for Havana soon since we need supplies, and pirate or not I don't think anyone should be left here to die. If you wish to join us I'll consult with the crew this afternoon, and they'll decide your fate by the evening."

I was surprised by her words, and I nodded my thanks and she smiled in return.

"I'll send Zaria to inform you of the details, since she seems to be rather fond of you."

"I think it's too early to say that."

"With Zaria it's the earlier the better, whatever you've done she seems to be devoted to you."

Avery moved away and I lost my chance to reply to her. She took a deep breath and waved goodbye to me, then she walked back towards the canopy from whence she came.

My thoughts turned to our last conversation after she left, where I told her that I would remain the same if I ever returned to civilization. With or without their help, I had to repay the bloodshed that was dealt to me. Piracy might be dead for now, but as long as Fletch and I live it can return, it just needs a new face to lead it. I took off my hat and bandana and a few locks of brown hair fell out afterwards. If I was to travel with them I'd have to shed these items to conceal myself; and I'm not sure what Fletch would think of Avery's offer, but at least he'd be able to rest; and he'd be able to rest on a ship instead of an island. The day may have finally come, where I could leave this island as either a free man or a dying one. Havana was not a place that was particularly fond of pirates, but it would be good to see how it's changed, even though it would not help me with my own endeavours. I often wondered how the world had moved on from piracy, even if these claims of its demise were not yet true.

A stinging pain came from my shoulder while I brooded, and I would need to treat it soon since I'd not yet had the chance to do so. I glanced back at the camp and Fletch was missing, and it was strange to learn this, since he was lying on the ground not so long ago. I hoped he was ok, but the young redhead was always tough, not much of a fighter, but he could take hits. I moved towards my bed and unsheathed my weapons from my belt, they were battle weary from my days at sea, and if I was ever to return to society then I'd need to replace them.

I laughed to myself after saying that, replacing weapons when I had no coins in my possession to do so, I almost sounded like a citizen, and that was a scary thought. While my thoughts swirled around inside me my stomach suddenly growled, and I remembered that I hadn't eaten anything since last night. These wretched women were costing me my lifestyle, and my thoughts turned to the dead boa that was still lying in the abandoned stick shelter. I'd never eaten snake before but then again I rarely saw them to begin with, and if I could get used to the taste of crab then I suppose I had no excuse but to try it. I tried motivating myself to go back there, then a few moments later Fletch arrived before I could. He was hobbling and clearly sore, but he looked cynical as well, however he was moving well for someone who'd almost been beaten to death by sticks. I moved towards him and his brown eyes were filled with sadness and disappointment.

"I went scavenging for food after you left, and I saw some crabs but found these instead."

There were four coconuts in his hands, which was normally a decent haul for us, so I didn't understand why he was so dissatisfied.

"If that's what you found then why are you so cynical?"

"Because it took forever for me to find these! Our food supply is shrinking Casper, the crabs are uncommon, the coconuts are rare, and the fish are often impossible to catch."

"Don't worry, I've found us another food source, but I need you to remain calm about it."

Fletch waited for me to continue.

"You remember the old stick shelter? The one that man used or made during our early days here?"

"Yeah I remember, why?"

"Well… that place is safe now, because I killed the snake."

"You went back there! What were you thinking pal? Do you remember what happened last time we went there?"

"Yes of course I do, I still have that image embedded in my brain, but… we could remove the source of that image now, by eating it."

Fletch didn't like where this was going, but while he stared at his miniscule coconuts his stomach suddenly growled, so his decision to eat snake had already been made for him.

"I guess I can't argue anymore, I hate you," said Fletch jokingly.

I laughed afterwards and his defeated expression only encouraged me, then he hung his head in defeat while I tried recomposing myself.

CHAPTER 6

A Desperate Time

After a vexing morning and physically laborious afternoon, I engaged in some weapons training in order to kill some time before dinner. It was almost dusk and Fletch informed me that dinner would be ready soon. Earlier in the afternoon Fletch and I carried the boa back to our camp, but we agreed to only eat half of it for the meantime. During lunch time we dipped the meat into the coconut milk to try and improve its taste, but unfortunately there was no improvement. We ended up using all of the coconuts Fletch had collected even though we shouldn't have, but we were desperate to get the taste of snake out of our mouths. I never thought that I'd prefer crab to anything else in life, but I guess there's always something worse and something better out there. When we'd finished preparing and eating what we had set aside, I set out to look for the Serpent's encampment, or ship.

I had no bearings to help me with this search, but I did have some ideas for where six crewmen could eat or sleep at. The cove was my first thought, since that was where Fletch and I had spent our first night, and neither of us had been there for weeks, so it was possible that they'd be staying there. I also had the thought that there was no encampment, which would be a problem for Fletch and I, but it was worth investigating while I had the time.

I made my way through the trees and bushes until I could see the shoreline, and I stopped walking when I discovered nothing. The island had four distinct areas which defined its various sections. To the north was the first of the islands two reefs, which connected to the shoreline and had a thicker canopy of palm trees inhabiting it. To the south was the larger second reef, which connected to the main beach and then past it's shallows you'd find the nearby cove. This is where we ended up on our first day here, and it became our main hunting ground for the majority of our first week also. To the east it was more open, since it comprised of smaller trees that were barely a meter high, and its sand was also different, because it was smoother and softer than the regular stuff. The west was where most of the grass could be found, and it's where our stranger and snake once lived.

The grass barely reached my ankle there, and yet that thing had managed to conceal itself from us, it was unheard of. Our first viewing of the creature was awful, and we were already late to the scene as it is, but the first time we saw it… was when it strangled and killed our mystery man. With some internal inspiration we stopped the creature from eating him, and eventually the snake fled after we charged at it repeatedly. We buried him near our crew's graves as a mark of respect, then we gathered up his belongings and left his shelter alone.

I arrived at the cove and there were voices coming from within it, and I quickly searched for cover while I listened in on what they were saying. I crept into the shallows next to a rock, then waited on their next words.

"Captain! You can't expect the crew to be comfortable with this, two pirates aboard our ship? It'll stir up conflict if you do," said a woman's voice.

"The risk is there no one is denying that, but if we leave them behind then we're condemning them to death. Things have changed, and they should be allowed to see that," said a voice belonging to Bellamy.

"They lost that chance when there ship sunk into the sea, and if we take them back then we'll be labelled accessories to their crimes. We've already committed piracy by stealing this ship! So if we associate ourselves with them then we might as well become pirates ourselves," said the woman's voice.

"What if they worked for us? They have a vendetta against the colonials just like we do, so with the last of the pirates on our side then perhaps they could protect us from them," chimed a third voice belonging to Avery.

"Nobody can protect us from the colonial's captain, there authority is absolute; but perhaps we could make a peace offering with them, and use the pirates as payment for better terms with Kingston," said the woman's voice.

"Negotiating with them is like negotiating with a king, what they can't take with words they'll just take by force," said Bellamy.

"So what's your suggestion then? To allow Kingston to be dictated by its corrupt governor and his fat pockets? It's because of him that we lost our place in Kingston; and the pirate's didn't help matters. The only way we can get what we want is if we barter with them, I don't like the idea but we just need enough from them to start over," said the woman's voice.

"That won't save Kingston from its corruption, but you're right we do need coin, and that's why I suggested that we head for Havana," said Avery.

'What would we do in Havana?" asked Bellamy.

"Start over, we could find work there as cargo shippers, or maybe at a theatre, or we could be shopkeepers. All of us have backgrounds, and if we pool them together then we could still have a future for all of us. We'll have to make sacrifices, but it's attainable, I know it is," urged Avery.

"No one would be after us in Havana, so it's plausible, besides we tried an island and it didn't work out, so why don't we give another city a go?" asked Bellamy.

"We'd have to check it out first, and your forgetting one thing Bellamy, pirates are very unwelcome in Havana, so there's no way that we could take them there; if we failed to convince them of our intentions then we'd be strung up right alongside them," said the woman's voice.

I waited for a reply and listened intently for it, but it never came. A rush of footsteps suddenly left the cove, and there was an annoyed thud as someone struck a nearby rock. I remained still while the waves splashed onto my tattered clothes, and there seemed to be no more discussions so I adjusted my position and tried to lay eyes on the woman who'd left.

A couple of minutes later they passed me by, and I quickly ducked out of sight while they did. I spied on their movements and remained cautious while doing so, then Avery and Bellamy emerged, and they talked amongst themselves. When they finished they regrouped with the third woman, who was waiting for them at the longboat. She was very tall and carried a large axe along with two smaller ones, but apart from that I couldn't identify her. The trio of women were about six yards away, and the third woman hopped into the boat and beckoned for the others to join her. They calmly rowed away from the shoreline, and when they were far enough away I emerged from hiding. A few moments passed while I spied on them, then I tried figuring out what to do next.

If I could follow them then I might learn where there ship is located, but I'd have no way of reaching it unless I swam. Our wreckage was disassembled shortly after we arrived here, but would it be possible to reassemble it? We have the rope for it, and we could find the wood, the question was did we have the time? I doubt it.

The longboat rowed towards the east, and I followed it as best I could on land. Several minutes passed while I raced across the sand, and I ran into a cluster of shrubs and bushes. I ran until I lost my breath, and I lost the boat as well. A while later I searched the area, and instead of finding the boat, I found something bigger. Roughly three hundred yards from shore was a ship, and its grey sails came into view while I moved closer. The Serpent had been found, and it was finally within reach. Its figurehead was a queen carrying a sceptre, which made me curious about its origin. Its features were standard, it had a brown timbered hull and black painted rails and sides, all except for its sails, which were probably a feeble attempt at masking its identity. Being a schooner there was a small array of cannons on board, and there were three on its portside, so I assumed that it was a six gun ship.

A few minutes passed while I observed it, then the longboat came into view. All of a sudden I was shaken from my thoughts, and the images disappeared as I almost hit Fletch with my sword.

"Sorry mate, my mind was running rampant and I shouldn't have let it, I'll be more careful next time."

Fletch raised his eye brows then shook his head.

"Dinner is ready when you are."

The leftovers of the boa suddenly filtered into my nose, and my heart sunk afterwards, all though perhaps our rationed bread would help us with its flavour. I put my weapons away and quickly washed myself with our barrelled water, then Fletch unveiled his pistols, and he noticed my eyes diverting towards them.

"You or I are going to have to use them soon, so I brought them out even though I know you don't want me using them."

"I'm not ready for that yet, we agreed to only use them for a desperate time."

"We're close to one Casper, and there our only advantage against the Serpents crew."

"We have to be on that ship tomorrow otherwise we're done," he added.

"You need to rest up first, since you're in no condition to fight them; but if you're feeling better tomorrow then perhaps we could formulate a plan."

"Let's hope there still here tomorrow, but even then we'll still need a way to reach there ship."

"What about the longboat? They beached it near the cove today, so maybe if we hid we could steal it if they come back tomorrow."

"We'd still need a distraction, something quiet but effective."

"The slingshot: it's our only option, I don't want any casualties unless it's necessary, so I'll draw them out and you take them out."

Fletch bit his lips doubtingly, but he seemed to have no alternative.

"I'm not the best shot with the sling shot, what if it breaks? Then I'll be useless to you without my guns."

"Use your bayonet then, no shots unless you have to, I want to be clear about that. Besides... you're the firing squad remember? What are they to you?"

"Not anymore I'm not."

A few moments passed and we remained quiet while we bit into our boa meat, and it still tasted terrible, but at least I was almost finished with it.

"I know it's been hard for you here, and I get it believe me, and we weren't friends back in the day but we still wanted the same thing; to preserve man's natural freedoms."

"I still want that Casp, but being here for so long has flat lined that freedom, I mean... the new world has total control now."

"That remains to be seen, we have the resources to challenge them we just need to get to them."

"Your referring to the maps aren't you?"

"Yes I am, and you agreed a while back that they were piracy's best chance at survival, and they could cover our essentials, a hideout to live in, and perhaps a ship to live off."

"Casper you have to stop doing this! If the maps provide us with what we need then we have to use them for survival, not revenge."

"Without revenge what's the point of survival!?"

Fletch fell silent, then continued eating his boa meat. He disliked it just as much as I did, but he gorged through it as quickly as he could. When we'd finished we drank our coconut siphons dry, hoping to wash away any traces of boa left in our mouths. We laid on our backs afterwards to watch the night sky, and it was something that we'd do regularly if we could ever remember too.

There were a good quantity of stars out tonight, and there various colours wowed me.

"I wonder if any of them are rooting for us," said Fletch.

"What do you mean? There just stars mate."

"Yeah but I heard things back in Nassau, about stars and planets affecting people in different ways, sounds stupid I know, but for some reason it stuck with me."

I didn't respond to Fletch's strange comments, instead I focused on one particular star, and all though it was stupid I found myself quietly pleading with it.

"Well if there not, then we've got one chance to prove them wrong."

CHAPTER 7

Breaking Point

I awoke to the brisk chill of the morning, and Fletch felt it too. Coldness was unusual for this islands climate, but I suppose today was an exception. We got up and sought out our stored food, and we realised that after today that would be the last of it. Our water barrels were also low, and it had not rained for nine days. Before falling asleep last night I had some doubts about the plan Fletch and I had discussed, and I didn't think that the two of us would be enough to defeat the Serpents crew. I wanted to tell Fletch that we should call it off, but I already know what he would say.

'We have to try Casp, even if it's the end of us.'

"Leave Zaria alone, she's helped us so we should spare her if possible."

"What if she attacks first? We can't afford to go in half-cocked."

"I'll worry about that if it happens, but unless that happens don't hurt her."

Fletch sighed but nodded and agreed to my request, he wasn't on board with it, but he would honour it nonetheless.

We finished off the rest of our food, then Fletch took the lead and we set off towards the shoreline. Our plan was the same as when the Serpents crew first arrived, except this time we wouldn't hide. I was confident that I could hold my own against a few of them, but if Fletch didn't help me then I'd quickly get overwhelmed in no time. Several minutes passed then we arrived and ran straight into hiding, and I hoped with all of my faith that they'd show up. Fletch scurried towards a group of shrubs located next to a tree, while I shielded myself next to the log that I'd used from before.

Many minutes passed and there was no sign of them, it was just quiet, quiet and empty. Birds hovered over the reef further out, but other than that there was nothing. I surveyed the horizon until I gave up moments later, then I walked back towards Fletch.

"We should head towards the east, that's where there ship was last located so we should start there."

Fletch nodded and we took off into that direction, all though Fletch struggled to keep up with me. I ran at full pace until my legs gave out, and Fletch caught up with me and he was just as tired as I was. A few minutes passed while we caught our breath, then we moved on until we arrived at the location. The three hundred yard anchorage was vacant, and the surrounding sea was empty, it was gone.

Fear started settling in my mind, and I think sorrow started settling in Fletch's.

"We have to keep looking, we can't assume the worst yet so it has to be here somewhere."

Fletch and I split up and searched the island far and wide, then for what seemed like an hour we searched until we arrived back at the shoreline. Neither of us spotted anything along the horizon, and neither of us had any hope of leaving this place. Our lives appeared to be over, and the two of us would die here in a matter of days. I had no words of comfort to give Fletch, and he had none for me, so we headed back defeated.

Our lack of energy would make the journey even longer, and when we returned to camp we both slumped against our enclosures. I reflected on the grim circumstances we now faced, and a dark thought emerged within me.

With no rations for the night we would have to hunt for longer during the day, or take the risk of hunting during the night instead. If it didn't rain soon then we'd also be facing dehydration, which in the past was manageable, but if we had to exhaust ourselves more during the day then our chances of survival were slim. A few minutes passed while I remained silent, then my guilt rose to the surface.

"I'm sorry Fletch, I should never have got involved with those girls; I thought I could use them to make peace with the others, but I was wrong."

"You should've killed them when you had the chance, they attacked you remember!? If Maroo was here he would've told you the same thing."

"But they were just runaway girls, practically kids Fletch, we might be pirates but even that is too much."

"Well your naval man sentiment has caused them to do this to us, caused them to do this to me!! If you had just killed them then we would've had two less crewmen to worry about."

I remained quiet and tried thinking of ways to defend myself.

"Regardless of what you did or didn't do it doesn't matter now, we're stuck here thanks to you, and we'll never get another opportunity to leave."

I had to change the subject somehow, otherwise if Fletch turned on me then we'd both be dead men.

"We should go out for a hunt, since sitting here in our misery isn't going to help us now, and we need a distraction from this."

Fletch didn't answer, but he got up and supposedly readied himself.

I turned to face him and Fletch armed himself with his pistols, and this concerned me, since he never took them when he went hunting.

"Come on! It's gonna be a dreary day and I'd like to put it behind me," urged Fletch.

I followed his lead and grabbed our fishing spears before departing, then I quietly handed Fletch his, and he took it without looking at me.

Upon arrival Fletch moved closer towards the water, and instead of preparing his spear for the hunt, he pulled out his pistols and turned to face me. I looked at him with confusion, then he hurriedly threw one of them at me.

"We're not going hunting anymore Casper, we're not gonna do anything anymore, this is our last act, and it's time we fulfilled our month long promise to one another."

"Now's not the time for submission Fletch, we're still alive for now and if we could just last a little longer than maybe something will happen for us. I know we made a promise to one another, to die together if it was the end, but I don't believe it's the end, I can't."

"We've been here for a month Casper! And that's the only ship that has come here in all that time, have you checked the horizon? No other vessel has even come close. We try and grab their attention, but they always sail away in the end."

"I know it's grim, but I want to see this through till the end, and you should too, don't you want to be able to say that? To say that you kept to the path no matter what."

"If there's no one to say that too then what's the point? At least if we do this now we'll be free from this place."

He aimed his pistol at me, then pointed it to the one at my feet.

"Prepare your shot Casper, we have to make it count."

I stood motionless, looking at the pistol while a single tear formed in my eye, then I looked at Fletch.

"Come on Casper! Pick it up and prepare your shot."

I paused then grabbed the pistol, and instead of picking it up, I threw it at him.

While Fletch was distracted by my throw I tackled him into the ground, hoping to reason with him afterwards.

"You need to get a hold of yourself! We don't have the time or the energy for this, so put the gun away."

"Your just too weak or stubborn to do what's right, and if we wait any longer than we might not be able to take each other's lives."

Several moments passed while we wrestled with one another, then Fletch pushed me off.

"I wanted us to go out together! But if you won't follow through on your word, then I guess I'll have to do this myself."

Fletch kicked towards my thigh and I blocked it, then I counter attacked with a kick of my own; which struck him in his opposite leg. Fletch was slow in recovering from it, and he shifted his fighting stance regularly. Before piracy I once trained recruits into becoming soldiers for the Kingston navy, and thanks to that I became adept at close combat.

It's been a long time since I've been in a fight though, and I wasn't familiar with Fletch's fighting, so I didn't know for sure if he was good or not; I just assumed that he wasn't. Fletch punched towards me with a flurry of jabs and straight punches, and I blocked two of them and the third hit me square in the stomach. He struck me with a back fist to the side of the head after, and I instantly fell to my knees. He drove his knee towards my face while I was down, and I blocked it and hit him in the groin.

While Fletch was injured I moved away from him, and I rose to my feet and prepared for retaliation. A minute or so passed where I couldn't move due to my wounds, and while Fletch recovered I hit him with a jab to the nose, causing his dirt layered appendage to bleed; then I straight punched him in the jaw

Fletch knelt into ground groaning in pain, and I lifted my leg up and slammed it onto the back of his neck. He crumpled into the sand afterwards, and he struggled to move which gave me some time to recuperate. When I was feeling better I hobbled over to collect his pistol, then I turned around and Fletch desperately willed himself to his feet. He clutched a handful of sand while he stood, and while he grimaced in pain he suddenly lunged at me. He threw the sand into my face and I shielded myself from it, then Fletch crashed into my arm with his shoulder and a sudden sharp pain followed.

I stumbled to the ground and agony instantly shot up my arm, and I tried nursing it but the bone rattling feeling was too strong. There was nothing that I could do, nothing but endure and suffer. I watched Fletch while I desperately tried managing my pain, and he collected his pistol and reacquired the other one that he'd tossed to me. Despite his current advantage Fletch was unstable on his feet, and he struggled to stand upright, though he gritted through it and remained tall.

"Please Casper! Just accept that this is it, it's over for us; so it's best that we just end it here."

I looked into his eyes and only fear and desperation looked back at me, there seemed to be little that I could do to change his mind, he was committed to this, committed to forfeiting his own life as well as mine; despite everything that we'd gone through together. I held out my hand and Fletch handed me his other pistol, it seemed that I had little choice, this is what he wanted, whether I liked it or not.

"If you are so committed to death then I will give it you, but I will not join you willingly, so if you pull that trigger Fletch… then you'll be dying alone."

Fletch's frustration increased, but he still held his pistol at me.

"Please Casper, this is your last chance," he pleaded.

A few moments passed while our eyes locked, and tears formed in all of them. Fletch and I breathed deeply, then I closed my eyes and waited for him. I waited for him to fire, and I continued waiting… until I opened them. Fletch cried into the sand on his knees, his eyes overflowing and his face filled with shame. I stayed quiet while he poured it all out, and I tried to hold it all in.

I expected one of us to break today, how could you not when you're stuck on a tropical prison like we were.

CHAPTER 8

Self Isolation

It was early noon, and Fletch was finished with his outburst so I took him back to camp, all though I did it without giving him a choice. While Fletch's guard was down I attacked him with his own spear, and I struck him repeatedly until he was beaten into unconsciousness. It was hard to justify such violence, but I needed to self-isolate him. It took twice the time and effort to return because of this, but when I returned I dropped him next to the nearest tree. I removed his guns for safekeeping but allowed his dagger to remain. I left the camp and went looking for a patch of sand to bury them in, and I located a spot and quickly dug and buried the pistols. The bayonet would be much harder to conceal, but I located another spot and buried it next to a bush. At least if it was harder to hide it might be easier to find, but somehow I'd likely have issues anyhow. I drew a circle in the sand with my dagger to try and help me find it later on, then when I was finished I went and retrieved my fishing spear.

I headed back to camp and took a lengthy drink, and after I'd drunk from my water barrel I estimated that I had about one or two drinks left inside it. If I was desperate I could drink more from Fletch's, but stealing from another pirate was a crime, even if we were castaway ones. With my thirst quenched I looked at Fletch one last time before leaving, then I moved towards the North-West side of the island. The briskness of the morning continued seeping through me like an unpleasant smell, and while I was hunting that would be an unpleasant affliction to have. I recalled Fletch warning me about the scarcity of food on the island, so I'd have to try a different hunting spot for today.

Upon arrival I surveyed the reef in front of me, scanning its clear waters for some kind of sign that this was where to be right now. Ripples and stillness awaited me, and I surmised that I'd have to go out further, unless I wanted to be stuck with measly sardines for the day. I removed my jacket and hat, then proceeded towards what I assumed was freezing cold water. My legs didn't react to the temperature change, but when it reached my waist it was hard not to flinch; then I regretted my decision.

The brisk wind continued blowing me around, and the bone chilling water seeped through me like air. I hoped that I would find food soon, and I hoped that the islands climate would improve, but at first glance, I didn't feel optimistic.

Many minutes passed and they felt like years inside this torturous liquid, but I had to commit to the long haul, even if it became absurd as time moved on. Several minutes passed while I tried skewering salmon that were swimming close by, and my frustration was building as five of them had gotten away from me. A sixth one lingered and I moved towards it and prepared my thrust, then the vermin bolted before I could finish my advance. I was no stranger to this sort of feeling, and neither was Fletch, but on a day like today, this was just too much for anyone to bear. I scoured the reef to see if there was anything else I could catch, but there wasn't, it was just sardines or coral, along with all the sand that I'd stirred up from hunting.

I waded furiously back towards land, then threw my spear angrily at the grass. It didn't reach that far due to my technique and lack of energy, and instead it just harmlessly clonked onto the sand.

While leaving the freezing cold water behind I was welcomed mercilessly by the cold wind instead; and I needed to return to camp to warm myself, but the evening was drawing near and I had no food to return with.

I rested on the sand to try and recover from the numbing fatigue, and the cold wind prevented me from enjoying even a smidge of relief. A few minutes passed then I slowly willed myself to my feet, and I thought back to my earliest days here. On the second day I tried treating my charred face with anything I could, but there was no chance of helping it here, and I'd be stuck with these scars forever. The commodore's barrage of cannon fire was responsible for my disfigurement, and after that I had to put up with Fletch's childish taunts for the rest of the week. I know he was just trying to lighten the mood, because Fletch knew as well as I what kind of hell-hole we'd just found ourselves in. I walked towards the grass which divided the reef from the mainland, and when I reached it an unfortunate sight awaited me.

A snake lingered up ahead, and I tried remaining still while it slithered away from me. Its pattern caught my eye: green, brown and black, I groaned terribly, as I remembered it was the same as the one before.

My guess was that this was its young, and there were three other snakes just like it nearby. They were in my way of returning to camp, and despite their small size I was still afraid of what they might do to me. I couldn't figure out how they were here since I'd killed there parent... then it hit me, they must have another one nearby. I remained quiet and still, then observed them while hoping that they would leave the area, but they lingered, and I was losing patience. I drew my sword as a precaution, then carefully proceeded my way around them.

They watched closely while I moved, and I leaped in order to get clear of them. When I landed there was a sudden reaction, however it wasn't from them. A loud hissing sound drowned out the other snakes, and another parent revealed itself. My heart sunk as this parent looked even bigger than the last one, and it lunged towards my leg and I kicked it away with a sweeping motion.

The creature was unfazed by my efforts, and its young joined its parent in pursuing me. I swung my sword at the reptiles to keep them at bay, and I moved slowly in order to avoid further aggression. A while passed while I retreated, and the snakes stopped following me; instead they watched me with exotic and weird head movements, and I continued retreating, then sighed while they seemed to calm down. Suddenly I tripped on a nearby stone, and I cursed to myself for forgetting about it. The sudden fall caused another reaction, one that I was most afraid of.

The snakes slithered towards me after my fall, and I swung my weapon at them, and the three younglings bit into my arm as a result. I almost shrieked in agony as there small teeth hooked into me, and I bashed at them with my other hand, until the parent came towards me. Its large jaws sunk themselves into my injured wrist, and the shock hit me like a plank of wood; and it was only instinct that kept me from fainting.

I bashed at the younglings again to get them off me, and I used everything I had until they let go. Even without them the pain of the parents bite still drained me, and I was too weak to fight them, and I grew weaker by the moment.

My consciousness started fading, and I attacked the parent and it readjusted its bite and kept going. A few moments later it let go, and I fell to the ground with a thud. The last traces of energy left me once I was released, and my consciousness faded also, along with the dripping blood from my arm. The snakes left me and fled into the grass, and I quietly prayed that I wouldn't be there next meal; just the poor fool who'd provoked them. My vision deteriorated, then everything went black and I fainted.

I fell into a dreamlike state, and I was transported onto the deck of a ship. The ship was a sloop with yellowish colours mixed in to the timber, and that was a trademark for many Spanish vessels in today's world. There were no cannons, but four black swivel guns were on board. Two were located near the helm, while the other two were located further along the bow. I assumed this was the cheaper alternative for dealing with men like me. A single cabin was located nearby, and a mysterious figure approached, a blurry and unidentifiable one.

"You've been working on this boat for hours, do you even remember the last time you took a break?" said a man's voice.

"Captain? Is that you?"

"There's nobody else, the rest of the crew have gone on a little expedition: I thought you would've joined them."

"I think I've drunk enough after my times in the Kingston tavern captain."

Captain Maroo chuckled, and his appearance remained indistinguishable.

"Those that fight and kill for their liberties always deserve more than those that don't, never forget that Nait, it is at the essence of who we are."

"Yes captain."

"My crew was sceptical of bringing a naval man on board there ship, but I convinced them only because they were curious, curious to see if the enemy could become our friend."

I hope you're worth the interest I've shown you, but I'm sure a survivor of Governor Manson will be worth all that," Maroo added.

"What do you mean a survivor of Manson? He's not responsible for my loss."

"Isn't he? My mistake, I thought he was in charge of Kingston."

I fell silent, stumbling on any reply that I could've had.

"The privileged rule this world and that saddens me, but the pirates were always there to challenge that, some of them did it for the wrong reasons, while some did it for the necessary ones."

"Revenge is not a necessary one, and as one of the last of the pirates you have a rare chance to redefine what they are, don't throw that away captain… think about it first."

"Think about what?! The skull and crossbones have always represented freedom, and to its enemies it would be freedom or death; since death from a free man was a fulfilling end to an unfree one."

"Maybe, but that philosophy could be corrupted by hubris."

"It will only be corrupted by disbelievers, disbelievers or deserters, in other words traitors of the black."

"The black? What's that?"

"The black flag, the one you and I swore to, the only black that matters."

I suddenly awoke and the pain from my arm returned. Blood soaked the sand beneath it, but at least I could move it along with the rest of my body. I crawled towards the reef in the hopes that the water would revitalise me, and the cold wind continued blowing, making it harder for me to move. The evening was upon me now, and there was little light for me to rely upon. A few minutes passed then I reached the shallows, and I continued towards them until there cold sensations awoke me. I screamed while the salt water entered my wrist, but at least the pain would keep me from drifting off. I sat in the shallows and shivered from the cold, and I washed myself in the reef and allowed its waters to cleanse me. I held back curses, then exited the reef and stumbled back towards shore.

Panic suddenly set in mind, and I remembered that Fletch was out there all alone. He was a better hunter than I was, but would he be able to manage on his own? Would I? I didn't know. Against the elements and the unseen, it was a constant stress that ate away at me. But my fears for his safety were pointless now, since I was powerless to do anything. I would be foolhardy to try and find him after dark, and leaving this beach would be even worse. Fletch was at the mercy of Mother Nature now, and if she chose to become cruel, then my fears for him would become very real by sunrise.

CHAPTER 9

A New Path

It seemed like morning or noon, but I was caught in a dream that I couldn't pull away from. The dream took me back to the deck of the Revenant, where splintered wood surrounded me, and streaks of blood had splashed across the ships railing. Fire and panic spread all around me, and in the midst of it all I made my way towards the captain's quarters. Cries and shouts echoed nearby, but I couldn't help them, since the chaos prevented me from doing so. I entered the captain's quarters and retrieved the maps, and they were encased in a tube, and when I touched them the dream changed. Captain Maroo appeared nearby, and he was in the same state as I remembered him in, but this time… a shadow moved towards us.

"You can't do anything for me, so if you have my maps you must go Casper," said Captain Maroo.

"I can't go alone captain! I can't do this without you!"

"Yes you can, I did the best I could for as long as I could, but in the end this would be all that awaited me."

"Then I'll find them, I'll find them and make them pay!"

"No Casper! If you seek them out then you'll lose everything, you have a different battle to fight now, and you must do it alone."

The captain moved towards the mast painfully, and sat himself next to it and let out a huge groan of pain.

"The maps will lead you to a hideout, one that was financed by me and my former allies, you must find and protect it; it could be your only sanctuary now."

"This was too be our haven someday, but now it will be yours," added Captain Maroo.

"That's the plan!? To hide! There has to be more to it."

"There is, you must survive, survive and rebuild, live the life that none of us could, because if you don't then some colonial slug will do it for you."

"But we were so close, so close to a republic of thieves, if we give that up then we're nothing, we'll be remembered as nothing."

"We'll be remembered as free men, and that's not nothing to me, but our time is over, and I should've accepted that long ago."

The shadow suddenly emerged from the smoke, and to my horror two large women approached us, and they were armed with large axes. The first was a burly blonde woman with fair skin and blue eyes, while the second was a burly redhead, with pale skin and hazel eyes that looked like black.

"You must choose a new path now Casper, a new life, so leave this ship, and leave all of this behind, please promise me that," urged Captain Maroo.

I paused and struggled with his words, then the two women arrived and they immediately raised their axes. The redhead and the blonde swung there axes towards Maroo's face, and he cracked a brief smile before the blades tore into his skull. Afterwards they moved onto me, and I yelled in horror until I suddenly awoke.

Sweat dripped off me and I breathed heavily, then my arm flared up and I groaned in agony. A few minutes passed while I calmed myself and endured my pain, then I looked around and somehow I was back at my camp.

"You're ok Casper, your safe," said a boy's voice.

I turned and Fletch lay on his bed nearby, he was ok, all though internally I wasn't sure if that was the case.

"You've been out all morning, I went looking for you earlier and brought you back while you were dreaming, you were talking in your sleep."

"So what is it now?"

"Just past noon, I think."

I remained quiet, I must've been in way worse shape than I thought, and to be out for that long was concerning.

"When I found you I thought that you'd succumbed to the elements, but you're heavily injured so would you care to explain that?"

"Yeah, we had a tough day, that's all there is to explain."

"No it isn't, you attacked me Casper? Why!? Why would you do that!!? I spent the whole night scared and cold because of you."

"You were broken Fletch, I had to try and isolate you until you were recovered."

"Recovered? I'm not sick Casper, I just had a moment of weakness! It could've easily of have happened to you."

He was right, it could've happened to me, but it didn't, and I intended for it to stay that way.

"I've bandaged your wrist and caught some salmon for us to eat; once you feel better you can eat your share, otherwise I'll leave it out for you while I'm out."

"Where are you going?"

"To find your maps, we won't need them anymore since we'll be dead before we can use them."

"Those are the captain's maps, there the only thing left of him and you're going to destroy them?"

"Just because you have dreams about him doesn't mean that I do, he's gone Casper, and perhaps it's time we accept that."

I almost gasped at his words, and I couldn't believe what I was hearing, but I was in no condition to stop him.

"The Serpents crew was the only shot we had at leaving this place, and now they're gone, along with any chances of survival."

"You don't know that, without those maps we'll have nowhere to go."

Fletch sighed, and stern indecision engulfed both of his eyes.

"If we're gonna get out of here then we need to get our acts together, which means we need to stop fighting one another and start working together; neither of us will survive this alone, so I need you at your best, and in return I will try and do the same for you."

Fletch struggled to look at me, and it seemed like he wanted to leave but couldn't, so he stayed.

"You'll need protection until I can uncover your guns, so take my sword since I can't use it, my arm won't allow it."

Fletch hesitated but retrieved it from its resting place, then he pointed its tip towards me.

"If my guns are lost because of you, I'm going to carve you up with this."

A few moments passed, then the tension subsided, and Fletch lowered the weapon and presented me with his attention.

"You should uncover the maps anyway, they've been buried for long enough."

"I'm going for a swim first, after that I'll bring you your maps."

"Thank you Fletch."

'Of all the pirates I could've been marooned with, I had to end up with the naval schmuck," joked Fletch.

I forced a smile, then Fletch left without warning.

When he was gone my thoughts returned to the nightmare, along with the maps and the hideout that they led to. Would it still be there after all this time? That was a question that kept rattling around inside me. Neither of the maps mentioned a name for the location that we were supposed to travel to, all though both of them were marked, however one was marked more than the other.

The dream was so real even though it wasn't, and captain Maroo never told us about a hideout, at least not through words. This might explain the markings on the maps, but if there was one then why were the multiple markings? Unless there was more to it. One map had two locations circled on it, while the other only had one, I didn't understand the purpose of this, but perhaps it was some kind of test. This must've been a part of Maroo's secretive ways, where only he knew where to go and everyone else would have to follow.

Was it possible that he was still alive? Did he leave the maps to me as a test? To see if I could find him someday, No!! That was insane, he's dead, and there's no way he survived.

It was Fletch and I that asked him to sail here, and the crew didn't understand why but Maroo chose to trust us over them in the end. I wanted us to have a stockpile on land, in case we were sunk in our next battle with England. After battling two pirate hunters I thought the crew would've agreed with me, but they didn't. The fools thought that we could run and hide forever, and I thought Maroo felt the same, but if these maps were correct then I guess I was wrong about him. I still had my doubts about what I was supposed to do if I got there, and Fletch had made it pretty clear that he didn't want this squandered in any way; so even if I figured it out, I was still lost.

Fletch wanted to survive and leave it all behind, Maroo wanted to hide and rebuild, and me... well, I just wanted revenge, but maybe it was too late for that.

My thoughts broke as cannon fire went off in the distance, I tried ignoring it then it went off again, and this time it seemed like it was closer. I wanted to investigate but I was still weak and sore from my ordeals, and I'd have to wait for Fletch, who was hopefully on his way back. The cannon fire continued and it quickly intensified, then there was an explosion which came from further out. The daylight diminished around me, and the evening drew near, bit by bit it seemed. I was hoping that this would be a short night, but perhaps the dreaded day had arrived, and perhaps my reunion with the new world was here; and if Fletch didn't return soon, then I'd have to face it alone.

CHAPTER 10

The Choice

I waited for what seemed like an hour, and Fletch never returned from his swim. I stayed on my bed for the entire time trying to soak in every moment of rest that I could get. I could go and find the maps myself, but I was worried that my condition would hinder me. A cloud of smoke appeared from the northern part of the island, and I grew restless, so I had to do something. Fletch would understand, I just hope that he wasn't in danger. I retrieved my dagger and scanned the area around me, Fletch's salmon was nearby, and I'd need to eat it before heading off. I drank whatever water was left inside my barrel, then I gorged on my share of the fish, and my condition improved slightly. The maps were buried in a separate location from our camp, and they were difficult to preserve during the attack, and even within its tube the water still damaged them in places. It was time we started using them, instead of just staring at them like an exhibit.

I left the camp and returned to the patch of sand where I'd buried Fletch's pistols, and I figured it was best that I bring them whether I found Fletch or not. A familiar circle in the sand helped remind me where to look, and a couple of minutes passed while I uncovered them. I hoped that the sand hadn't damaged them, because if so Fletch would certainly be displeased. I moved towards a bush once I had them, then I poked into the sand with my dagger until it touched something that resembled a weapon. Fortunately I was right, it might be harder to conceal but at least it's easier to find. A few minutes passed while I uncovered it, then I brushed and shook the weapons of any sand that remained. It had been years since I'd held a firearm, I used one in the navy of course, but as a pirate I'd never used one. The weapon never sat well with me, it was too… convenient.

I ventured back towards camp and a few moments passed until there was movement from within it, then I ventured closer until a familiar face greeted me.

"There's been an explosion and cannon fire coming from the northern reef, I haven't checked it out yet since I wanted to check on you," said Fletch.

"Do you have the maps?"

"I do."

Fletch unveiled two dark brown cylinder tubes, and he threw one of them towards me.

"You've got my guns I see, I'm afraid they don't suit you."

"I haven't held a firearm for years, you're partly to blame for that."

"I apologised for that incident, I thought I could beat him."

I shook my head then dismissed it.

"I'm gonna eat my share of the salmon, then I suppose whatever water is left I'll drink as well."

"That'll be it for sustenance then won't it? There's nothing left after that."

"Yeah, there'll be nothing left."

Fletch gorged on his fish and water, then while he did I unravelled the map he'd thrown to me.

A strangely shaped island was imprinted on it, and large stone henges were also illustrated. This was the circled location, though there was no name, just markings. For memory Fletch's map had a menacing looking cove on it, one with protrusions and oddly shaped rocks. This was the other circled location, though like this one, there was no name. Non circled locations were also finely illustrated, like a grassy island that glowed, all though a black x had been imprinted within it. A red x generally meant treasure, but a black x was unfamiliar to me.

Fletch finished his fish and water, then retrieved his guns and carried my sword with him as well. He would have to fight in my stead for the time being, but I still carried my dagger. I could use it if need be with my other arm, but I doubted that it would bring much comfort.

We set out towards the northern reef, we each had a map with us, and Fletch took the lead while he had the sword. We made our way through the thicket of trees and bushes, taking care while we did, since the remnants of daylight were almost gone. Fletch fiddled with his pouches of gunpowder and shot, and he made sure that his guns were in good nick while he ventured towards the reef. The night arrived and we quickly prepared torches before continuing, then when we were lit, we kept going.

"We'll head to the northern reef to locate the source of the smoke, then we'll check out the other areas nearby."

"Understood, but if it's clear, then we should head back, ok?" asked Fletch.

"Ok, but only after that."

Fletch continued leading, and I followed him into the unsettling darkness ahead. A hissing sound came from nearby, and I shivered as my memories turned back to the boas. The hissing grew more frequent, and I tried blocking it out afterwards.

"Take it slow Fletch; that boa that we ate has a family nearby, and if we're not careful then we'll both end up with snake bites."

"Understood, but be ready in case we're forced to fight."

From the illumination of our torches there was no sign of the reptiles nearby, but we remained vigilant, then continued walking. A few minutes passed while we trekked, then the hissing stopped and I was relieved that only the sea replaced it. Numerous crabs scurried across the land while we searched, and they were all insect sized and therefore useless if we considered eating them. Several minutes later we reached the end of the mainland, where the reef and its sands awaited us.

We entered the domain and the smoke's source appeared up ahead, and we ventured closer and neither of us could believe our eyes. A burnt and blown apart ship lay in front of us, and its flames were still burning, and it was only a few hundred yards from shore. It would be impossible to identify at night, and we steered clear of it since its sight was so ominous. I tried ignoring it but its flames kept echoing in my ears, and soon the fire itself occupied my thoughts. All other sounds quieted as the fire replaced them, even the tide which I could barely hear while we walked.

"We should turn back Casper, there's nothing here but the ship."

"We should look for a little longer, at least until we reach the end of the beach."

Fletch grunted in protest, but continued looking while we walked towards the end of the beach.

"We don't have time for this Casper, we should head back and rest for the night: we can return in the morning."

"Someone might come looking for us though, and they'll be injured and alone out here."

"Whoever that someone is will probably be dead, if they came from that ship there not gonna last long."

Minutes later we arrived at the end of the beach, and only the tide kept us company, along with a subtle breeze that swished past us every now and then. The atmosphere was still, and there were no signs of life nearby.

"Let's head back, your right, there's nothing here."

There was silence between us while we turned back, and a few moments passed and voices suddenly spoke. Fletch heard the whispers as well, and we marched curiously towards them. Several torches suddenly lit and emerged along the shoreline, and we continued advancing while the voices grew louder. Fearful cries uttered nearby, then pleas for help; they sounded like women, and we approached the source of them. Six women were restrained and knelt into the sand before us, and my heart dropped while I looked at them. Several figures suddenly stepped into the light after, and before we knew it, we were surrounded along with the captives. I reached for my dagger and I was interrupted before I could draw it.

"Don't fight, or you'll die quicker than the women will," warned a female voice.

A large blonde woman suddenly emerged from the shadows, and to my horror she was like the one from my dream, burly and fearsome all round. She carried a large axe on her being, and it was almost a perfect reflection of the one she'd used in the dream.

"The commodore would like to talk to you and your comrade, and as you can see you are outnumbered, so I would suggest that you comply," said the blonde woman.

"Who are you to order us around? What is your purpose here?" demanded Fletch.

The blonde woman remained silent, then more footsteps quickly approached. Fletch was suddenly yanked away from me and replaced by an older and more imposing woman.

A middle-aged brunette approached me, and she wore rectangular glasses along with a grey coat, my memory suddenly kicked in, this was her! This was the source of my suffering, along with Fletch's. I seethed with anger as the images returned to my mind, and my temper boiled while they replayed themselves.

"I'm impressed that you survived our last encounter Mr Nait, but I did not expect to see you with a friend as well, that is truly extraordinary," said the commodore.

"You're the one that sunk the Revenant! Our lives have been lost because of you," said Fletch venomously.

"That's true, I am the one that ended piracy, and I will do it again if you don't keep quiet."

A crewman grabbed Fletch and prepared to strike him, then the commodore interrupted them.

"Keep him restrained but uninjured, we're not here for violence, at least not yet."

"Have you come to finish the job? Is that why you're here? To finish off two pirates with a crew as large as yours."

The commodore slapped me across the cheek with a firm cold hand, and my face quickly flared up due to the force.

"The reason I've come Mr Nait is to ensure that your survival is kept a secret, which is why these six women are here instead of Havana."

"I can't have them preaching about dead men that should've stayed dead," added the commodore.

My heart accelerated with her words, and my brain spun around while I tried thinking my way out of this.

"As I said before I'm impressed that you survived, but unfortunately the new world won't share my sentiment, so I must ensure that they never learn of it."

When she'd finished I tried to speak, and the commodore slapped me again and this time she hit me near the eyes. I cursed quietly while I recovered, then the commodore waited and I gazed at her while she looked at me with her stern brown eyes. The eyes told me that I should stay quiet, so I did.

"Instead of killing you however I wanted to offer you a choice, a choice that no other pirate has received, are you interested? Are you curious? Are you ready to hear it?"

I anxiously turned to Fletch, then I turned to the female crew, though none of them were looking at me. Fletch wrestled free of his hold and attempted to escape, then the blonde woman struck him with the butt of her axe, painfully knocking him into the ground. An eerie tension followed, and I could feel it in the air as it seemed that everyone was waiting for my answer, but I figured that she preferred me alive, so I moved against her.

I kicked the commodore in the thigh and rushed towards the mainland, then I turned around and Fletch attacked her crewman also. He desperately dashed towards me after, then when he caught up with me we ran for it.

It didn't take long for our adversaries to give chase, though half of them stayed behind so at least that gave us a chance. We reached the mainland and slowed down while we brush past the tree's, we were injured enough already, so I didn't want to risk any more cuts or scrapes. I wasn't sure where to go after, and the pursuing crewmen weren't slowing down. We reached a more open fielded environment, then my first instinct was to retreat to the camp, but I couldn't risk the hunters finding it; otherwise it would be destroyed by sunrise tomorrow.

While we kept running our chasers caught up with us, and I still had no ideas on how to lose them, so I turned to Fletch.

"I don't know where we can go, how are we gonna lose them Fletch? There's nowhere for us to hide or disappear too."

"I know, but maybe we can slow them down, or at least make things difficult for them."

I racked my brain trying to figure out what he could mean, what could slow them down here? Or at least make them think twice about following us? I couldn't figure it out.

"The rock walls Casper, they're tough to climb but we could lead them there, it'll be dangerous for us at night, but it's our best chance at slipping away or losing them."

I got a vague idea of what Fletch meant, and he was right, they were dangerous, day or night.

"All right then, rock walls it is, at least we'll all be in danger then, just hopefully not for the entire night."

CHAPTER 11

Slipping Away

We continued running despite feeling exhausted all over, and if we stopped now I doubted that we could get going again. Fletch and I adjusted to a jogging pace and our pursuers did the same, then a few minutes passed and our objective came into view. Large brown rock walls appeared nearby, and we reached the shoreline and stopped to take a breather. Our pursuers drew near and they stopped before reaching us, then the four of them rested while we were nearby. Fletch and I moved and our legs were unsteady, and while we continued urging them we tripped and fell onto the sand. I sucked in the brunt of the impact, then I remained still and allowed the coolness of the wet sand to relieve me. I didn't want to get up, I wanted to stay here and relax, even if it was ill advised.

Moments later I moved into a kneeling position, and I turned to see the pursuers hilariously tumble into the sand. No one moved after that, since the chase had taken everything from us, and I'm sure none of us wanted it to continue. We all had objectives though: so only the strongest would survive. Two injured men crawled towards us with swords drawn, and

Fletch brandished his pistols at them, and they quickly backed away like dogs.

"Your outnumbered pirate, even if you shoot us more will come for you afterwards; the shots will lure them here, so it's best that you surrender now," said the first man.

"We haven't done anything to deserve this, why are you here? What does your commodore want with us?"

The two men snickered and smirked, and I received no reply. Both men rose to their feet and Fletch responded.

"Stay where you are scum-bum, return to your lady now and I won't blow holes in your head."

"Weren't you listening tosspot? Shoot us and you'll only make things worse! So drop your weapons and come with us now... if you do that, the commodore may grant you mercy," said the second man.

There accomplices also rose to their feet, the first was a young fair skinned brunette with ragged hair, while the other was a gruff pale-skinned boy, whose face was covered with red marks.

I rose to my feet and met there gaze, then the two men pressed their swords against me. Fletch fired upon them and both men suddenly clutched for their chests, then they flopped onto the sand lifelessly. Their comrades saw what he'd done, and we immediately bolted towards the walls. The enraged crewmen quickly caught up with us, and Fletch was less fatigued than I was so I covered him. We approached the rock walls and Fletch prepared himself for the climb. The gruff boy engaged me with his sabre while I covered Fletch, and the angry woman did as well, with her two war axes brandished eagerly. Fletch dropped my sword before climbing, and I drew my dagger in order to protect him. I had to remain close to the wall in order to do that though, which would leave me vulnerable if they pinned me against it.

The boys sabre sliced towards my neck until I blocked it, then I pushed him away and the woman's axes swung towards me. I evaded her and she struck the wall, and she injured her arm then I kicked her into the rocks. I turned around to see Fletch close to crossing over, and I would have to try and scale it soon, since I didn't want to lose sight of him. I engaged the boy and he slashed towards me, and I blocked his blade and attempted a feint. The fool fell for it, and before he could recover I slashed his sword hand with my dagger, cutting him under the wrist while leaving him in agony as I passed him by. With him out of the way I focused my full attention on the woman.

She ran towards me and I attacked with a thrust that forced her into a half block, then while my thrust left her unbalanced I seized the edge that I had acquired. She pushed my twelve inch dagger away and I feinted her, then she stopped attacking, and I thrusted towards her elbow. She yelped in pain and I fled, then while she nursed herself I started climbing the wall. Fletch started his cross over while I climbed, and minutes later our pursuers returned to their pursuits. They seemed more focused on me now rather than Fletch, but there expressions probably concealed that.

While Fletch crossed over he stumbled slightly, however he made it to the other side until a sudden slipping sound caused him to fall. I couldn't help him until I made it to where he was, and he cried horribly and all I could do was listen. The two foes behind me quickly caught up, and I had to speed up which didn't help with my anxiety. I reached the top and Fletch was gingerly holding on for dear life, he was near the bottom, but he was in tremendous pain. It seemed that he was trying to recover before descending, but I was worried that he was risking too much with that idea. The boys hand grabbed my ankle before I crossed over, and I struggled to escape his grip. I couldn't shake him loose so I kept going, then the woman's hand grabbed it as well, which made it impossible for me to continue.

I unsheathed my dagger and swung it towards their hands, and they quickly let go then the woman unsheathed one of her axes. She hacked it towards my ankle and I narrowly avoided it, then I pulled myself towards the other side, however the woman grazed my ankle before crossing it. I recoiled fiercely and lost my balance, then my other foot rapidly slid down the rocks, and I was seconds away from slipping off entirely. I desperately grabbed the wall with my other hand, then the second, since the first was badly cut. Burning pain quickly grew inside me, and I had to find my footing soon, or I would fall a lot faster next time. I found something that wasn't the best choice, but if I moved quickly enough then I'd be ok.

While I continued descending my handholds suddenly cracked, and with nothing else to reach for I let go and prepared for the bad landing. Another handhold appeared and I reached for it, then my injured hand flared up, and I couldn't hold on any longer. I adjusted my body while I fell, then I landed on my shoulder and screamed in agony. My eyes watered, but I fought to keep them from crying.

Fletch was nearby and he seemed in relatively good nick compared to me, all though his knee was bleeding badly, and his arm appeared to be sore as well. I groaned, cried and cursed myself to my knees, then I cursed myself again since this had been a disaster for the both of us. But it wasn't over yet, and things would only get worse once the hunters were here.

A few minutes passed while Fletch and I nursed our individual agony, then I estimated that we had only a few more until the hunters were down here with us. I could barely move my shoulder while I worked through its pain, and it was the most incredible pain that I'd experienced in life. I'd have to rely on my snake bitten arm instead, there was simply no alternative once it came to combat. I hadn't tested it to see if I could swing a sword with it, but I imagine there would be some discomfort, but it had to be better than what my other arm was feeling. Fletch limped on his bloodied knee while I recovered, then he reloaded his pistols, which meant that his arm must be ok. He prepared his bayonet after reloading them, then the hunters swiftly approached. They were moments away from touching down from there descent, and I was too injured to stop them, however Fletch saw his chance to stop one of them.

Fletch fired at the boy and the shot passed through his neck, immediately killing him while he fell onto the rocks, leaving just the woman to deal with. Fletch switched over to his pistols since he didn't have time to reload it, but it was too late, the woman was here now.

"Save your ammo Fletch, we'll take her out with blades instead of shot."

Fletch appeared hesitant but switched back to his bayonet, then we approached her with caution. Fletch attacked by throwing his spare knife at her, though his technique was poor so instead of piercing her it just bounced off harmlessly. The woman grew angrier afterwards and the dreaded fight was upon us, with neither of us in good shape to fight her.

I drew my sword which Fletch returned to me earlier, and I used my bandaged hand to wield it, and like I thought, there was discomfort upon using it. It wasn't as bad as I expected, and if Fletch and I could end this quickly, then maybe I'd be ok for the time being. Fletch's arm appeared to be irritated as well, and he tried shaking it off but it seemed that using the bayonet would also take a toll on him.

"Your plan hasn't worked pirates, all you've done is caused yourself further pain, and they'll be more to come once the commodore has you in her custody," said the woman.

"You should've taken the hint lady, I've already killed three of your friends, so why don't you just leave us alone and go back to your English master," said Fletch.

"That won't happen, not until your pacified and captured by me," said the woman.

She prepared herself for battle, then attacked Fletch.

Fletch avoided her assault then she attacked me with a swift kick, which I weaved away from barely. I swung my sword at her and grimaced, then she locked her axe blades with my own and yanked my weapon away from me. She rammed the eye of her axe into my exposed shoulder, and I groaned intensely after its impact.

Fletch attacked her while she was focused on me, and he pierced her arm causing her to curse spitefully while she retracted it. She retreated and nursed her wound, then Fletch moved in while I stayed put. He thrust his bayonet towards her, then she sidestepped him and struck the attached tip. To both our horrors she severed the weapons tip, meaning that the attached blade was gone, and the weapon itself was now useless as a firearm.

Fletch retreated and rushed to reclaim the knife that he'd thrown earlier, and she advanced on him, and I lunged towards her. I pushed her back while Fletch was hopelessly out of contention, and we sized each other up in the meantime. Without Fletch's help I was vulnerable to this woman's skill, and I couldn't fight her with two weapons so I was even less confident than before. Reluctantly I drew my dagger, I had no choice now: I had to take the risk. My shoulder roared in pain while I moved it around, and my other arm hurt as well, with every attack I did with it causing it further pain.

I breathed heavily and concentrated on blocking it all out, it was kill or be killed now, and I've come too far to die here and now. She ran confidently towards me and swung both her axes in an overhead motion, and I moved in towards her and attempted to block them. I wouldn't be able to hold the block for long, but I just needed long enough to formulate a plan.

Her weapons crashed against mine, and I struggled with the weapon lock then adjusted my position. I moved my shoulder while holding it, forcing myself into a better spot to attack her. My arm was knocked back while I moved it though, and one of her blades skimmed across me, leaving numerous cuts across my forehead. The other one crashed against my skull, and the blunt trauma made me yell on the inside. I fought off its effects and tried keeping it contained, I had to remember what my plan was, and that was to hold on then strike back. The weapon lock ended and an opening came into effect, and I thrusted with my dagger and aimed it towards the crown of her forehead. The blade poked into her, but the impact was too weak to kill her, so I continued thrusting until it bled. I slid the blade down her nose after, then slashed the left side of her face. She screamed and retreated, then I grabbed her by the hair and weakly smiled as Fletch approached us.

Fletch plunged his knife firmly into the woman's throat, finally ending the battle, and all the dratted noise that came with it. I wish I could've seen her reaction, but I'm sure Fletch will indulge me with it later on. Fletch and I lay very still after she was dead, and we were overwhelmed by soreness and fatigue. I wished more than anything that I could just lie here for the night, but I couldn't, since there'd be more of them if I did. The woman's blood spilled all over my pants and hands, and the knife that had killed her was still stuck inside her throat. A minute or so later I moved the corpse away from me, then I offered the woman's axes as compensation for Fletch's bayonet.

"No, I'll take the boys sword instead, it's too personal to take the axes," said Fletch.

I helped Fletch walk with my uninjured shoulder, even though he didn't really need it. Both of us were very banged up, but I wanted Fletch to be more comfortable than I was, he was the youngest among us, and the least injured.

We walked towards the rocks and advanced further in, and other rock walls appeared nearby, but thankfully, we didn't need to climb them. We sat and rested behind a nearby boulder, then the landscape before us changed. A stone beach resided further ahead, and if we advanced towards it then we'd quickly lose cover. They'd be no more hiding after that, just running and running until we dropped dead.

"We'll have to hide out here for the night, and hope that none of her crewmen find us."

"What about in the morning? How are we going to return to camp?"

"We'll have to leave early, the longer we wait the more time it gives them to find our spot."

"So this is it then? We're leaving the Serpents crew behind? Assuming there still alive, are you willing to do that Casper?"

"Yes I am, this woman will do anything to protect her reputation, and she's not gonna stop, so we'll have to face her eventually."

"We don't have to face her, but you're right, she's not gonna stop, and neither will we."

"We have to do this together though Fletch, we have to be on the same side, otherwise there's no point in leaving here tomorrow."

Voices suddenly interrupted our talk, and they came from the other side of the wall. Even if they scaled it we were hidden, but there presence was enough to make Fletch and I nervous. If they found us in this state then we were dead, since there'd be no more fighting from us. I dozed off during the quietness until Fletch stirred me from it.

"I'll take first watch, you need to sleep Casper; you're no good to us like this."

I laid down on the hard surface and closed my eyes, and my pains kept me up so I tried ignoring them.

"They're gone Casper, I can't hear or sense any of the crewmen."

"Thank you Fletch."

I then attempted to fall back into rest.

Fletch removed his pistols from his belt, then gently placed them on the ground, probably to reload them I suppose. A pouring sound occurred and I assumed it was gunpowder, then the sound occurred again so I believed I was right.

"If we travel on land they'll almost certainly find us, and one of us needs to safeguard the maps," said Fletch

"So what are you suggesting?"

"I'll stay within sight of you until I signal that everything is all clear, then I'll cover your journey back to camp."

"You're leaving me? But I'll be caught? And if they find me then they'll use me to find you."

"You'll have to take that chance, but the maps need to be hidden, and you'll be easier to capture than I."

I wanted to protest further but Fletch's mind had already been made up, this was the plan now, whether I liked it or not.

"You can't climb with your shoulder so you'll have to swim back to shore, I'll climb the wall and cover you as best I can."

"Then I'd better get some sleep then, but wake me up when it's time to switch watches".

CHAPTER 12

Our Future

The dawn shined down upon me and I wearily sat up and examined the surrounding area. My body ached all over from yesterday's injuries, and I only managed to get a few hours rest at most. Fletch was still asleep so I carefully moved around him while I was awake, then my hunger and thirst took effect, and I'm unable to quench them. A few moments passed while I patrolled our environment, looking for any signs of scouts or sentries. I moved my shoulder around while I walked, and it instantly flared up in agony. The cuts on my hand and forehead didn't bother me, but if I got into the water then it'd be a problem in no time. Fighting would also be an issue, and like before I'd be at a disadvantage every time I acted upon it. I walked further towards the rock wall and the southern reef came into view, it was a few hundred yards away, which meant that I'd be in for a hefty swim once I started.

I returned to my resting place and sharpened my sword with my whetstone, a minute or so passed while I sharpened it, then Fletch started to stir. I continued sharpening in order to prevent him from oversleeping.

"I assume the area is clear? When you're finished we'll head to the wall and take a look beyond it."

"Yes everything is clear, once we reach the wall I'll enter the water and wait for your signal."

"You should probably let me go over first, I'll scope things out for you before you swim back to shore."

"Very well."

Fletch gathered his belongings then readied himself for the plan ahead. A few more minutes passed while I continued sharpening my weapons, then when I was done I placed them back on my belt. Fletch placed the maps underneath a boulder, then gestured for me to look away while he hid them.

"It's best that they stay hidden, if we're caught I don't want the commodore getting her hands on them."

"Hopefully they'll still be there once we retrieve them."

"They should be, there's no breeze or anything to blow them away."

"Are you ready? Without your bayonet you'll have to be twice as careful from now on."

"It would definitely help matters, but we'll survive, we always do."

Fletch continued limping on his wounded knee, and like my shoulder it was pretty banged up. We approached the wall and I surveyed the diving spots nearby, then I decided on one and Fletch started his climb to the other side. Fletch grunted frequently while he climbed, then moments later he made it to the top safely. He crossed over to the other side and disappeared from sight, then when he was gone I submerged my head into the water. The coldness cleared it of any fatigue I may have had, but the salt still stung even though I'd gotten more used to it.

I swam around the rock wall and my injured shoulder slowed me down, then I settled into a slower pace. I met up with Fletch and he headed towards shore, keeping his pistols in hand while he moved.

I swam towards a place to settle in while I waited for Fletch's signal, then I distracted myself from my shoulder pain by gazing into the water below. During the dawn I'd learned that the water here was always at its coldest, but I hoped that when I started swimming the temperature would improve. A warmer climate could do some real good for my body, but I would have to wait for Fletch first. I remained sceptical about the odds of our plan, but I admit having one of us on land was wise, and for Fletch I suppose that was better. I hoped that in the end both of us got off this island, because after everything that's happened, it simply had to be both or neither of us.

I continued watching near the rocks, then several minutes passed and Fletch called out to me. With the area clear I began swimming towards shore, but it was annoying that I'd have to travel slower than usual. I tried different swimming techniques to see which one was the most bearable, then I just free styled with one hand, and side paddled with the other.

Two things constantly pestered me while I swam, the first was the persistent pain of my shoulder, and the second was the constant chilliness of the sea. It bothered every part of me, and the tide continued moving me off course, forcing me to readjust frequently. The waves weren't very strong, but they hindered me every time they made impact.

Seagulls flew up ahead while I continued, and they flew towards the rocks in order to frolic and gather with one another. During my time here I'd learned to swim with additional weight, and it was something I'd needed to get used to while scavenging the wreck of the Revenant.

When Fletch and I had successful hunts we'd often go swimming together in the twin reefs, and when we had rainfall we'd also go swimming, and it was a beautiful experience for the both of us. All that time surviving and scurrying took a lot out of us, so it was nice to have some down time if we got any. The activities helped lift us out of our moods, and because of that, our spirits became brighter. I'd swam for about a hundred yards now, and my hunger and thirst quickly took over me. Apart from the birds it was quiet this morning, and they generally left as quickly as they came. I reached the halfway point and distance quickly became a challenge, my muscles ached terribly, and the water's temperature had not changed since I'd started.

I continued despite my bodies protests, and I focused all of my will on the shore and nothing more. Several minutes passed while I swam and swam, then I closed in on the shallows and lunged for the sands until I touched it. I dug my fingers in and rooted myself, I'd made it: I'd finally made it. I pulled myself through the water and grasped for the shore with one hand, then I continued doing so until I flopped onto the beach with a thud. A few moments passed while I lay there motionless, it was so relaxing to be on sand again, then I reluctantly pulled myself to my feet.

I unsheathed my dagger and looked around, Fletch was nowhere to be seen, and the beach was empty. A few moments passed while I continued searching, then voices came from the mainland. I prepared for combat and advanced towards them, there would be no hiding; I'd just have to trust in Fletch. A few minutes passed and I reached the mainland, then the voices grew louder until there were footsteps as well. Two gruff looking seamen revealed themselves, and I assumed that these were the commodore's men. The two men spotted me and immediately drew there weapons, and I waited for them to engage.

"We knew you would come here eventually, we located your camp so it was only a matter of time before you tried coming back to it," said the first seamen.

"Commodore Weiss will be very pleased to see you again, she has special plans for the both of you," said the second seamen.

They advanced towards me with swords drawn, and I quickly drew mine and waited for the first move. The first man thrusted towards my shoulder and I parried it away, then I quickly readjusted my stance. The second slashed towards my chest and I blocked it with my dagger, then my shoulder ached terribly. I pushed the second man away from me and slashed towards the first, and he blocked my blade instinctively and pushed me away from the both of them.

I was outmatched and there was no point in denying it, I just had to last long enough for Fletch to reveal himself. I slashed towards the first man and locked blades with him, then he pushed me away and his companion moved behind me. He slashed towards my shoulder and I struggled to block it, then he scraped against it with the tip of his blade. I squirmed and tried shaking it off, then he charged into me and pushed me into a tree. While I was trapped his companion approached me, and there was nowhere for me to go, and they pointed their swords at me.

"I surrender, all I ask is that you give me food and water before I leave with you."

"You're in no position to negotiate with us, so the answer is no," said the first seamen.

The second seamen released me, then roughly grabbed me from behind.

"Once you're on board our ship you'll be given whatever's required, but for now you'll go without, and you'll come with us to see the commodore."

"So Commodore Weiss, how long has that been in effect? I mean having a woman on board is dangerous enough, but having one in charge? Blimey! You English lads must be mad."

The seamen pushed me forward then started walking, and his companion followed suit.

"She was the one that tracked and killed most of your kind Mr Nait, I'd say she's earned her title after sinking your pathetic vessel," said the first seamen.

"But she didn't finish the job did she? I wonder what the colonials would think if they found out, I wonder what they would do if they learned that I was still alive."

The second man stomped on my foot in response and I grunted in pain.

"Be grateful that you're still alive, because if it were up to us then you'd be tossed into the drink right now," threatened the second seamen.

"But you'd still have to worry about my friend, and good luck trying to get to him."

"He's got nowhere left to hide and very few places left to run, it's only a matter of time before we kill him," said the first seamen.

Fearful quietness fell over me, they were willing to kill Fletch but spare me, why!!? Somehow I had to learn more.

"Why did you come back here? Or better yet why now? What led you here in the first place?"

"The insurgents did, we chased them here from Kingston under the governor's orders, but once they docked we spied on them instead of engaging them. We waited patiently until they were ready to leave, then when they did, we attacked them," said the first seamen.

A devilish smile crept across him.

"Pursuing them on the island would've required more time and effort, so instead we waited them out, then we ambushed them," said the second crewman.

"So that was the Serpent? You really blew there ship to hell back on the reef."

"Precisely, just like the Revenant before it, oh sure they tried to resist us and fight back, but they were too weak and too poorly trained to do so; then out of desperation, they gave you up, to try and gain clemency from our commodore," said the first crewman.

"They ratted me out? Just like that? And they call me a criminal."

"You are a criminal, the only difference is that you're a criminal without a crew, or at least you soon will be," said the second crewman boldly.

"He's still out there though, and eventually he'll take you both out."

"Maybe he will, maybe he won't, but in the end, he'll die here anyway, whether it's by us or by the island, he won't last much longer either way," said the first seamen calmly.

"So what's gonna happen to these insurgents? Or to me for that matter? Private executions? It doesn't have the same appeal as a public one."

"You'll live, for now anyway, as for the insurgents, well… most of them will die," said the second crewman.

"This seems like a lot of effort to keep me alive, she must've grown soft since we last met."

"The commodore has never been soft, but you'll soon learn that there are worse things in life than living or dying," said the first seamen.

I remained quiet while we continued walking.

A couple of minutes passed and we suddenly stopped, then Fletch emerged and the hunters moved towards him. Fletch shot the two men where they stood, and after opening up their chests they dropped to the ground simultaneously. I confiscated there weapons and Fletch reloaded his pistols in the meantime.

"There's no way we can leave here now, there's more of them around and I don't see how we can escape while there here," said Fletch.

"They know about our camp Fletch, and after those shots I'm sure they'll be on their way."

"With our ailments and injuries we won't be able to combat them, so what do we do?"

"I'm out of ideas pal, I need food, water and sleep: how are we supposed to get any of that with these mutts chasing us? We have to consider surrender, we might live if we do."

"I'm not sure what to consider Casper, but if we surrender: then we'll be surrendering our future, they want us alive but for how long? I'm sure we'll be dead even if we do."

"Maybe, but we'll never find out unless we try, and after everything we've gone through we have to survive, somehow, we have to live through this, we have to."

Fletch remained quiet then cocked his pistols.

"I've killed too many of them Casp, if we surrender it'll just be you that she spares, it's better if I fight them, then once I'm dead you'll be safe for the time being."

"No, I can't do this without you! You can't leave me after all that's happened, I won't survive."

"Casper Nait might not survive, but maybe somebody else will."

Fletch walked away and I grabbed his arm to stop him, and I desperately held on even though it was wrong.

"I can try and hold them off for as long as possible, but you must seek them out on your own, what happens next will be written in the stars."

"Your mind's made up isn't it? This is really happening."

"Our time's up Casp, but for what it's worth, it's been good."

"So you'll leave me for the stars huh? Well, tell me if any of them are still rooting for me."

Fletch smiled emotionally, then took his leave.

Two tears formed and escaped my eyes while I followed him, then while they did I struggled to keep pace. My ailments and injuries overwhelmed me, and I struggled to bear them and continued falling behind. Fletch continued on then noticed my delay moments later, and he turned just in time to see me collapse into the ground. Weakness and hopelessness consumed me, and it seemed like I was the one that was about to die instead of Fletch, who wanted to go out through bloodshed. Fletch arrived then lifted me up, and he struggled with the effort, since he suffered from the same ailments as I did. A few moments passed while Fletch tried again, then the effort became too great for him. He stopped and slumped next to a tree, then some voices moved towards us. I rolled onto my back to get a better look at things, while Fletch prepared himself for the coming conflict. My voice grew weak and parched, and I struggled to formulate words.

"You have to run Fletch, leave me behind and save yourself."

A man and a woman approached interrupting Fletch's reply, and my vision started to blur.

Fletch aimed his pistol at the woman, then was struck by a throwing axe before he could fire it. I struggled to tell, but I believed that the weapon punctured his throat, and even with my fading eyesight I sensed his body flop onto the ground. The two crewman then moved towards me, and I struggled with the thought of being alone with them.

"The redhead is dead, fool was just as weak as this one," jeered the man.

He lifted me up and carried me by my arms and legs, ensuring I was as uncomfortable as possible. A few moments passed then my eyesight blacked out, and my consciousness faded while the hunters carried me off. It was over.

CHAPTER 13

Blood Debt

I awoke to a strange new setting, and while I moved around a terrible feeling washed over me. My hunger and thirst still persisted, all though my fatigue was improved, alas not very much. I'm on a small bunk inside a cabin, and someone familiar was staring outside its window. I moved towards them and a voice interrupted me.

"Stay."

The figure turned around and Commodore Weiss revealed herself. The commodore wore a black coat instead of her usual grey, and inside of it was a concealed weapon, an epee sword. It seemed that the rumours about her were untrue, but nevertheless, the sword was impressive. The blade was like a needle, and its disclike handguard was spotless, the handle itself was black like ebony, and it glistened slightly until it faded from view.

"It's nice isn't it? The sword was a gift from Governor Manson, I got it shortly after I sunk the last three pirate vessels in the Caribbean," said the commodore.

"My crewmen thought that you were a knife person, since you ambushed us like one."

The commodore laughed and came towards me with food and water. Silence followed her while she did, and I learned that she wanted me to eat and drink before continuing. I feasted on one of the fruits that she'd brought me, then sculled some of her water to satisfy her.

"On the beach last night I tried reasoning with you, but after the deaths of my crewmen I'm now forced to make amends."

"Blood for blood has always been a pirate tradition, you killed all of my crew, so the deaths of yours should even us out."

"Well the crew doesn't see it that way, sure we killed your friend, but if they were in charge, you'd be dead alongside them."

"Then what do you want from me? I'm a pirate too, why would you spare me but not him? I don't understand."

"No I suppose you don't, but you will, if you do as I say."

"So I'm your prisoner then? You've kept me alive just to enslave me, you coward."

"You say that like pirates never did the same thing, your captain surely took prisoners at some point, but instead of profits it'll now be for blood."

I remained quiet in response, what was her intention? What would she gain from bloodshed? All this confusion ate away at me.

"My crew are now six men short, and because of this they have requested a blood debt from you, if you pay it and survive, you will be rewarded."

"Rewarded with what? You have nothing that I want."

"Life Mr Nait, you will be rewarded with life."

"An enslaved life, forget it, I'm not working for you."

"You don't have a choice, you can either stay here and rot, or you can fight, and possibly thrive alongside me."

"I don't want anything from you! Anything except your life, and any lives that dare to defend you."

"Well we're way past that now aren't we!? You'll never get that chance Mr Nait, so stop thinking that you will!"

"As long as I'm alive there's always a chance."

"Fool, doctors! You may enter."

Two women entered the cabin and they carried small boxes which they set down and moved towards me.

"These two women will tend to your wounds, then after their done you'll be escorted to the brig, where you will wither away until you die."

She walked out briskly and the two maids prepared themselves for my treatment. They started with my forehead, then moved onto my hand, then unwrapped my bandaged hand in order to peek under its deteriorating layers. They cleaned my wounds thoroughly then asked me to lie down, then they stitched me up and once they'd finished they packed up and left. When they were gone one of the commodore's crewmen walked in to fetch me, and they escorted me towards the brig. While I followed them my body ached from all the bandages and stitches that I'd been administered, and I struggled to cope with them, and I thought back to what the commodore had said.

She promised me a new life if I bled for her, but I had no idea if I should, all I know was that I wanted to kill her, her... and everyone that defended her. I drifted into hopelessness while

I followed, I was alone, and I wasn't sure how I was going to survive on my own. A hatch appeared and the crewman opened it upon arrival, then we walked down the stairs towards my new home.

Darkness immediately engulfed me, and only the hunter's lantern revealed anything resembling sight. The hunter continued walking and a few minutes passed until we arrived at a dank empty cell. I was forced into it and locked inside, then moans and pleas suddenly emanated around me. The pitch black hid them from me, and I was left to my bleak surroundings. The crewman left and quietness quickly followed, then I sat down next to the wall to reflect and think on my thoughts.

"You're the last one aren't you? The last pirate that they wanted so badly," said a woman's voice.

I turned and tried locating the mysterious voice, but the shadows were too thick.

"I am, they killed Fletch: they killed the only friend I had left in the world."

"I'm sorry, I'm sure Avery has regrets about what she did, but she was just trying to protect her friends."

"So your one of them? One of her friends? Did you support them attacking him like they did?"

"No, all though his attack was uncalled for."

"It was just a warning! Sure it was hurtful, but he had to do it in case you were an enemy."

"I guess so, but every action has a reaction, so they say anyway."

"It doesn't matter now, he's gone, and I'll be joining him soon enough."

"Why? You're still alive aren't you?"

"I'm not fighting for her, I'm not fighting for the woman who destroyed my way of life."

"If you don't fight then you'll die here, and your way of life will have died for nothing."

I remained quiet since she was right, but I wasn't in the mood for false hopes.

"Some of us aren't getting a chance to fight for her, instead we're getting sent back for execution; you should consider that before you rot away in here."

"What about Zaria? Is she getting sent back for execution?"

"No, worse, she's getting sent back for profit. The commodore hopes to make money off her from the governor, or some other interested parties."

"And I guess you, Avery and Bellamy are all sentenced to death?"

"Not me, she told me that I would have the privilege of watching my friends die."

"That's... horribly familiar, I'm sorry too."

"I'll be forced to fight for her anyway, because if I do I might be able to save myself, along with Daze and Leri, then if we live; we'll just be eternally imprisoned instead."

"For how long?"

"I don't know, but insurrectionists probably won't be leaving."

I stayed silent and tried processing what she'd just told me, this was worse than I could've imagined.

"What did she offer you? What was the worm that she threw into your mouth?"

"Life, she said that if I fought for her then I'd have a chance to thrive alongside her, so I'd have life, but it would be an enslaved one."

"It's still better than no life, and it's still a choice that you have time to make, you have to take it, you'll survive if you do."

"If I have to live under her thumb then there's no point in making that choice, survival doesn't matter if all manners of choice are taken away from you."

"So what will you do then? Stay here and die? Is that what you want now?"

"I don't know, I just need time to think and recover for the meantime, then I'll figure things out."

"If you won't fight for her terms than fight for a chance to decide your own, isn't that what piracy was about? To be free from laws and responsibility."

"It was, but we were forced into a life where you either followed the gold, or you hunted for it: that was the new world's precedent."

"That's a simple way to justify it, did you really believe in that?"

"I don't know, but I saw merit in it, and when it was spoken to me I didn't try to question it, I didn't try to question him."

"Him? Who's him?"

I sighed and contemplated my reply, then instead, I chose not to.

"I'm fighting to save whoever I can, and if you choose to fight then maybe we'll both live through this."

"Get some rest, it's like I said before, I need time to think."

"You won't get much of that here, but good night, and make your choice soon."

I moved myself onto the timber floor, and it dug into me while I tried getting comfortable. Sleep was like a distant thought, and my brain continued mulling over what it had learned. I closed my eyes and tried thinking on what I should do next, but nothing came to me. New life was the commodore's reward, but could I really trust her on that? She's spared me twice as of now, yet I still didn't know if she was honest or not.

My choices seemed to be fight for her, or fight for the chance to fight for myself, but did fighting really matter anymore? Now that I was alone in this world. I hated this situation, but it seemed like there were no alternatives: Fletch was dead, the Serpents crew soon to be, and if I did nothing, then I'd die also.

The question that still struck me was, what would I fight for? What was worth all the blood and death that I would surely face? Sentiment told me that it was Zaria, but I wished there was another. My options were limited, but doing nothing would mean that they'd evaporate right before me. A moment passed while my mind turned to Daze and Leri, then I quickly remembered just how much I hated them. The only option I had was Zaria, but it was a gamble, even if the alternative was to live and die under Weiss's thumb. The hatch door suddenly opened and two voices came towards me.

One of them carried a lantern while they approached, and they walked past me towards another cell. They banged on the cage and a prisoner suddenly stirred.

"It's time for your debt lass," said the first hunter.

She quietly rose to her feet, then waited for the door to be opened. The hunter opened then held the door while she exited, and I quickly reached out to them.

"Keep away from the bars pirate! Or we'll come in there and keep you away from them," warned the second hunter.

"I've changed my mind about the debt, tell your commodore that I've changed my mind, but I'd like to change the reward."

"If you live to see it that is," laughed the first hunter, followed quickly by the second.

"Will you tell her though? I'll start tomorrow if I have to."

"In your current condition you're in no shape for a blood debt boy, but I'll inform her of your change of heart," said the second hunter.

They escorted the woman away, and it was the tall axe woman from the cove. Her skin was tanned like mine, but it was foreign and most likely hailed from East Asia instead of England or Spain. Her hair was long and black, and it draped in a single ponytail, her eyes were brown and leathery, and her body was lean and athletic. When she was gone I lied back down on the floor, and I couldn't sleep so I tried meditating. The silence helped but the darkness didn't, I'd grown accustomed to doing it on the island, but its tranquil environments made it easier for me to concentrate. I missed the background noise as well, whether it was the waves, the wind, or even the birds, it all added to its atmosphere.

I cleared my mind and tried again, and it was difficult to hold onto, though I had to keep this luxury in order to stay sane.

I turned the tides back until I got what I wanted, and a memory of Fletch envisioned itself. It was during our first week on the island, and we'd just finished trekking the islands landscape. It was vast and difficult to memorize, but there was some joy to be had in trying. It was one of our better days on the island, and we were busy all week burying our dead, or sorting out our supplies, then scouring for alternate places to hunt or settle at. After what had happened we were both still very raw, and we still hadn't learned how to work together as of yet. Fletch and I barely talked with one another on board the Revenant, and he was one of the ships newest gunners back then. My role on the other hand had been accelerated, and instead of being on the vanguard, I was promoted to quartermaster.

It wasn't a role that I wanted, but apparently no one else was up to the task, and it became even harder when rumours spread about me succeeding the captain. Fletch and I were recruited in 1726, and only a few days separated us in regards to Maroo's service. We didn't become friends until a year later, and this was in the last three months of 1727. By this point the new world had become too powerful, and if we wanted to live, we had to change.

Most of the crew never believed that piracy was ending, and when captain Maroo finally accepted it, it was too late. His previous plan of running and hiding hadn't worked, but on the day of the attack we finally learned that this wasn't his real one. My memory stopped and I opened my eyes, then I let it fade from thought. I became calmer than I'd even been in the past week, and I quietly thanked the balance for this blessing.

The hatch door suddenly opened, and footsteps quickly approached. A lanterns light swiftly moved towards me, then it arrived and Commodore Weiss stood outside my cell.

"My crewman tells me that you've had a change of heart, but you think that you can dictate my reward to you?" Asked the commodore harshly.

"A new life under you is meaningless, but there is another reward that I will fight for."

"So what is this reward then? Freedom? You know that I will never grant that to you."

"No, but will you grant it to Zaria? Or grant a pardon for her and any crimes that she may have committed?"

"Pardons are no longer an option Mr Nait, and this debt has never involved them, so you're going to have to give me a second offer."

"Zaria then, if I fight and survive my debt, then you let her go no questions asked."

"I need her for profit, so no, but if you survive your debt then I'll let you leave this ship for good, you can stay on my island instead."

"Fine… I guess you win then."

"You'll be given time to recover from your wounds, after all my crew want strong opponents to fight, not weaklings, there's never any value in them."

"How long will I have to wait?"

The commodore smiled cruelly while she responded.

"You'll be given a week to recover, then after that, your debt will begin."

CHAPTER 14

A Taunt of Power

Four days passed since I was captured and imprisoned aboard the commodore's ship. I've remained in this cell ever since, and because of that I was oblivious to the ships routine. Yesterday Daze and Leri were moved into these cells as well, while I continued talking with the woman I'd come to know as Kaleen. Kaleen and the others had fought in vicious duels recently, and they all had wounds to prove it. Kaleen described them as brutal drawn out spectacles, structured to test you, and entertain others like never before. Daze and Leri had remained quiet ever since entering these cells, and they'd tried to deter Kaleen from speaking with me, too no success I might add. It was strange that she was, since she seemed so against me back on the island. But I suppose our current surroundings had changed things, so mistrust and resentment no longer mattered. Daze and Leri often tried provoking me, but when they did I always guilt tripped them with Fletch's death, which I partly did hold them responsible for. They stopped insulting me after that, and they stopped interfering with our talks as well.

"Who would you really fight for? If not for Daze and Leri who would be your first choice for this debt?"

"I would fight for Avery, but without Bellamy I would be scared that she'd fall apart without her, the two are like sisters, they can't be separated for long," said Kaleen.

"So where is Avery? Or Bellamy? Why are they not down here with us?"

"I don't know, but I assume there somewhere else on this ship, probably being subjected to worse things than us."

A bell sound rang and several voices shouted above deck, and I suspected that we'd arrived in Kingston. After she'd fought Kaleen told me more about this blood debt, or at least what she understood about it. The debt wasn't based on a normal blood debt's terms, and instead of revenge it was based on punishment. Instead of killing or dying for your debt, you had to suffer for it instead, which meant that you were tortured before you fought.

Kaleen was hesitant to go into much detail, but I got an idea of what sort of savagery I'd gotten myself into. The ship suddenly grew quiet, and a few minutes passed while our docking concluded. The hatch door opened and three hunters appeared and released the women, then they escorted them out and returned to release me. I was befuddled, and they beckoned for me to leave.

"We'll be watching you Nait, so be mindful of that while your free," warned a hunter.

"Stay in sight at all times, otherwise we'll drag you back down here by your ears," threatened another.

I left the brig last, but for the first time all week I was finally able to see the sea again. Three colonial ships were docked in Kingston's port, and from the deck they all looked to be a part of the commodore's fleet. I wandered and the hunter that released me kept a close eye while I did, while everyone else became preoccupied with disembarking.

The commodore led a group of hunters to the docks, and they had the Serpents crew in tow, except for Avery and Bellamy apparently. The commodore looked around as if she was looking for someone, but she couldn't find them so she quickly walked off into the distance. I figured that my time above deck was short, so I had to absorb as much of the surroundings as possible. The ship was painted grey instead of a usual brown, and its complexion was like smoke, making it seem dreary and hollow. The sails were white, and black dots were carefully spotted across them, making me think that there was some reverse symbolism at work.

Black cannons occupied the ships gun ports, and twelve of them stuck out even though I'm sure there were many more. I walked towards the helmsman's wheel which was painted with a dark brown texture, and there wasn't anything to see after that, but at least now I had a feel for the kind of ship I was trapped on. I moved towards the stern and stared at the bustle of Kingston, it had been many months since I'd been here, and it was strange to watch it all unfold in front of me. The noise and activity was still the same, and redcoat rats still patrolled off into the distance. Persistent merchants continued chatting up anyone fortunate, or not so fortunate to pass them by, and the commonality of this seeped into me. It was a world that I would probably never see again, but at least the views were nice, while they lasted anyway.

White timbered buildings still inhabited the city, and I imagined its sandstone looking manor was still intact. Large networks of markets and shops lingered nearby, and I think the tavern was near them, but it was hard to see off into the distance. It had been so long since I'd drank rum, but perhaps it was good that I'd had a break. If I ever got to drink it again, I would never take it for granted, never. A few moments passed while I observed the view, then a hand touched my shoulder, and I turned to see the hunter standing behind me.

He signalled to me that it was time to go, and I followed him back to the brig. When I reached my cell a huge heaviness fell over me, and a moment or two passed while I was locked back inside it. There was no one to keep me company now, so I sat down against the wall. I thought back to my better days, and my mind gradually stumbled towards Maroo. They were memories that I didn't want to revisit, and I tried sleeping instead of dwelling on them.

4 days later

The days couldn't have been more boring if they'd tried, but after learning some juicy news perhaps they'd finally start turning themselves around. Two days ago I was summoned to the commodore's cabin at night, and she wanted to inspect me after all this time.

"The governor of Kingston is coming aboard soon, and it is a special occasion that I am inviting you to," said the commodore.

"You will be invited under certain conditions, and if you agree to them then all will be well," added the commodore.

"I've also failed to find a buyer, so your maroon looking friend might be safe for the time being," said the commodore bitterly.

She paused then continued.

"The governor was fixated on your captain when he was alive, and Alva Maroo was a man that was greatly feared by him. I was tasked with hunting him down after his hunters failed, and that came with great personal cost to me."

The commodore dismissed me and my reply, and I turned to leave and held back my aggression.

"Do not reveal yourself to the governor, while you are on this ship you are a ghost, and when it comes to the outside world, Mr Nait no longer exists," warned the commodore.

She summoned me again on the next night, and this one was far more demoralizing than the last.

"Take off your clothes Nait, including your hat and bandana," ordered the commodore.

I gritted my teeth in rage, but I was in no position to argue with her. She set aside new clothes for me while I stripped, then forced me to wear garments that her crewmen no longer wore. Unclean smells entered my nose, and it seemed like these coverings hadn't been washed in weeks. I was given some of my usual apparel back, but it was either in a different colour or a different look. After I'd finished dressing she burned my clothes right away, then she showed me my weapons, which she'd cruelly had all this time. I was furious, but if I lashed out then everything would go wrong for me. All I could hope for, was that when my blood debt began, I could humiliate her in a similar fashion. Her visits were just a taunt of power, one that I'd had a taste of back on the island.

The quarter deck hatch suddenly opened, and footsteps quickly walked towards me, a hunter arrived outside my cell, then looked at me expectantly. He unlocked the door and I walked out, then he led me towards the quarter deck hatch. He unlocked it and then escorted me above. We ascended to the ships main deck, then I was led towards the commodore's cabin. He let me in then immediately closed the door behind me.

Zaria resided close by, and her brown eyes were fearful and unsteady. She said nothing upon my entry.

"As you might've guessed we are hosting the governor today on board this vessel, and the two of you are going to attend to our every need, is that understood?" Commanded the commodore.

"Yes commodore', said Zaria quietly.

She turned to me and all I gave her was a nod.

"The crew will be occupied by tonight's feast, and the cook will have his hands full with all the blood shed that will be spilled tonight."

"Bloodshed? Who's fighting or dying on your ship this time?"

"The Serpents captain and quartermaster of course, the main instigators of the wretched insurrection, yes we have a couple of ladies that can die for our dear governor today."

Fear quickly spread across Zaria's face, then she turned to me, and I became unnerved.

"The governor feels uneasy about a public hanging, and he only just reinstated some law and order here, so I offered him another solution, and he gladly obliged."

"Won't that be a short occasion though? Executions usually only last a short while."

"That's true, which is why it won't be an execution, instead it will be an exhibition match, to the death; the results will still be the same, but we've made it… more entertaining."

An amused smile crept across her, and I bit back my fury before it could take a hold.

Venomous thoughts bottled up within me, and by god I wished for the day where I could unload them: unload them all on this wicked excuse for a woman. But then again, perhaps the governor was just as responsible for this, after all, he was no friend of mine. He's the one that put the hit out on Maroo and his allies, and he was just as much of an enemy as Weiss was.

"Once this is over we can set sail from here, and once this is done Kingston should become orderly once more."

"Is there anything else we should know commodore?" asked Zaria.

"Yes there is one more thing, Once Mr Nait here starts his blood debt you will become an integral part of it as well, unless your sold off of course; but be mindful of that my dear, for his fate will be the same as yours."

"I suggest you watch the match closely Mr Nait, in order to fully absorb the severity of any sins you may commit," added the commodore.

She dismissed me after, and kept Zaria while I left, and she looked even more scared than before.

CHAPTER 15

Spectacle

The evening approached, and instead of returning to my cell I was asked to wait on deck. The governor was expected to arrive soon, and I couldn't wait to see his snivelling hide try and come aboard. A few minutes passed then the commodore emerged, along with Zaria who seemed relieved to be outside again. The commodore sported a navy blue attire, with her coat and pants taking on an admiral blue sort of complexion. I suppose this was what she was supposed to wear, at least when she was in the presence of proper men and women of status. Her brown hair and glasses had been cleaned, and she looked like a proper stiff of the English crown. She remained silent upon seeing me, then turned to one of her crewman.

"Go and welcome the governor, make it the best welcome you can, otherwise I'll throw you into tonight's game's."

They scurried off instantly, and disappeared from sight. A slight chill lingered in the air tonight, and the sun started setting in the west. It seemed like we were still an hour or two away from its departure, which was a pity since there'd be nothing left to look at afterwards.

Zaria approached me, and no one seemed to mind while she leant in and whispered.

"Why are you still alive? The commodore was obsessed with hunting you down and yet here you are, why?"

"I don't know, but I imagine it's not for compassionate reasons."

"She kept me and the others imprisoned because of you and your friend, there has to be a better answer then I don't know."

"There isn't, so if that's all you came to find out then you might as well head back."

"That's not all I wanted to find out, I want to know why you've committed yourself to a blood debt, and why I seem to be a part of it?"

"Because I was convinced too, and because you're the only one that tried to help Fletch and I: you're the only one that saw us as men."

"I still saw you as dangerous men, but you shouldn't have done that, you won't survive what's ahead of you."

"We'll see, piracy wasn't my first exposure to violence, before it I was once a naval man: so I've seen a thing or two when it comes to death."

"You have to call it off, if you must fight then fight for something else, don't get me involved."

"It's too late for that, besides if anyone deserves freedom here it's you, the colonials could easily mistake you as a slave, then they'll throw you in chains if you remain here."

"I won't be able to get away from them, the insurrection and the Serpents crew was my only shot at getting away from them."

"Whatever you had planned could still be achievable, but if you don't accept my help then you'll have no future: mine is already forfeit, but yours could still be saved."

"I don't believe that, especially if I'm sold tomorrow."

"That's one possibility, but it's not the only future that's open to you, not if you let me fight for it, please, it's the only thing that can keep me going."

"There must be something that you want in return, a pirate always wants something in return."

"All I ask for is your eyes, observe everything that you can so that if we talk again, we'll know more about the ship, the crew, and hopefully the commodore herself."

"This is so dangerous, I don't know if I can do this."

"Just make the most of it, you can do this, you have to, otherwise we've already lost."

"But what if I'm chained to the commodore's service? What if instead of slavery in Kingston I'm just enslaved to her?"

"Well that's a what if, and if that's the case then we'll find a way to use that."

"Do you truly believe in this plan? How can you believe in anything after what's happened to you?"

"I believe in balance, and in the certainty that the future is like sand, it always shifts eventually."

Zaria smiled with a slight awe in her face.

"Do you think they would've made it? The Serpents crew, do you think they would've got what they wanted in Havana?"

"You rarely get what you want, but they would've got something a lot better than what they've got now."

Zaria's reply was interrupted by conversations from the docks, and she and I assumed that the governor had arrived.

We subtly moved away from one another, then waited for our guest to come aboard.

The governor was a bulgy man, and he had a large round belly that logged around in front of him. He wore a silly blonde wig also, which made him look outrageous and almost womanly. He wore a green coat and white pants, which probably matched his hair if I had to guess. The soldiers helped this pathetic excuse for a man come aboard, and I smirked when he almost stumbled. He took little notice of Zaria and I, then scoured the ship upon arrival. His soldiers kept a close eye on him, and the commodore whispered to one of her crewmen. They shot off towards the docks, then headed towards one of her fleet's ships. The commodore signalled for me to approach, then signalled for Zaria as well.

"Get us some refreshments," she said quickly.

It was a shame, I would've liked to of overheard their conversations, but I suppose I would have to wait until later, when the nightmare began.

Zaria and I headed below deck, and we navigated our way around various crewmen while we did. We searched for the cellar or the kitchen, then asked a nearby crewman for directions. They pointed us in the right direction and a few moments passed until we reached the cellar. It smelled like bad breath, but I uncorked a bottle and had a little taste.

"What are you doing!? If someone spots you drinking that they'll throw you back into the brig," scolded Zaria.

"I just wanted a little sip, I haven't had this stuff for months! Besides it's worth the risk."

Zaria snatched the bottle off me and glared at me with her scathing brown eyes. I didn't take it to heart, and a few moments passed then she calmed down. She was quick to anger it seemed, despite seeming gentle at first. I grabbed a second bottle as a precaution, then we made our way back towards the main deck. A chant started to form while we climbed the stairs, and this quickly prompted me into wanting to know what was about to happen.

We reached the quarter deck and handed the liquor bottles over to the commodore, who dismissed us instantly. She poured a glass for herself and the governor, while Zaria and I walked towards the ships railing. I looked down below to see what all the fuss was about, and Avery and Bellamy were shackled below us. They were covered in bruises, and Avery appeared stoic while Bellamy looked scared.

A few minutes passed then two other crewmen joined them, and I feared the worst upon seeing them. Two large women stood behind them, and the first was the blonde that I'd met back on the island. The second was a stranger, all though she had similar features to her companion. She was a redhead with dark hair and a burly physique, and she carried an axe, one just as large as her counterpart. Both of them were dressed in leather clothing, all though the clothing looked more like armour than fashion. The redhead had pale skin and hazel eyes, and I immediately became alarmed as she was the woman that I'd seen from my dream. Both of them had somehow materialized, and somehow my consciousness had warned me about them.

It was like my worst nightmare had just become real, but instead of my captain it would be Avery and Bellamy instead. The chanting continued alas with brief pauses for drinking, then the prisoners were released by their captors. The monstrous women handed them swords, then they backed away after they'd armed themselves. Zaria struggled with her anxiety, and I couldn't help her, since I wasn't keen on taking their place. A few minutes passed while the chanting and drinking continued, then the commodore and the governor moved to address it.

"Loyal crewmen! Tonight we take the final step towards Kingston's stability, and with the death of these insurrectionists, we shall once again know order," said the commodore.

The crew cheered in response, while a few shouted in praise, then the commodore continued.

"As you have all requested, the governor has agreed to an exhibition match, a fight to the death between hunter's, and the hunted; after all, who doesn't want a little entertainment tonight!?"

The crew roared with enthusiasm, and the governor approached and they fell into silence.

"I would like to thank all of you along with your commodore for your efforts, you have helped resolve a very unfortunate mess, and you have done Kingston and England proud today; so thank you, and enjoy yourselves."

He moved away from the railing and the simpletons clapped in response. The commodore signalled for the match to start, then it did.

I moved to take a look while Zaria appeared reluctant to watch, and the commodore took notice of this.

"Go fetch us some food maroon," she said quickly.

Zaria reluctantly jogged off.

The four fighters were surrounded by cannons, barrels and weaponry, and the area was cramped with them making it tricky to fight in. The gun deck was a bad spot to be in, and it didn't help that two of them were pitted against such large and fearsome opponents. The hunted would have to keep their distance, otherwise they'd be destroyed.

Avery and Bellamy eyed their opponents carefully, then they feinted towards the redhead. The redhead resisted there feint then slashed towards Bellamy. Bellamy avoided the assault and stumbled into a nearby cannon, encouraging the redhead to follow her. The blonde attacked Avery, and slashed towards her in the same way as her counterpart did. Avery avoided it, then thrusted her sword towards her opponents arm. The blade pierced into her and Avery retreated and moved towards the redhead, who was almost upon Bellamy. The crowds cheering and jeering drowned out much of the battle, but if Avery was any kind of fighter, then she'd have to prove it here and now. Bellamy seemed hopeless against her opponent, so much of this fight would rest with her captain. The redhead swung towards Bellamy and Avery blade locked with her before impact, then she held on, and struggled with the effort.

Moments later Avery was shoved into a cannon by the redhead, and her opponent re-joined the fight, and smirked upon seeing Avery lying on the ground dazed. She rammed her axe towards Avery's face, and Avery dodged and she struck the cannon instead. She roared in pain while her hands struggled with the impact, and Avery moved away and kicked her in the face. The redhead suckered Avery and tackled her into a nearby post, then she banged her head into it leaving her groggy and heavily injured. She whimpered and fell to the ground, and I became concerned about her condition. Bellamy slashed towards the redhead while she was distracted, and the redhead parried it away without concern. Avery was helpless to help her, and she could only watch as her friend tried to get an advantage over them. The blonde recovered then re-joined her companion, and she advanced on Bellamy.

Avery urged herself to her feet, and the blonde bludgeoned her and she fell to the ground. The blonde charged towards Bellamy while Avery watched, and the redhead engaged her as well. The blonde hacked Bellamy's sword away from her, then the redhead sliced towards her ribs. The blade tore through her skin like parchment, and she screamed horribly, forcing me to cover my ears. Zaria returned and witnessed the screams of her dear friend, and I wanted to look away, but I held my nerve. The monsters didn't seem finished with her yet, and they smiled while Bellamy tried retreating from them. Avery rose to her feet with sword in hand, as if she'd been spurred into action by the screams of her friend. She looked groggy and sore, but I'd never seen a more determined fighter in years. The redhead noticed Avery's recovery, and she moved towards her without fear. She attacked Avery with an overhead swing, and Avery blocked it while the blade inched closer towards her. The impact brought her to her knees, and the axe inched closer and closer until she smoothly slipped out of the blade lock.

The redhead thrusted towards Avery's thigh with a blunt thrust, and she struck it savagely then immediately reattacked. She slashed towards Avery and she avoided it, then out of desperation, Avery rushed at her. She wrestled with the redhead who was caught off guard by Avery's recklessness, then they continued grappling with one another. Avery bit into the redhead's arm, then pushed her away and slashed towards her with her sword. The redhead blocked her with her other hand, then Avery skimmed her fingers with the tip of her sword. The redhead cursed in pain and Avery kicked her in the jaw, angrily knocking her into the ground.

Avery advanced then stopped, and the blonde held Bellamy by her hair.

The blonde released Bellamy and smashed the pole of her axe into the woman's face, supposedly knocking her out instantly. Avery's expression turned to horror, then into fury while her friend's fate remained unknown. Avery advanced towards her and the blonde stomped on Bellamy's face, leaving her further injured while she lay at the woman's feet.

The blonde charged into Avery and she stood her ground, then she knocked her into a nearby wall. A few moments passed while I lost sight of the duel, all though Avery's groans told me all I needed to know. The blonde planted Avery headfirst into another cannon, effectively ending her then and there. Moments passed while Avery appeared lifeless, then she looked up to me while the blonde's axe descended upon her head. Cheers and laughs were replaced with vigorous rounds of applause, then the crowd turned and excitedly talked amongst themselves. The blonde inspected Bellamy after the fight, and upon seeing no signs of life she let her be and assisted her redhead companion.

Despite being an unpleasant spectacle to watch, at least I got some insights into what to expect when my time came. With all the noise, violence and emotion I'd forgotten to check on Zaria throughout the fight, and she cried upon seeing the corpse of Avery.

I moved towards her and the commodore intervened, and I immediately disguised my concerns.

"Quite a fight wouldn't you say? Now you have some idea of what you will be in for once your time comes," said the commodore.

"Will I be fighting them? Because if I am then you might as well just kill me now."

"Oh don't worry you won't be fighting them, there only for special occasions, since there my enforcers. There my weapon of choice for crew disputes, or punishments."

I stayed silent while the hulking figures below remained fixed in my eyes.

"Remember Mr Nait, my crew wants this not me, I want you to live, I want you to thrive alongside me."

"That's surprising, considering I don't want the same for you."

"You should, because without me you won't survive here for long, after all, you wouldn't want to die without getting your imaginary revenge now would you? You wouldn't want to die as nothing more than Maroo's disciple on board this ship."

"I'm not his disciple, I'm just the man he chose to defeat convicts like you."

The commodore's aggression took a hold of her, then the governor arrived and she eased it away. The commodore signalled for her crewmen to take me back to the brig, then I was quickly escorted away. While I walked Zaria lingered in a corner by herself, and the governor noticed her nearby.

"What about the maroon commodore? Perhaps she should fight in the next exhibition match," said the governor.

I became furious after the governor's suggestion, since Zaria would have even less chance of surviving this savagery than the others.

I was escorted back into my cell, then I was left to process the mess that I'd just witnessed. I felt little for Avery's death, but she didn't deserve this, even if she did sell me out to the commodore. I don't know if Bellamy was still alive or not, but they'd probably still kill her if she was regardless. She was no match for either of those behemoths tonight, so giving her a mercy kill was probably the best thing that she could get right now. I had to get off this ship somehow, and I had to believe that Zaria would stick around long enough for her to help me with this.

CHAPTER 16

Memories

I awoke to the sounds of a distressed woman late at night, and I turned to investigate while two hunters came into view.

"Come with us girl! You're going to the brig whether you like it or not," said a hunter.

"You shouldn't have resisted the governor! You should've fought when you had the chance," said another.

Zaria came into view, and it appeared that she was the source of the distress. She was forced into a cell upon arrival, then locked inside it and left alone. She appeared to be hurt, both physically and emotionally, though I remained quiet. It was late and I wanted to sleep, and I'd already spent much of this week trying to get used to the timber floor. Remarkably I missed the sand, or I'd even take regular old dirt right about now. The hunters left and it grew quiet, and everything seemed ok. I pondered on how long it would take for something else to happen here, and it was a good distraction while I lulled myself to sleep.

Zaria mumbled to herself while groaning and sobbing, then she moved into what I assumed was a more comfortable position. She mumbled again while softly speaking to herself.

"I can't believe he did that to me, why would the governor force me to fight for him? And why did I resist? When I knew the governor would hurt me if I didn't?"

She paused then mumbled again.

"I have no choice now, I have to help Casper if I want to have any chance of leaving this place. But why doesn't he hate me? Why is he still fighting for me when I left him behind just like the others did?"

Zaria moved herself then stayed quiet, though she whispered frequently throughout the night.

Despite the uncomfortable surroundings it was peaceful here, and the tide swayed outside along with a faint breeze that blew infrequently. The atmosphere was perfect, and it guided me towards a much needed rest.

The next morning I awoke to an unusual quietness, there was no noise above deck, and Zaria was still asleep in her cell. Her wounds became visible, and it seemed that she'd been beaten or bashed for her defiance. I couldn't ask her about it, so I dismissed it from my mind. There was swollen bruising on both her cheeks, and her arms were bloodied, which made my blood sizzle with anger.

I put my ear to the wall to see if we were still moving or not, and we were stationary, yet I was puzzled as to why that was so. There were faint voices coming from the docks, so we were still in Kingston, but why? I moved away and thought about something else instead, then I decided to meditate and I moved myself into position.

I closed my eyes and concentrated on the peacefulness around me, then a few minutes passed, and I achieved serenity. My thoughts turned to Fletch, then to my captain.

For a year we sailed the seven seas together, and Fletch and I were a part of the original crew that had emerged during piracy's return in 1725. My place with them didn't begin until October of 1726, when my time with the colonials suddenly came to an abrupt end. I didn't know it back then, but I ended up meeting one of these crewmen at this time, a time where I was at my weakest, while they seemed to be at their strongest. Before I met Fletch I met a man named Alva Maroo, the newest face of piracy back then. Our first encounter was a strange one, since I was still reeling from the loss of my job. We met in a tavern where I was still a colonial, or at least still dressed like one, and he tried provoking me with his rhetoric's.

"What's the matter son? Did one of the tavern girls turn you down today!" laughed the old captain.

I didn't respond to his insult, even though I would've under usual circumstances.

"You're a stink in a stink free zone lad, why don't you leave and take your smell with you," taunted Alva Maroo.

I continued ignoring him then he came over and sat down beside me. Alva looked to be in his mid-forties at this time, and he looked weary and tired, yet he still had this gruff and chiselled feel about him. He had a short brown beard and pale blue eyes, and when I looked into them, he quickly learned that he had me.

"Perhaps you've finally learned that English taxes and wages are not for you, have you woken up lad? Have you seen what kind of hell you've dug yourself into?"

"Taxes and wages never bothered me, I liked my job: recruiting and training men was something that I was good at."

"Ah so that's what you were huh? A conduit between boys and men, taking them from the streets and preparing them for the hells that awaited them at sea."

"It seemed rewarding at first, helping men to fight for England's cause, sure we were strong and powerful already, but we'd only stay that way if we kept watch over that power."

"And now England has betrayed you? Just like it betrays everyone in the end, that's it right? You've learned the most important lesson of all, never trust royalty."

I breathed deeply then took another sip of my drink, and while I contemplated my reply Maroo cut me off.

"Jobs only benefit one person in the end lad, and it's never going to be you or I, because in that world, you're always expendable, your always cannon fodder even if you think you aren't."

"I wish I had learned that sooner."

'Aye, as do we all lad."

Alva got up to leave, and I stopped him out of confusion.

"Why did you tell me all this? What am I supposed to do with it?"

Maroo smiled and shrugged his shoulders.

"Whatever you want lad, but if you're looking for a greater existence, then keep your eyes out for more men like me; someday we'll be the future for this place, this place, and perhaps others as well."

He left the tavern and I thought about what to do next. At the end of the week he found me again, and this time he was alone, which apparently wasn't so last time. He told me that many of his crew had rebelled against him, after they'd learned that he'd partnered up with an unknown captain. His crew suspected that they were a fake or a fraud, but Maroo had done it anyway.

On that day I was forced to make a choice, and I chose to defend him from their wrath. The confrontation appeared in my mind, and it was Maroo and I against several other Revenant crewmen.

"You're gonna standby a boy that you met in a tavern less than a week ago? are you mad captain?" asked a Revenant crewmen.

"This boy has nothing to do with this, this is about you not trusting in me."

"We don't need a partner! You had one before and it only lasted a short while, then you fell in love and look what happened there," said another crewmen.

"Don't mention her!" Snarled Maroo.

"I'm telling you we can do this ourselves, we have enough allies, and we don't need any more captains," said a third crewmen.

A fight broke out then I learned the truth about him, and once it was over his crewmen lay beaten in front of us. I was told a story once about how captain Maroo sacked the city of Kingston, it was many years ago, but the shocking part of it, was that he took nothing. There was plenty to seize yet he and his crew took nothing, instead, Maroo attacked out of sport, choosing violence over plunder. Later on I met this captain that he'd partnered up with, an unfit man by the name of Thornton. He didn't seem like a real captain, and I had my doubts about Maroo's decision. Eventually I shared the same suspicions as the crew: that this captain felt like a placeholder, like they were being used by someone else. I raised these concerns with Maroo, but he dismissed them.

After a year of sailing with him all the pirates that had propped up followed his lead. Whether he was on deck or not, no one dared to oppose the man that had solely resurrected piracy from the grave. No one knew how he had done it, but it was remarkable that it had come back stronger than before.

Despite piracy being held together by two captains, everyone knew that Maroo was the backbone of this alliance; but I was still left to wonder, who our real captain was in the shadows. When 1727 arrived I was urged more and more to find out who Thornton really was, and who was controlling him. More of the crew became suspicious, but when I asked Maroo about it he again still denied it. Our numbers dwindled and all conversation about Thornton or our real captain started disappearing, instead I was left to try and find out what our captains plan really was.

The weeks passed by and Maroo became more reclusive and harder to talk too, and I suspected that something had happened, something that was changing him day by day. By the end of October I was forced to talk with Fletch, who was still a newcomer at this point, and was one of the less regarded people among the crew. Nine of us were left at this point, and he was the only one that shared my opinion of the captain. In November we took action against Maroo, while he refused to budge from his plan of running and hiding. The second hunter attacked us afterwards, then after its attack Maroo's mind seemed to change a little.

It didn't change fast enough though, because the third hunter came and nearly killed all of us. I harboured deep resentment for Maroo, even though he changed my life with adventure and plunder. He threw me a lifeline when the navy severed mine, and he offered me a renewed freedom which I'd never known in my past life.

But the man had secrets, dark secrets which were hidden away in that mind of his. Something in there sabotaged all that he had created for himself, and because of that it all withered away and died with him.

Everyone seemed to like him though, except when he sacked Kingston for sport. He had won the crew wealth many times in the past, and made the Revenant feared all across the Caribbean. But he had secrets, secrets which to this day no one has uncovered. Even when pirate hunters were coming after us the crew was still with him, but he was mostly lucky on those days that they were able to fend them off for him.

The memories passed and my true reasoning's returned to me, none of this mattered anymore, all that mattered was that I attain my revenge. My will was gutted, the deaths of Maroo and Fletch weighed heavily on me, but there was still a fire that refused to burn out. The maps were gone, and with it the hideout that they led to, and my clothes and weapons were gone also, which made me question as to whether I was actually me or not. My name wasn't even real anymore, it was just an echo inside me, or inside this ship. I opened my eyes and tears formed within them, my heart beat tightened as well, and its aches quickly seized a hold of me. Zaria suddenly awoke, and it was too late for me to stop now, so I didn't hide it while Zaria took her first glimpses at me.

CHAPTER 17

An Unsanctioned Act

I recovered from my emotional moment then moved to sleep for as long as I could, the hatch door then suddenly opened, and the sounds of crewmen woke me up. Hunters quickly came towards me and moments later they approached my cell, they glanced at Zaria also, then released us both simultaneously.

"What's going on? Are we going somewhere?"

The hunters remained quiet, then they escorted me out of my cell. They led me towards the main deck and when I arrived a large group of crewmen awaited me. They looked at me expectantly while they formed all around me. I don't know why, but they all stared at me, like I was a worm that they wanted to devour. A circle suddenly formed around me, and I was pushed into the centre of it by the hunters. Some crewmen nearby stood guard over Zaria, then one of the hunters approached me.

"The commodore has business in Kingston, so she has left us in charge of you, but she has strict orders not to kill you. We must follow them but for now we will bend them while she's away," said the hunter.

"I'm afraid I don't follow."

"The maroon refused to fight last night when she was ordered too, so you will give us the fight that she denied us instead. Then your battles will determine both of your fates."

"So what you're going to kill her? I thought the commodore wanted her for profit."

"She does, in fact she's out right now trying to find a buyer, but if she fails then we want to have a solution waiting for her when she gets back; hence this event that many of us have organised."

"The commodore said that I'd have a week to recover from my wounds, but even then, I would expect that I'd be given some notice before I fought for her."

"True, but we've grown impatient, and many of us don't like the way that she treats you, it feels too… personnel, so we're gonna soften you up, so that we can kill you quickly once your debt is due."

"So what are the terms then hunter? If I lose my fight does Zaria die as punishment?"

"Oh it'll be more than just one fight, but yes, if you lose any of them then she will die," said the hunter coldly.

The crew chanted when he was finished, and the hunter took the lead while they all joined in with him. A minute or so passed then another hunter stepped into the circle with me, and I guess they were my first opponent. A lean muscular man drew near, with blonde hair and two slashes to each side of his face. He was unarmed, so I assumed that I was fighting him hand to hand, and he wore brown and white clothes, while eyeing me rabidly with hazel eyes. He lunged towards me with a left hook punch, and I narrowly avoided it then moved myself to the right. I kicked towards his right foot and he blocked it and countered with a kick of his own. His blow caught me in the ribs, and I was winded while I tried easing myself back into the fight.

He advanced on me and I threw a left jab towards his nose. The jab struck him, and he stopped and retreated for the time being. He eagerly regrouped for another bout, then I threw a straight punch towards his face, and he avoided it and moved away. The hunter grappled with me from behind and I drove my elbow into his stomach, then I pushed him into the ground. Frustrated he lunged towards me, and I rammed my knee straight into his incoming head. He was left completely dazed after impact, and I grabbed his head and smashed it into my knee again. I elbowed him in the neck then he collapsed in defeat. The hunters stopped cheering when the fight was over, and the leader intervened while they stopped.

"Be patient, he's still got some fights to go, so let's not be sour over things just yet."

The crowd murmured to themselves and they seemed to be in agreement with the leaders words.

"Darrel, it's your turn, end this," said the hunter.

A tall slender man emerged from the crowd, and he had short brown hair, and funnily enough, a damaged nose. A part of his nostril had been removed, and it looked like a pistol wound had shot it off.

Darrel noticed me trying not to smile at his disfigurement, and he instantly became angry about it.

"Pirates did this to me! Now pirates will pay for it!" Shouted Darrel.

"Not this pirate I assure you."

The hunter roared with aggression, then attacked with a back fist towards my head. I avoided it despite the big man's size and length advantage, but the motion unsettled me.

I moved closer towards him and the hunter grabbed me by the shirt and lifted me into the air. He slammed me into the deck then choked me furiously, and the other hunters became worried.

"Darrel! We can't kill him, the commodore was very clear about that, you have to release him now," said the hunter.

"Just let me choke a bit longer! Pirate must suffer as I have suffered."

His grip was too strong to resist, and I quickly succumbed to it, it was almost impossible to breathe, and if he didn't release me soon then I'd die.

"Darrel!! I'm gonna count to five then your gonna release him," urged the hunter.

One, two, three, four, five! Do it now Darrel, or you'll be thrown into the brig in his place," added the hunter.

He held on, then a few seconds later he released me. I caught my breath then Darrel slammed my head into the deck angrily, and I sensed blood dripping from it after.

I coughed and spluttered heavily, and I was groggy and bleeding while I recovered. I inhaled and exhaled quickly, and I did this until my breathing returned to normal. My head and neck ached constantly, and I had no desire to get up off this deck. The hunter pulled me up moments later, then Darrel was escorted below deck.

"Pirate dog deserves death! Why doesn't commodore let Darrel destroy pitch faced man?"

Even while he was below he still yelled curses aimed at me.

"Let the pirate rest for now lads, then we'll reschedule his fight with someone else, someone who's preferably not so unstable," said the hunter.

While I recovered I walked around the ship, trying to regain my bearings for the muck ahead of me. A few minutes passed then I was called back into the circle, and Zaria watched me with deep concern. She should be concerned, both our lives rested with me, and I leant on the railing for a little while longer, then returned to the circle at the hunters request.

A black haired woman with dark skin awaited me, and she was skinny up top but had very stocky legs down below. They were almost like horse legs instead of human ones.

"All right Indy, have at it," said the hunter.

Indy leapt towards me with leopard like speed, and she kicked towards my face and I dodged just in time. She swept towards my legs and I partially lost my balance, then she fiercely kicked my knee causing me to fall while I tried recovering. Her stocky legs were painful and powerful weapons, and it was like being kicked by a deer instead.

She leaped up for another kick, and I intervened and struck her in the leg beforehand. My kick didn't seem to faze her though, and she countered with another front kick. I blocked the attack and it wounded me upon impact, and somehow I had to think about how I could stop her from using those legs of hers. If I couldn't stop them soon then I'd be too sore to fight against her, and Zaria would be dead if that happened. She kicked towards my ribs and I caught her leg, then I yanked her towards me. I elbowed her in the face upon reaching her, then she crumbled to her knees. She clutched her mouth and nose painfully, which probably bled if I had to guess, then while she was down I moved behind her. I kicked her in the back of the head, then while she recoiled in pain I grabbed her by the hair. I yanked her into my knee, then while she squealed I planted her head first into the deck. I eyed the hunters menacingly, then stepped away from Indy.

I walked away from the fight to nurse my injured limbs, and while I recovered the crowds cheering and jeering quieted. Several moments passed while I recovered, then Indy slowly rose to her feet. She struggled to stay there, though the crowd cheered while they were unsure if she would rise or not. Minutes passed then Indy stood firm, and while she adjusted I kicked towards her. She grabbed my leg and the kick connected into her stomach, then she sucked it in somehow, and held on by biting into my leg. She couldn't grip it the way that she wanted too though, and she released me and slumped back into the ground. I moved towards her and readied myself for a final blow.

"STOP!" Shouted a woman's voice.

I turned to see the commodore board her ship, and she looked unhappy at what she was seeing.

"You have all partaken in an unsanctioned act of violence! You have disobeyed my orders!! And worse yet, you have not only released the pirate, but the maroon as well; perhaps I have been locking up the wrong people," scorned the commodore.

"We were denied a fight last night by the maroon commodore, we thought it would be ok if the pirate gave us one instead," pleaded the hunter.

The commodore tried relaxing herself, and her enforcers were less than pleased with them. They brandished there axes eagerly, waiting for the slightest hint of the commodore's wrath.

"Why is the maroon free if you just wanted the pirate to fight? Did you intend to punish her as well?"

"Well, we thought it would be fun to place her fate in the hands of the pirate, if he lost then she'd die, but if he won, then she'd live."

"You thought that did you? You blithering fool! The maroon has already been punished, and does not need to be subjected to this spectacle. Put her back in her cell, then report to my cabin for punishment," scathed the commodore.

"Yes commodore, I'm sorry for disobeying you, I just wanted to make things right with the crew," pleaded the hunter.

"My enforcers are in charge of making things right with the crew, you knew that, and yet you still undermined me! But your right, you will be sorry," threatened the commodore.

The leader skulked off and took Zaria with him, then he disappeared from sight. The commodore then turned her attention to those that remained.

"The maroons fight was an unexpected request, one that shouldn't have been made but it was. We all know that we have to please the governor, which we did by punishing her for her defiance, but that was the end of it! So whose idea was it to carry out this treachery?"

Silence followed, and the commodore wasn't having any of it. She signalled for the enforcers to approach the crew, and they eyed there crewmen carefully, looking for any signs of guilt to pounce on. A minute or two passed without any confessions, and she and the enforcers grew restless.

"It was me commodore, Bobby and myself who you just sent away organised the whole thing," confessed a young brunette woman.

The enforcers smiled, then backed away.

"Vivien, well you know that I had clear plans for the pirate and the maroon, so you'll be sharing in Bobby's punishment when he gets back."

She nodded sadly, then the commodore approached me. Her two enforcers also approached me, and they watched me just as closely as they watched the commodore.

"How many fights were you put through Mr Nait? This is your one chance to punish us for our misdeeds."

"What about the maroon? I want to know what's going to happen to her first."

"Don't worry about her just answer the question!" Warned the commodore.

I eyed them sternly, I was tempted to lie in order to get the most out of this, but the risk of being caught was too great, so I reluctantly went with the truth.

"Three, technically two since my second opponent tried to kill me, but I fought three."

The commodore sighed heavily, then vulgarly stared at her crew.

"So... instead of a fight for a fight, you decided to add two more into the mix, well, because of this the blood debt is now invalid. The terms have been broken, and the victim is now free."

The crew protested in anger, and the enforcers quickly intimidated them into submission. Moments later the dissent finally settled.

"To make things fair everyone will be subjected to a fight tonight, because as I've said many times before, there is no value in fighting the weak."

Protests returned and the commodore didn't care, and the enforcers attacked anyone that didn't keep their mouths shut.

"Dismissed!! Back to your stations," ordered the commodore.

The enforcers spurred everyone into settling and returning to their business, then it was just the commodore and I who remained. We walked towards the ships railing for privacy, and the bustle of the ship died down.

"Are you injured? It seems like you fought well."

"It's Casper by the way, not Mr Nait, and I'll be ok, as long as I get to hurt those savages."

"You must understand Casper, I've asked them to do a difficult thing, to show leniency towards a crewmen of the Revenant, to show mercy towards a follower of captain Maroo. I understand there discord entirely."

"If you understand then why didn't you prepare for it? I was almost killed today, and your orders barely prevented that. Next time they might forsake the consequences."

"There won't be a next time, from now on you'll stay in my cabin, and you'll remain there until we reach our destination. This is not a request."

"Where are we going? If it's another port for profits or trading then please just return me to the brig."

"We're going to an island, perhaps we'll discuss it this evening, but for now, let's just say it's a place that we could all use right now."

She walked off while her enforcers eyed me closely. I walked towards the commodore's cabin which raised a few eye brows along the way, and the enforcers quickly warded them off and I opened the door and immediately closed it behind me. I walked towards the bunk that I had awoken on before, all though there was more that I wanted to do while I was here. I needed rest for the time being, and it was better to rest here than on the floor of the brig.

CHAPTER 18

A Walking Death

It was almost evening while I looked through the commodore's window. I'd spent much of the afternoon resting on her bunk, and it was hard to leave when you'd been deprived of such comfort for so long. I was unsupervised so I looked around her cabin without concern, but my search did not illuminate my understanding of this woman. There was a small painting stashed in the corner of her cabin, and it depicted her with a young boy, who I assumed was her son. There were books on her shelf but they were few, and one of them was labelled the art of duelling, while another focused on seamanship. There was a third book which seemed to be a story book of some kind, probably for her son if I had to guess. There were tools on her desk which included a spy glass, a compass, and funnily enough, a whetstone. There were also notes and letters from the governor of Kingston, and Governor Lee Manson had even put his seal on them. I had no idea why, but I assumed it was for ill intent.

While I read through the letters an old bounty came up amongst them, and it belonged to Alva Maroo, Manson's confessions were on it stating that he'd grown frustrated with Maroo outsmarting him, so he planned to put a hit out on him. I remember the massive witch hunts that he used to use to intimidate the city, as well as the public beatings that he used against anyone that was suspected to be with Maroo. This applied to anyone that knew him before 1725, so whether you were a past or present friend, no one was safe from his persecution. Other letters confirmed that Manson's original two hunters had failed to kill Maroo, and instead were killed in their own attempts. There was also an enquiry letter which showed the commodore's true name, and it also showed that there was still one pirate crew left unaccounted for. The crew's captain was named Neagan Bonnet, a name which sounded familiar to me. There was no other information about him, only that he had been missing for some time.

There were now three names that I could hold onto, all though right now I only cared about one. The cabin doors suddenly opened, and I raced towards the bunk just in time for the commodore to see me lying upon it. Strange sounds came from the bunk after I'd landed on it, and I was in an awkward position while the commodore seemed confused by my actions.

"I assume you had a good sleep? Must be a lot better than the floor of the brig."

"It is, though I'm unsure if I'll be sleeping on it for much longer."

"Most definitely not, you'll be on the floor next time, or maybe the chair if I'm feeling generous."

"There was no one outside my door when I awoke, no supervision whatsoever, aren't your crew concerned about that? About your treatment towards me?"

"I'm renowned enough now that they've learned not to question me anymore, besides, I've secured there futures, I've ended piracy and we can all walk away prosperously because of that."

"Your letters say otherwise, Governor Manson says there's still one pirate crew left unaccounted for."

"Ah you read that did you? Well there's no substance to that statement, besides, I did what he wanted, now it's time for what I want."

"What does someone like you want? Power? Wealth? What gets you out of that bunk in the morning? There doesn't seem to be anything left that you could need."

"I need peace Casper, I need normal, and that's what we're heading towards right now."

"Well I need you punished for what you did! You left me to die on that island when you could've killed me, but instead you left me looking like this! Now you've imprisoned me, like I'm some kind of trophy."

"What you need is peace Casper, and you won't find any if you keep treating me like I'm your enemy. I gave you life, twice! You'd best remember that before you insult me."

I approached her and she pulled out a knife, then she held it to my face while I emanated my anger.

"It's true that I left you for dead, and that's because I thought you would be. But now I'm offering you mercy. Your captain and crew are gone Casper, and I'm not proud of that but if it wasn't me then it'd just be someone else."

"So what does that mean? That I should be grateful to you? You're delusional."

"You haven't seen what I've seen, the pirate bodies hanging from the streets, the constant witch hunts in cities or towns, and the brutal floggings for anyone who tried to speak up about it. Ever since Maroo brought it back three years ago things have been worse, Maroo didn't care about any of it, but I did, and I couldn't go along with it any longer."

"So you joined up with them? You let them carry on with their mistreatment towards the misjudged, towards the wronged."

"I joined up so that I didn't become a martyr to my own son, I joined up so that the man I once loved didn't get strung up in a square for monthly entertainment."

I fell silent after her revelation, and shock followed in its wake.

"I was like you once, I was inspired by Alva Maroo back in the day: so much that I tracked him down and joined up with him. We became close in 1725, and for a time we were seen as a power couple in the pirate world. But a year later that started crumbling around us, so I tried pulling him away from it, and I failed."

I processed her words carefully, and they shocked my brain, then my mind dwindled, dwindled towards the one mystery that remained unanswered.

"It was you then? You were the captain behind Thornton? Behind the placeholder that Maroo teamed up with? It was all you?"

The commodore remained quiet, and she looked at me without words.

"You sabotaged our world!! Destroyed not only mine, but his as well."

"I had too!! But it wasn't enough to stop him, so I joined the colonials, and condemned half of my crew to join them."

"You sacrificed their lives to hunt my captain!?"

"I sacrificed their lives to stop him! And I promised myself that I would stop him, nobody else, just me. Despite everything that he'd done I wanted him to die with dignity instead of dejectedness, he deserved that, in memory of what we had."

I lashed out towards the commodore in rage, and she slashed me under the nose, causing a trickle of blood to drizzle down my mouth and chin. I cried in pain and retaliated against her, and she kicked my injured knee and I slumped into the ground hopelessly.

"You may have lost Maroo and the Revenant Casper, but at least you lost them on my terms instead of England's. Instead of being strung up in a noose or lost at sea, Maroo is now buried in the ground where he belongs."

I stayed quiet while I nursed my injured face, and I used my toque to stop the bleeding, then the commodore dropped a rag in front of me. I used it instead, then when I'd finished I threw it at her desk. The commodore put her knife away and concealed it in her boot, the crew was right all along: she was a knife person after all.

"So what does this mean for me? Am I just a thing to be concealed from the world? Something to be hidden away? That's not mercy, that's a walking death."

"You're a ghost that I choose to preserve, a last bit of string that ties me back to the old world. I didn't realise it back then, but it's good to have something to remind you of what this was all for."

I was dumbstruck and infuriated upon her response, her words were like a twisted nightmare, one that I was forced to bear forever it would seem. What happened to this woman? Too much from the sound of it, but it wasn't enough to saint my anger. I was alone in the world now, where as she wasn't, she had a son, a crew, a position of power that most could only dream of; where as I was left with nothing, nothing but defeat and despair. My mind overloaded with thoughts, and my head suddenly ached because of it.

"Maroo cared about you Casper, but before you it was me, and you ended up filling the role that I'd vacated. The only difference is that you wouldn't have been enough for him, but I would've been, if he had chosen my love instead of his war. He would've lived if he had, and if you'd just stayed out of it then you would've been happier, you wouldn't have been hurt like I was."

"You lie! It's more likely that Maroo chose a pirate's life over a false romance, if you truly loved him then you would've stuck by him, but you got scared: so you betrayed him. You betrayed him, and you betrayed the black."

I rose to my feet and the commodore approached me, then she unsheathed her knife and held it towards me, looking very tempted to use it.

"You're making this very hard Casper, I don't want to kill you out of respect for what you've suffered, but you're making it more and more tempting by the minute. I've seen enough blood to last me a lifetime, and if you were a better man than I would've thought that you'd feel the same."

144

"I did the best I could with the time I had left, there's not many people in the world who can say that, but Alva and Fletch were two of them, and you're the devil that killed them both."

I shoved the commodore into her desk, and instead of provoking her, a sickening smile suddenly formed instead.

"The crew want your blood, fine, I'll give it to them, drop by drop, day by day, until you have none left to bleed. It might not satisfy them at first, but once they see the misery in your eyes, they'll come around. Then! Once you reach my island, everything that you've lost, will be nothing!! Compared to what they have taken from you."

"Hunters!"

Seconds passed then two hunters answered the commodore's call, and they waited outside her cabin.

"Tie Mr Nait's hands to the desk, he'll remain here for the night, but it will be the longest night that he can remember."

The hunters left to go fetch some rope, then while they were away, I desperately searched the cabin for anything that I could use. The commodore watched me while I searched, and I disguised my intentions while she did. The hunters returned several moments later, along with my short time frame for searching.

They punched me in the chest upon arrival, making me low enough for them to bind and restrain. They tied me in rope cuffs then tied them to the nearest desk leg. When it was done the commodore dismissed them, and she walked out of the cabin leaving me alone while she closed the door behind her. It was silly of me to provoke her, but at least now we understood each other. If I am to suffer in her clutches then so be it, I'll prove to her once more that I'm stronger than she knows. She seems to have a code that she thinks makes her better than me, but if I survive what's ahead, then I'm sure the truth will be revealed. I have her name as well as the name of two others to fuel my anger for what's ahead, and in this environment, anger is all that I need. Revenge will be mine one way or another, and if I can't have her life, then I'll take her son's instead.

CHAPTER 19

Escape

It was just past dawn and the commodore awoke from her bunk. I'd had a few hours' sleep at most, and its effects were already wearing me down. I moved myself into an upright position, while the commodore prepared herself for the day ahead. My stomach grumbled in the meantime, and the food and drink that I'd been given was enough to live on; but I suspected that I'd been withering away ever since I arrived here. A few minutes passed then the commodore came over and severed my bonds, and when I was free she untied my hands as well. She helped me to my feet and said nothing, then she left the cabin while everything around me became heavy. My body wanted to lie back down again, though I resisted it, otherwise I'd be stuck there. Two hunters suddenly entered the cabin, and they escorted me out immediately.

"We'll talk more tonight Casper, since I'm sure we still have much to discuss. But for now you'll remain in the brig until I summon you."

I was too sluggish to respond, and the hunters took me away before I could think of a reply. Walking was a huge effort, and while we approached the brig the hunters dragged me until I reached my cell. Upon arrival I was thrown in and locked inside, all though a part of me was glad to be lying down again. The other part of me whinged in pain, as the impact hurt and diminished my condition. A few moments passed then I forced myself to my knees, and my vision was cloudy, and Zaria's cell appeared to be empty, leaving me alone. I had no idea where she could be, and my mind couldn't function due to the overwhelming fatigue inside of me. Wherever she was I couldn't think well enough to try and guess. Sleep was my only option now, so I just had to hope that I was feeling better in an hour or so.

I awoke however long after, and my mind and body seemed considerably improved. I don't know how much time had passed, but I didn't care, because I seemed close to normal again. While I regathered myself I sensed movement nearby, there was no mumbling or talking, so it didn't seem like pirate hunters. I waited and more sounds occurred, and I speculated on who it could be. I couldn't come up with an answer, so I waited for it to reveal itself.

"Casper," whispered a woman's voice.

It rang familiar until its familiar face revealed itself.

"It's good to see that your still here, it would've been a disappointing boat ride if you weren't," said Kaleen.

"You sailed here? But you were sent off to prison, how'd you get out?"

"It seems we were sent in on the right day, because the prison became disorderly the day after we arrived. A prison break was attempted, and because of this we were able to get out."

"We? Who's we? Oh wait, don't tell me."

"They said they'd help me with this then they'd part ways with me, I tried changing their minds but they wouldn't listen."

"That's fine with me, but why did you return? You could've been free yet you sailed here, to save the pirate? Surely they don't approve of that."

"Both of my friends were murdered by the commodore, and I can't forgive that, so I didn't know who else to turn to. Against reason I decided to try you, did I make the right choice?"

"If we can get out of here, I'll see to it that you did."

"Good, then we better hurry, because if I'm not back in time, then the other two will leave without us."

Kaleen set cloth and oil beside her, which made me curious about what she was planning. Kaleen wrapped the bottom of the brig door with cloth, then squirted it with oil. I moved away from the door while Kaleen unravelled a flintlock pistol, then she used it to ignite the cloth. She set it ablaze and the fire sizzled and rose.

"Wait, don't move yet," said Kaleen.

Moments passed while the fire quickly spread, then it covered the cell, and I wanted to protest her plan.

"Charge at the door, do it now!" said Kaleen.

I ran and crashed into it, and the door held prompting frustration from me.

"Try again, ignore the pain and crash through it: trust me."

I charged at the door again and there were voices above deck while doing so, then I crashed against the iron and it crumbled beneath me. I grimaced as some burns singed my arm, then groaned again as the impact wailed inside of me. My shoulder stung but I was free, at long last. We moved towards an exit and a pirate hunter came down and saw us. Kaleen immediately grabbed and held him by the shirt, then she pushed him into the fire. He didn't burn from it and he reached for us, then I kicked him back into it and we ran. He screamed and this told us his story, and I didn't feel any guilt whatsoever.

We raced towards the gun deck and there were voices which had taken notice of what was happening.

We opened a gun port out of urgency, then prepared to climb out towards the sea.

"My mother's sloop is close by, but we'll have to swim for it," said Kaleen.

I agreed with her then she climbed through, and she dropped into the sea below. I followed her lead then dropped in also. While I descended Kaleen swam close by, and I resurfaced beside her, then immediately shivered while doing so. We nodded to one another then dove again, and I followed her lead while we swam for our lives. My time on the island had thankfully improved my diving skills, but I was still weak when it came to holding my breath, all though my underwater swimming had vastly improved.

I dived for twenty seconds then resurfaced, and Kaleen seemed to be the better diver between us, all though I kept pace with her despite this. I continued my pattern of diving for twenty seconds then resurfacing for five, and in those five seconds there were angry shouts coming from the commodore's ship. I continued swimming with Kaleen until she spotted the sloop, then she led me to its docking point. Several minutes passed until I reached it, then Kaleen was helped aboard by Daze and Leri. I boarded moments later, then remained quiet while I tried recovering from the coldness of the sea.

"We did what you asked Kaleen, once we're ready let's get out of here," said Daze.

"We need to return to my island, I have some supplies there that could help us."

"You mean Twin-Reef Island? Why? You were stranded there remember?" said Kaleen.

"I have a map there that could lead us to a new home, it's a hideout that my captain and other captains financed before they died. No one knows about it so it'll be perfect."

"Perfect for you, we're not looking to hide out, we're looking to rebuild our lives. If we can reach another port then we'd be able to do that," said Leri.

"She's right, Leri and I aren't interested in a life on the run; we just want to settle down and start again," said Daze.

"I don't think that's an option anymore, if the commodore finds you again then you won't survive next time."

"That won't happen, because Kaleen will get us far away from her," said Daze.

Kaleen remained quiet, and brooded instead of responding.

"Since it's my sloop I vote that we return to Twin-Reef Island, I can get us there in a few days, and the sloop will have enough provisions for the journey."

"Do you have weapons? We might need them at some point."

"We have a few swords and muskets that we took from the colonials, but I'm afraid we have little to spare," said Daze.

Leri reached for something behind her, and she threw a dagger at me, laughing mockingly while I received it.

"That's it!? There has to be more."

"I can toss you another dagger if you like? But the real weapons will stay with us," said Leri.

I sneered at her, then examined the dagger.

"All right enough is enough, let's set sail for Twin-Reef Island, before the commodore learns of our location," said Kaleen.

Kaleen adjusted her main sail and lifted her makeshift anchor out of the water. Then she took up the sailing position, and the sloop started moving.

It seemed as though the commodore's ship had not spotted us, and a few minutes passed while they cleared out of our trajectory. Once we were safe from there clutches I examined the dagger again, wanting to pass the time and be alone for the moment. It had a slight curve at the end of the blade, and the handle was black instead of the usual brown I was more accustomed to.

"So what's your name pirate? Since we'll be sailing together for the next few days?" asked Leri.

"It's Casper, and that pirate that you almost killed, his name was Fletch, remember it well cow pat."

"That was uncalled for, we did what we thought was best for us, his death isn't our fault," said Kaleen.

"Maybe, but you sure as hell didn't do him any favours."

"We didn't expect a commodore to be so interested in castaways, after all, you're supposed to be dead," said Kaleen.

"I would've been, if you had gotten your way. Or if the commodore had followed up with hers."

"What do you mean? It seems like she left you there to die," said Kaleen.

"She could've killed me before that, but she didn't, then she left me to die. But now she's not interested in killing me."

"After that escape I'm sure that's changed, we might've just used up the last of her compassion," said Kaleen.

I didn't have a reply, so I acknowledged that she could be right.

"Do you know her from somewhere? Is she working for the governor?" asked Leri.

"I'd never met her until Twin-Reef Island, but it seems our paths were always close together. She was a pirate once, then a pirate hunter, but now, I'm not sure what she is."

CHAPTER 20

Life before the Sea

With the morning behind us I took over for Kaleen, and she requested rest after successfully rescuing me. Daze and Leri had been quiet ever since we left, and they chatted amongst themselves while watching the horizon with interest. I wanted to learn more about them, so I moved towards them to try and foster some peace.

"Where will you go if you leave us? I'm sure it would be safer if you stayed with Kaleen and I."

"With Avery's death we feel that it's better if we run, we'll start over just like she wanted, and we'll go to Havana just like she hoped for," said Daze.

"It's a long journey but it's a good place to start over, hopefully in a city that's less corrupt," said Leri.

"It's a safer place but it's still got its share of injustice, are you sure you won't reconsider? I'm sure Kaleen could use the help."

"We're not fighters like her, we'll just be a liability if we continue alongside her. Besides, we don't have the same goals, not anymore," said Daze.

"She's your responsibility now pirate, she's lost her friends, her relationship with her mom, and any chance that she may have had at living a normal life in Kingston; so you better make all that sacrifice worth it," said Leri.

"She's not the only one who's lost things, but she saved my life, even though I'm a pirate that still means something."

"Commodore Weiss has a fleet behind her, a fleet Casper! How do you plan on getting through that? This vendetta that you both have will not end well," said Daze.

"Maybe not, but I don't have a past life to return to, piracy was all I had, without it I might as well be dead."

"You must've had something before piracy, can't you give that another try? Even if you were a castaway," said Leri.

"No I can't, because there the reason I joined up with piracy."

"Well maybe it's changed, give it another try, if not in Kingston then somewhere else," said Daze.

"I'm not giving the Kingston navy another try! Not on your life, or anyone else's. Besides, it's too late for that, it's too late for me."

Both girls fell quiet after my outburst, and a few moments passed then I tried changing the subject.

"Why did you follow Avery? If she and her friends committed insurrection then why did you help her? Shouldn't you have done the opposite?"

"She was a voice for Kingston's mistreated, she spoke up, she interfered, she incited, and when things reached breaking point, she led. Bellamy and Kaleen helped but she made the people feel important again, regardless of their status in society," said Leri.

"So what happened then? If she did all this then how come only six of you were on board that ship? What about the others?"

"They were killed, the governor came in and put down all resistance. Avery and Kaleen fought against him, but eventually they had to flee, just like the rest of us. It seems the commodore was assigned to capture us, and well, you know the rest," said Daze.

"Yeah, you led her straight back to Fletch and I."

"If you had left us alone then she wouldn't have learned about you, Avery had to give you up, it was our only chance at clemency," said Leri.

"That words means nothing to her, she'll do anything to protect her reputation."

A lone dolphin suddenly jumped out of the sea, and we all paused to admire the joyous occasion. The dolphin followed us and Daze and Leri seemed thrilled by its movements, then a few more of them joined in and they all jumped and splashed in unison.

"How much do you know about Governor Manson? As a pirate I never gave him much thought, but my captain did, and as a colonial my dealings with him were limited."

"He's a classic monarch, he demands everything be done in a certain way otherwise it'll be redone until he's satisfied. He also likes to preach about his laws, making sure everyone follows them to the latter," said Daze.

"He doesn't sound that different from the other governors, does he still go to the establishment often? Or does he go somewhere else now? I'm only asking so that I can keep track of him."

"We used to work at the establishment where he often visited, but that was years ago now, after we lost our jobs there we stopped caring about the governors habits," said Leri.

"Did you work for an associate of his? Someone with close ties to him? Or was it just a regular hotspot that he liked?"

"The owner had close ties to him once, but with his death we only ever dealt with his son, Neagan Bonnet," said Daze.

"Did you say Neagan Bonnet? He was in the commodore's letters aboard her ship, but he's a pirate, how could he run an establishment? It doesn't make sense."

"A year after we lost our jobs we learned that Bonnet had gone missing, we were approached by a shrouded figure who made it happen, and that was the end of it," said Leri.

"But who was the figure? Or the original owner? Why is this all smoke and mirrors!? Damn it! I'm sorry, that was inappropriate."

"That's all we know, we never learned the figures identity, and the original owner, well… it was rumoured that he became a pirate," said Daze.

It seemed like tracking this man down was impossible, and I pondered on this while I brooded. Daze and Leri assessed the troubled looked on my face, and they waited, then spoke many moments later.

"We're gonna swap with Kaleen now, since we need rest as well. Considering you're our best fighter I think we need you on watch for as long as possible," said Leri.

"As long as I get to sleep at night that's fine, but I've been awake since dawn, so I know a little about tiredness as well."

"You'll get your rest at night, the only question is, what are we gonna do at night?" asked Leri.

"Depends on what the ship has, I'll ask Kaleen about it later."

We farewelled each other then the girls approached Kaleen, who they stirred from sleep while quickly explaining themselves as to why. Meanwhile a Spanish schooner appeared close by, it was better than an English one, but any contact with other ships would be a nerve-racking experience for us all. A sharp wind suddenly came into effect, and Kaleen quickly leapt into action in order to keep us on course. The schooner didn't pay us any attention, but I still hoped that its course didn't intertwine with our own. The wind passed and everything returned to normal, then Kaleen came towards me, and she spotted the schooner as well. Kaleen said nothing while it sailed nearby, so I spoke instead.

"After Twin-Reef Island I guess we'll be heading to Havana next, I hope there's enough supplies for the journey."

"We could stay at Twin-Reef Island for a day or two, fish, scavenge, but after that I'll have to honour my promise to them," said Kaleen.

"You didn't answer the question, will we have enough supplies to reach Havana? You might have to drop them somewhere closer, like Port Royal."

"Port Royal is too close to Kingston, and I doubt they'll agree to that. If we can find extra food on Twin Reef then we should be ok, all though water could be a problem."

"If we reach Twin Reef there might be some water left in my water barrels, assuming there still there of course."

"You should be more concerned about whether your map is still there, if it's not then we have nowhere to go, and we need that desperately, otherwise this is already over."

"It'll be there, I just hope that this hideout is everything that I hope it will be, it has too; otherwise it wouldn't exist."

Kaleen didn't respond, and moments passed while I stayed quiet.

Birds flew across the horizon during the silence, and the atmosphere was peaceful, as the birds, the sea, and the ship contributed to it.

"I lied when I said I had no one else to turn to, before I came looking for you I sought out my mother. I hadn't seen her for months, and she was my last tie to Kingston."

"Is she ok? Did something happen to her before you…"

"She's alive, but she's afraid of me, so afraid that anything I say to her is rejected. She's a physician who helps people, so was I once, until I betrayed her."

"You fought for people in Kingston, that's what Daze and Leri said, you and your friends fought against colonial injustice. That doesn't sound like treason to me."

"Yeah I fought against colonials, and I killed my friends because of it. I was the one who suggested it! but instead of doing it alone like I should've done, I got them involved; I convinced them to kill like I did, when I should've just let them live their lives."

"Fighting against authority is never easy, but you survived it and now you've learned from it, not everyone can say that."

"I learned what the price of freedom feels like!! It feels like holding your best friends body after they've drowned! After you've fished them out of the sea alone. Then you look for your other best friend, but you know that deep down, there gone too, probably dumped into the sea as well."

Tears streamed down the poor woman's face, she tried controlling them but she couldn't, and they quickly flowed continually.

I took off my shirt and offered it to her as a tissue, and she took the sleeve of it gratefully. She turned away and wiped her tears, then when she was calmer she turned back around and finished wiping her eyes. I put my shirt back on to conceal my wounds. Kaleen's clothes were tattered and messy from her ordeals, and her dark blue garments were torn and spotted with holes. Her large brown eyes were frazzled, and her long black ponytail was disorderly. Her east or south east ethnic skin seemed ok, but it was far from its optimal health.

"Before I became a pirate I was once a colonial, I trained boys into becoming men, and I made a difference in their lives; but it turns out I was only prolonging there suffering. They didn't want to be there, and the system made them feel the same way, but in the end I did the best I could with the time I had left; That's all any of us can do, and it's all that's required when it comes down to it."

"But you tried helping them in an environment that couldn't care less, there's not many people who would do that."

"I was different back then, more innocent, and less damaged."

"So was I, except that I thought this would work, it felt right, it felt like…"

"Destiny, it felt like destiny."

"Yeah, it felt like destiny."

I walked away from her then turned around.

"Since you fought against colonials in Kingston would you be able to duel against one more? We could use the practice."

"I'm not supposed to give you a sword, the other two won't like it."

"It'll just be for this, I'll get my own somehow, and maybe they can join in later on."

Kaleen looked conflicted, then a few moments later she obliged.

"It would be a nice break from the scenery, and it would be good to keep us on our guard."

A minute or so passed and Kaleen handed me a sword, then we prepared ourselves for our duel. Leri awoke moments later, then she saw what was about to happen.

"What are you thinking Kaleen!? You're giving him a weapon and planning to fight him as well, put them back," demanded Leri.

"We're just duelling each other Leri, we're going to need practice when we encounter the commodore and her crew again," said Kaleen defensively.

"We told you before that the pirate doesn't get any of our weapons! They belong to us, so unless he duels you with that knife then you'd better put that sword back," scathed Leri.

"What have I done to you huh!? Did I rob you at some point? We're just trying to pass the time here. Besides, I heard that Kaleen fought colonials in Kingston, so I wanted to see how good she was."

"Well once you get your own weapons then maybe you can find out, but for now, think of something else to do!"

"Maybe you should duel me instead? Let's see how good you are without your friend to back you up?"

"I don't need to prove anything to you, but since Kaleen doesn't seem to understand your threat level, we're going to move the weapons."

Daze woke up moments later and saw what all the commotion was about. Leri was handling it, through scolding just like she usually does.

"Who put you in charge of the weapons anyway? Shouldn't it be Kaleen? Considering this is her vessel? Your authority is mute on this matter."

Leri snatched the knife off me in retaliation, and she pointed it at my face before storming off with all the weapons. An awkward silence followed in turn, and we all separated while the tension remained. It would be a long few days it seemed, since another power struggle had been created just like before.

CHAPTER 21

War

Dusk arrived and we finished our meals for the day, then Kaleen organised a game of cards for the girls. While this happened I sat alone in a corner of the sloop, fiddling with the knife that I'd recovered from Leri earlier. I reflected on past events, but also reminded myself that I'd need rest sometime soon. The commodore occupied my thoughts, and I wondered what she was up to, would she come looking for us? Or would she continue sailing towards her island? As much as I wanted to kill her, I had no idea how I would do it. I'd been told repeatedly that she was too big, but there had to be a way. I was no assassin, I'd killed before of course, but I was more accustomed to just inflicting pain upon others. Maybe that's what I would do, after all, I'd dreamt of it back on the island. Torturing the commodore was something that kept me alive back then, but now that I know she has a son, perhaps hurting him would be even better. His suffering would be an alternate path for revenge, but I'd have to make sure that she was unable to stop me from achieving it.

When I first became a pirate I tried bringing my naval morality to my brethren, in order to save them from becoming savages. Civilization already believes we are, but I refused to be labelled as one. We were the men and women of old, the free men who kept what was theirs and gave nothing back: it was simple, it was fair, and it was natural. The women on this ship are the ones I used to fight against, two of them I literally had, they were the enemy, and yet here I am alongside them. Despite their opinions they weren't far off from my world, they still think that there higher beings, they still think that fate will fall into place for them; but they'll soon learn that there wrong, because fate falls into place for no one.

I lied down and overheard Kaleen explaining the rules of her game to the girls. A few moments later stars formed in the sky, and I couldn't help but stare at them. I remember Fletch telling me about the stars on that fateful night, and I wondered again which ones would hurt or help me. It was a surprise to learn that a former gunsmith apprentice from Nassau took such an interest in this sort of thing; but maybe there was a hidden wisdom to it all. I closed my eyes and the noise from the girls died down, then several minutes passed until I rested. I could hear the sea inside my mind, and I imagined the hideout atop it.

It was one of the last things I had left to look forward to in this life, and I tried picturing it atop crystal clear water. Seaweed green grass also appeared, along with a tavern and a dock. Would there be any remnants of civilization at all? I hoped so. I imagined a house, or at least a hut of some kind to put things inside of, I would need something like that, something to make me feel alive again. The girls suddenly grew loud, and

I struggled to hold on to the paradise that I was envisioning. A few moments passed then I awoke, and I shook off any lingering tiredness that remained. Kaleen came over to check on me, and she waited while I regathered myself.

"Would you like to play a hand?"

"Sure, I guess I can give it a go."

"You'll be taking on both of them, and the game is called war, which is as bloodthirsty as the real thing; from a card games perspective that is."

The objective of the game was to acquire all of your opponent's cards, and you do this by splitting the deck in two, then overturning the top card of the deck. Whichever card has the highest value wins, then the winner adds both cards to their pile. But if the cards value are equal then war occurs, which means two extra cards are added in. The first is played face down while the other is placed face up, meaning whichever face up card is greater wins the whole stash. It seemed simple and fun, and I'd heard of this game in the past but never actually learned how it was played. I was up against Leri first, and she seemed very interested in the game. Daze was behind her, and she too watched with interest. Kaleen shuffled the deck multiple times then rapidly dealt out the cards with precision; Leri and I eyeballed each other while she dealt, then when she was done we readied ourselves for the game.

Leri flipped over a jack of diamonds, while I flipped over a two of spades. In the second round I flipped over a queen of spades, while Leri revealed a five of hearts. In the third round Leri flipped over a king, while I revealed a four, and in the fourth round I flipped over a queen, while she flipped over a six. In the fifth I won with a ten, then in the sixth she won with a jack, it was so back and forth that it seemed like it could be anyone's game. Several rounds later Leri and I triggered our first war, since we both flipped over an ace. I had two more pairs than Leri, but this war could potentially change that. We flipped over our cards, and unbelievably, this led to another war.

We each overturned two's, then as a result we repeated our last motions. I flipped over a jack while Leri flipped over a five, and she was devastated, since this gave me a huge advantage going forward. Leri won the next few rounds, but by the end I had eight more cards than her. Leri was sour after losing to me, and she made it very clear to everyone nearby.

"I want a rematch!" shouted Leri.

"No, you lost Leri, now it's Daze's turn if she chooses," said Kaleen.

"No thanks, we'll do our own thing now," said Daze.

Daze and Leri wandered off to their own part of the Sloop, and Kaleen smirked at me while Daze mumbled under her breath.

"There not one for games I suppose, they prefer results instead of probability."

"I don't think it's that, I think they just couldn't handle the thought of losing to you," said Kaleen.

"Am I really that bad? I've done nothing to them, in fact it's the opposite."

"There difficult at times I admit, but they have qualities as well."

"Like attacking pirates without reason? Oh yeah, there's some fine qualities for you."

"I hope your being sarcastic about this? I'd hate to boot you off my ship."

"After rescuing me that would seem like a waste wouldn't it? But of course, I'll continue to play nice."

Kaleen nodded in thanks and gathered up all of the cards, then she shuffled and put them away.

"I don't suppose you'd be up for a game? I could use a more skilled opponent before I sleep. A game or two could benefit you as well."

Kaleen continued shuffling the deck without answering, then she placed them on the surface in a fierce show of confidence.

"My mother and I used to play this often when I was growing up, these cards were passed down to her by my grandmother, and they've been with us for as long as I can remember."

"So does that mean that you'll play? As a way to remember her? Maybe this deck of cards is more than just a game for you."

"It was a treasured tradition, something that brought us together in times of need, but now it seems that our relationship itself has become war. We're on different sides now, and we're both taking losses, but who's going to end it I wonder?"

"If we survive long enough then it will be you, once we have what we need then you can try again with her."

Kaleen began dealing out the cards for both of us, then a minute or so passed until we each had our respective piles.

"You better be right about this map Casper, because if you aren't then it will be hard for me to keep you here."

"If you maroon me then you'll have no one to help you, and after those girls are gone, you're going to need that."

"Well hopefully it won't come to that, otherwise that would be very unfortunate for both of us."

Kaleen smirked, then placed her hand on top of her pile.
I placed mine on top of my pile also.
"Are you ready for war pirate?"
"I'm ready for war, insurgent."

CHAPTER 22

The Revelation

The next day arrived, and Kaleen woke and informed me that it was noon. I'd slept in longer than I thought, and I was a little embarrassed because of this. We were almost at Twin-Reef Island, and we were only a few hundred yards away from it. Everyone had their weapons at hand, which seemed odd but I kept that to myself. I lied down again since I wanted more rest before we docked, and fatigue waned on me, so I wanted as much energy as I could get before leaving. Several minutes passed and Kaleen dropped anchor, then we all waded towards shore. We split into two groups upon reaching it, with Daze and Leri heading off to find supplies, while Kaleen and I searched for the maps. Silence followed while we walked across the sand, and I turned to look at Kaleen who had her hand closely resting against her sword. Perhaps she was serious about her threats last night, and if so, I hoped I was strong enough to answer them.

A strange splashing sound came from further off shore, and it seemed like an animal was nearby, but I couldn't be sure. The weather was warm and breeze free, just how I liked it, unlike my previous days on this island. We reached the rock walls and Kaleen suddenly stopped, and I turned around to find out why.

"We're gonna swim around those instead of climbing them, it'll be quicker and safer, since the weather is calm," said Kaleen.

I didn't try and argue with her, and Kaleen removed her pistol then headed into the shallows. I'd done this swim many times before, and on a calm day like today, it would be nice despite the deepness beneath you. I entered the water and my drowsiness improved, then I swam and I struggled to keep up with her. It may be quicker than the rock walls, but I wish she'd chosen climbing instead. I stopped trying to keep pace with Kaleen, though she didn't seem to notice. A few minutes passed and Kaleen found a spot to pull herself up on to, then she exited the water and noticed that I was lagging behind. She gestured with her arms for me to swim faster, and she seemed restless while she waited for me nearby.

A few minutes passed then I powered towards her, reaching for the rock as it slowly drew nearer. Kaleen grabbed my arm and heaved me onto the rock, then we rested in the meantime.

"Do you remember which rock you hid it under?" asked Kaleen.

"I've got a decent idea of where it is, but you might have to work with me a little."

"As long as it's there then there shouldn't be a problem, but if it's not, then things will get messy."

"There's no one else here so it shouldn't have gone anywhere, but let's get started."

I dried myself off in the sun along with Kaleen, then when we were dry we set off to look for the maps. We arrived at the furthest section of the rock walls, and I searched under the boulders hoping that Fletch had hid them like he said. Several moments passed and I looked under a boulder that I thought was the correct one, there was nothing there, and my heart sunk in horror. I searched under the others in case I was wrong, and like the original, there was nothing there. I searched the remaining area until I'd covered the surrounding space, the maps were gone! And I pondered furiously on what could've happened to them. Did the commodore find them? Did Fletch lie or destroy them? Did the weather blow them away? I wish I knew. While I pondered Kaleen realised that I'd failed to find them, and her frustration quickly seized a hold of her. She drew her sword instinctively, then gradually lowered it.

"I freed you with the hopes that you would have something to offer! But it seems that I was deceived, because you have nothing! Do you? No maps, no allies, no resources, nothing! I was foolish to waste my time with you," said Kaleen.

I couldn't respond, maybe she was right, maybe I did waste her time, it was a hard thing for me to contest right now. Kaleen breathed heavily and a few moments passed while she tried composing herself, then she pointed her sword at me, probably contemplating whether she should use it.

"When the other two find out about this they'll vote you off my ship, and I won't be able to defend that."

"Give me a reason why I should defend that," added Kaleen.

"Because they're going to abandon you after Havana, do you really want to be alone after that? Let me find another way to help you."

"I'd like to believe that Casper, but I don't: so don't bother coming back, because your life is here now, back where it belongs."

Kaleen shook her head then waved goodbye, and she kept her sword fixed on me as a precaution. I was powerless to stop her anyway, because without my own sword I'd have no chance against her. When she was comfortable she dived back into the sea, then swam towards the shore. I wouldn't be able to keep up with her, so I had to think about how I could keep myself from being trapped here; again. My only option was to seek out Daze and Leri, and there's no point in searching for the maps any longer.

Fletch's body could still be on the island as well, and if his body was still intact, then I had an obligation to bury him with the others. My mind sunk into hopelessness, but if I acted fast then perhaps I could preserve it. I dived into the water then swam towards the southern reef. There was a pebbly beach that I could've walked on, but the swim seemed like the more comfortable option. Several minutes passed and I arrived at the reefs shallows, and it was warm upon arrival. My body ached while I traversed the water, and it seemed that my imprisonment was taking effect upon my body. It was no longer used to the strains of swimming, and the days aboard the commodore's ship had diminished whatever strength it had left. My chances of finding Daze and Leri were slim, and if they were already back at the ship then I was finished, but I had to try, otherwise I was finished regardless.

My hope is that my camp is unfamiliar to them, so I would rely on luck while I went looking for them. A jellyfish suddenly appeared nearby, a small bright blue one which scared me half to death while I swam towards the shore. My body wailed from all the swimming that it had done, and I became hungrier by the minute, but I had nothing to remedy it with. I reached the shore and the pale crabs greeted me, which didn't help with my growing hunger. Water was also a concern, and I hadn't had any for quite some time. I lied on the sand and rested, then I tried focusing on my breathing, while my heart beat frantically. A minute or two passed then I pressed on, and I walked towards my camp, hoping that someone, or something, was still left there to be found. I walked slowly despite the urgency, and while I headed inland I kept an eye out for snakes. My thoughts turned to the evening when the family of boa's attacked me, if things had been different then I could've been dead from that weeks ago.

The bites had long healed by now, but I still hadn't forgotten the pain that came with them. Something up ahead interested me, and while I moved closer there were patches of blood on the grass nearby. There was no one around but I still wondered, was this his blood? Did these drops belong to Fletch? And if so, where was his body? My instincts told me that we were close to where we ran on that day, but I couldn't tell for sure. Maybe the hunters took his body, but that seemed unlikely so I dismissed it.

I searched for any signs of additional blood nearby, and a few more drops appeared, but there wasn't a trail or pattern of some sort. I continued looking around and more droplets stained the sand, which made me wonder if Fletch had been carted away by someone. It seemed that I would be unable to bury him, it seemed that I had been robbed of a final farewell.

I mulled over his loss: then my growing hunger and thirst distracted me from it. I was craving those crabs that I'd seen earlier, and I was tempted to scour for some coconuts, so that I could smash them and gorge myself on their liquids. My fatigue continued hindering me, and the full effects of my past imprisonment took a hold. Living off the bare minimum was not ideal, and it was another thing that I would curse the commodore for. I may have been free of her plans, but I would be feeling the side effects of them for quite some time. It was terrible, this was the worst possible moment to be weak in, and yet here I am, struggling to think, struggling to survive. All the past conditioning that I had committed my body to over the past month was gone, like it was all in vain. I recovered and planned out my next move, even though there was only one move to make.

The only move was to return to my camp, and hope that Daze and Leri were still there. If they were I could talk to them about Kaleen, but if they weren't I couldn't afford to search the island for them. I didn't have the energy, and frankly, I didn't have the time. My body was like a log, every step that I took was an effort, and every thought that I had was a weight, with each one becoming heavier and heavier by the minute. I continued moving towards the camp and I slowly willed myself into its direction. I gazed up at the sky while I walked, and three clouds occupied its space. With whatever I had left, I hoped that that wouldn't be the last thing that I saw on this day.

My thoughts returned to the jellyfish, and how I nearly ran into one once while I swam in the reef weeks ago. I became frustrated with the crabs also, since I could've used a plenitude of them a week ago.

They were small and miniscule for memory, but a handful of them could've sustained me for hours. I no longer wore boots so moving across the sand became easier than before, so long as I watched where I stepped anyway.

I trekked further inland until the old campsite came into view, and the voices of Daze and Leri were close by. I was too zoned out to listen to what they were saying, and I couldn't see them anywhere, but I didn't care, so long as I made it to them intact. I arrived and quickly keeled over next to the campfire, desperately fending off my stomach pains. Footsteps approached me while I was on the ground, and I couldn't find the strength to see who they belonged too.

"Why are you here Casper? You're supposed to be with Kaleen," said a voice belonging to Daze.

I tried responding but my voice was sore and parched, and my mind wouldn't cooperate with me.

"What's happened to him? Has he been attacked or is he just unwell?" asked a voice belonging to Leri.

I rolled onto my back and Daze and Leri were only a few yards away from me.

"He looks exhausted, and perhaps sick, maybe we should grab Kaleen," said Daze.

I raised my hand in protest, then moaned instead of speaking.

"We're supposed to head back once we've acquired everything, we don't have time to nurse him back to health," said Leri.

"Did you forget that he helped you after we attacked him before? We may dislike pirates but he still deserves some proper care; but if you won't do it then I will," said Daze.

"Ok fine, just calm down all right, ask him what he needs and we'll go from there," said Leri.

Daze knelt beside me and repeated what Leri had said.

"Food, water, please, I need..." my next words turned into croaks, but I think they understood my meaning.

"You found some coconuts right? Offer him some," said Daze.

"All right, I guess we can spare a couple."

Leri went to go grab them while Daze remained alongside me, looking more concerned than ever. Her faint blue eyes surveyed me constantly, and her sun tanned face creased continuously with concern. Her bright blonde hair provided comfort to my wellbeing, and it always glowed and brought me warmth when I looked upon it. It reminded me of Bellamy's hair, except Daze liked to alter it every so often.

Leri brought the coconuts and hacked away at them, then a minute or two passed and she offered them to Daze. Daze poured the liquids into my mouth, and they were refreshing despite the small quantities that they offered. I ate the contents inside as well, and a few minutes passed while I consumed two coconuts worth of food. My mind and body was still weak, but I didn't expect that I could rely on these two for much longer.

"We need to return to the ship to drop off these supplies, but we'll send for Kaleen to come and collect you when able," said Daze.

"Kaleen doesn't want me to come back, she's angry at me because the maps I said would be here aren't."

"Well that's unfortunate then, because it's her ship, and whether we like it or not she calls the shots," said Leri.

"But if I can't come back then I'll be stuck here, you have to convince her to let me back on, I'll die otherwise."

"Yes you will, but she freed you with the hopes that you would become a valuable ally for her; and it seems that you weren't, so this has nothing to do with us," said Leri.

"I helped you when you were dying! You owe me for that."

"We just helped you then, and we gave you what you needed, so now we're even, but I guess we can spare you one last favour," said Daze.

"Coconut," said Daze to Leri.

Leri looked uncertain about the request, but she threw it towards Daze, who then threw it towards me.

"Consider this our farewell".

And they left me without looking.

I laid still after they left, then I forced myself to sit upright. I reached for the coconut and looked at it, wondering if this would be the last thing that I ate today. My last chance had failed me, and unless I found an alternative soon, I would die here. To survive I would have to make difficult choices, but could I live with them after they'd been made? Who would I be? There was no answer for me to cling to. Giving up felt like a loss, because if I gave up, then what was left to look forward to? A life where I accept all the suffering that was dealt to me? A life that has nothing to keep me happy? It sounded so empty.

I looked up towards the trees and into the sky, and my guess was that it was close to sunset. There was little time left, but I needed rest, no matter how badly I wanted to move again.

I laid down next to the campfire, hoping that I could clear my head of all the problems that plagued it; but once I was rested I would need to act, and I would have to fight them, I would have to fight all of them if I wanted to survive.

CHAPTER 23

Letting Go

I followed Daze and Leri until they spotted the sloop, and I couldn't see it as well them, but I assumed it was their based on their reactions. All I had on me was a coconut and a dagger, which would have to be enough to take down these two insurgents. My rest had helped me, along with the coconut juices and flesh, but I would need stealth if I wanted to survive against both of them. They stopped walking and rested while bickering amongst themselves. I waited behind a nearby tree and contemplated the actions I was about to take. This was the day, the day that I finally let go of the naval man within me. Both women turned around and I threw the coconut at Daze, striking her in the back of the head and knocking her into the ground. Leri screamed in surprise, and I used her distress as an opportunity to advance on her.

I hid behind another tree while Leri examined Daze, and she looked into the direction of the attack. Leri readied her musket and I had to wait until she got closer. She looked around nervously, searching for any signs of danger, then she shouted in frustration. She returned to Daze's side, and I crept away while using the shrubs as cover. I watched her closely, and moments passed while I planned out my next move. I threw my dagger at Leri as a distraction, then charged at her, and she deflected the blade away with her musket. I reached her and grabbed a hold of her weapon, then we wrestled with each other for control of it. Leri fired the weapon into the air then kicked towards me, and I blocked it and countered with a kick of my own. Leri reached for the coconut and I kicked her again, then I pinned her into the ground.

"You monster! Coward! How dare you attack us like this."

"You've left me no choice! You should've helped me when you had the chance."

I stomped on her neck then quickly reached for the coconut.

"I offered you friendship and you rejected it, I offered you diplomacy and you abused it, savagery is all you deserve now."

I bashed the coconut into Leri's face, and she cried then I did it again. Blood spurted from her mouth, and she wailed terribly. I wanted to kill her, but it would be better if I frightened her, then she'd never disrespect a pirate again.

Leri's eyes quickly filled with tears, and she whimpered while trying to cover her bloodied image. I went to check on Daze, and I checked her pulse and thankfully she was still alive. I plunged my knife into her thigh, to make sure she wasn't a threat if she awoke. I then returned to Leri, who was quietly begging for her life. She'd have it, she just didn't know that yet. I cracked the coconut open on a tree while Leri continued with her pleas, then I drank and ate its contents while pondering on Kaleen's whereabouts.

"Kaleen will finish you off Casper, she's fought many men and won, and you'll be no different," muttered Leri.

"There's always someone who's different."

I placed the coconut remains near Leri, then kicked her goodbye before leaving. I retrieved Daze and Leri's swords while departing, then I buried a musket and one of them for safekeeping.

I could've used the musket against Kaleen, but with only one shot I didn't want to risk missing. I advanced towards Kaleen's sloop, and several minutes passed until I reached it. It was tempting to just hop in and disembark, but I didn't want any nasty surprises today. A thought suddenly hit me, the supplies were with Daze and Leri, and if I wanted to retrieve them then I'd have to deal with Kaleen first. Several minutes passed while I waited in the sloop, then there was movement up ahead, followed by a tragic cry. Kaleen arrived and checked the bodies for signs of life, and her sword was still in hand, and while she was focused on them I prepared for departure. I quickly raised the anchor from the shallows, and Kaleen saw me and ran straight towards the sloop. I searched for any additional firearms and a single pistol remained on board. Kaleen closed the gap between us, then while I cocked the pistol Kaleen dove into the shallows.

I waited while she was submerged, and she moved around and I struggled to get a clean shot on her. A few moments passed then her patience won out, and I discarded the pistol and drew my sword instead. Kaleen launched herself onto the deck then quickly got to her feet with sword still in hand.

"You're willing to attack anyone to get what you want, even innocent girls."

"You've left me no other option, I want my revenge against the commodore, and I will not be stranded here again."

180

"It's where men like you belong, away from the rest of the world."

"At least I served the world at some point, all you've ever done is cause it problems... you really should've just been a pirate."

"I don't steal and murder like you! I've only ever helped and protected people, sometimes at the cost of others, but at least I've done what's right; until recently."

"You're helping and protecting people that want to abandon you, and then your gonna fight someone who has everyone on their side! How do you plan on doing the right thing then? Without me you're going to fail."

"No! I thought I needed you, but I was wrong, it'll be harder alone, but I'll do it without a pirate's help."

"Then you're a fool, and it looks like only one of us is gonna get what we want."

I slashed horizontally towards Kaleen's ribs, and she blocked it and shuffled away.

"Why didn't you kill them? You had the chance too yet you didn't take it, you could've improved your odds."

"There pacified and that's all that matters, as long as that remains then they don't need to die."

"But if I kill you now then you'll have achieved nothing."

"I'll have slowed you down, and even if you win you'll have to carry them back to Havana alone, and questions are bound to arise if you do."

Kaleen yelled and lunged towards my belly with a thrust, and she narrowly missed it. I parried her blade away then kicked her in the knee causing her to trip. She retreated and I advanced on her, then she swiftly rolled away and got back up.

"This is your last chance Kaleen, surrender or suffer, you won't win this."

"That's what you think."

We moved towards the cabin doors and I slashed towards her, and she blocked it then countered with her own. I fended off her slash and we stopped, and we waited for the other to strike. I slashed again and this time I put more force behind it, and this surprised Kaleen however she adjusted and nimbly evaded out of peril. I slashed towards her head and again put more force behind it, but the attack wore me out and she blocked it effortlessly. I couldn't open her up, and I was growing nervous about my energy levels.

Kaleen sensed my fatigue and thrusted towards my rib, and the blade pierced some of my clothing while narrowly missing me by inches. I parried her blade away and kicked towards her stomach, and she avoided it then charged into my shoulder. It barely moved me, but the action was enough for her to reposition herself for another attack. Kaleen slashed towards my neck and I blocked it, but it was stronger than I expected and the force put me under pressure. I pushed myself away from her and lured her towards the mast, then I thrusted towards her knee. She parried it and counter slashed, and it grazed part of my neck. I recoiled while it stung, but it wasn't serious so I was lucky. Upon delivering the slash Kaleen fiercely swung her sword at me, as if the sight of my blood had enveloped her.

Her slash grazed my forearm, and my block failed while her sword overpowered it. I struggled to concentrate, and the non-stop fighting drained me, as I seemed incapable of blocking or parrying. I retreated and she pursued me towards the front of the ship, where only the bowsprit or the sea awaited me. I moved around the bowsprit while Kaleen closed in, then I lunged towards her and we engaged in a blade lock. I pushed her into the mast and quickly kneed her in the thigh, then I kneed her again and this time I put more force behind it. She recoiled in pain and crumbled into the ground, then I grabbed her by the hair and rammed her head into the mast. The impact seemed to stun her, and her sword fell out of her hand. I slumped next to the ships railing, sensing and hoping that Kaleen was defeated. I reached for my neck wound and cursed while I tried wiping the blood away, then I assessed my forearm and thought about what to do with it.

I tore off parts of my clothes to treat both wounds, and when they were wrapped I closed my eyes and rested against the ships railing. Several minutes passed then a strange sound suddenly disturbed my peace, and I looked to investigate and Kaleen reached for a nearby lantern. I willed myself to my feet and Kaleen grabbed it and threw it at me.

I raised my forearms and the lantern crashed against them, though the broken glass fragments cut into them. Drops of oil also spewed into my eyes, blinding me from seeing what would happen next. Moments passed and I could only see for a few seconds at a time, and I could see Kaleen nearby, who recovered her sword.

"You did better than most I'll give you that, but it's time for you to depart, return to the island now, or I'll finish you here and now."

"I can't, I won't!"

I moved towards her and she slashed me across the chest, then she picked up another sword. I yelled from the fresh cut and tried nursing the trickling blood that had emerged. It continued flowing over my hands, and I couldn't contain it no matter what I did.

"I don't want to kill you despite what you've done, but please just go, and maybe you'll live another day."

My eyesight improved and she pointed her sword towards me, while carrying my own in her other hand.

"What about the other's? You can't carry them back and hold me off at the same time, you'll have to decide between them or you."

Kaleen groaned and she had to know that I was right, if she helped them then that would leave her vulnerable to me later on.

A figure suddenly walked towards the beach, and I exited the sloop and it appeared that Leri was moving towards us. She was carrying Daze with her, and she was struggling with the solitary effort.

"Maybe you're wrong, maybe I won't have to expose myself."

Kaleen waited beside me while keeping her sword poised against me at all times. Leri walked closer towards us, but how long would Kaleen wait? And how much did Leri have left? It all rested with her now. Leri continued moving then stopped, and the effort seemed to be taking a toll on her. She noticed that Kaleen wasn't going to help her, and that mustn't have helped with her struggle. Kaleen remained quiet while watching Leri, and she barely moved except for the rare sword adjustments of her arm.

A few minutes passed then Leri reached us, and she dragged Daze while panting heavily; her feet were also wobbly, and they seemed like they might collapse if she kept moving them.

Her brown eyes were stained with redness, and her lightly freckled cheeks were swollen and bloodied. Her dark brown ponytail was knotted, and her athletic physique was battered and weary.

"You need to carry her on board Leri, once that's done we'll depart for Havana," said Kaleen.

"Why did you spare him!? Look what he's done to Daze and I."

"That doesn't matter, just take her aboard so that we can get going."

Leri grunted then obliged, and she continued carrying her friend towards the sloop. Leri struggled to lift Daze upon arrival, and Kaleen grew nervous while watching her. Leri lifted her towards the railing and dropped her, then she splashed into the water below. She tried again and dropped her once more, then she boarded the sloop instead. She grabbed Daze and pulled her out of the water, then she pulled and pulled until she heaved Daze over the ships railing. Daze thudded onto the deck heavily, and Kaleen moved towards the sloop, keeping her sword pointed at me while keeping my sword sheathed in her belt. I wanted to stop her, but without my weapon I had no chance against her. She boarded the ship and took the helm, then she sailed away and there was no point in watching her leave. I was already in a hopeless situation, and watching her would just waste time. At least the supplies were still here, all though there were barely any left. I washed my wounds in the shallows, then tried focusing on what to do next.

I headed back to where Daze and Leri once lay, and I located the supplies that they were carrying. I also retrieved the musket that I'd buried before, along with the spare sword. The knife was gone but its extracted blood still remained, and I analysed the supplies and tried thinking about how I could use them. I had barrels, I had rope, and I had planks, so my best chance was to build a raft. With no food or water my only option was the sea, and it was time that I let go of that fear, it was time that I faced it instead. There would be no more waiting and surviving this time, if I wanted to live, I'd have to do it myself, and I'd have to start now.

CHAPTER 24

Blue Nightmare

An hour or so passed and I prepared the raft with the remaining supplies. I'm glad that I'd buried the sword, because without it cutting and rationing the rope would've been a nightmare. It consisted of two barrels, along with a few planks of wood tied to them by the rope. It was very small, only four planks wide, and there was little room to sit on, but it was all there was. I used a stick and a cloth to create a flag that could help me determine the wind's direction, and it was the closest thing I had to a bowsprit. I hadn't tested it yet, so if it didn't float then all was lost. Traces of a storm brewed over the horizon, and I was eager to leave before it arrived. I quietly spoke my farewells to the island, then I pushed the raft towards the sea. It wasn't heavy, but it was challenging to move due to my condition. I reached the shallows and things became easier, then a few minutes later I moved into the deep.

I moved onto the raft and grabbed the fishing spear to use as a paddle, it stayed afloat so far, all though I didn't feel secure quite yet. I paddled and paddled, then a few minutes passed and the raft started sinking. I quickly worked to salvage the barrels and the rope, and I left the planks behind and swam back towards shore. I should've known better, I was no raft builder, and neither was Fletch, so this plan was always an unreliable one. I could still use the barrels since they would float, but I would have to retie them together and either sit in or on them for the entire voyage. I pondered on this plan, then I reused the rope I had and created what I hoped would suffice. I still had the spear with me, so I had a paddle which I would need. I moved the raft back towards the shallows, then I hopped on once it was far enough out. This time I was more confident about staying afloat, all though I would have to paddle harder because there wasn't much speed to go on.

Non essentials remained on the empty barrel for safekeeping, while the spear and I was all that was in the other one. Several minutes passed while I paddled out of Twin-Reef's waters, and being so far away from it seemed unnatural. My arms ached and I rested, then my hunger and thirst returned. The wind picked up while I recovered, and it carried me north or maybe North West. Without my flag I couldn't be sure. I suddenly grew cold from the increased wind, and I tried rubbing myself to keep warm.

I paddled again and looked back to see how far I was from Twin-Reef Island. The storm seemed to be forming more and more by the hour, and if it struck me then I doubted I could survive it. The ocean was empty and almost quiet despite the gusts of wind, nothing was in view, which was something I didn't expect. I continued paddling until I grew more fatigued, then I put my spear away and laid in the barrel. I closed my eyes and tried resting, but it was an uncomfortable rest. My hunger and thirst continued bothering me, and it remained like a pesky fly or a bee. It interrupted my thoughts, and soon it would be all that occupied them.

I turned my mind towards Fletch and remembered some of the things that we did before the island. Last year Fletch gambled away my pistol, all though he claimed that he didn't know it was mine. He lost it in a wager to another crewman, then that crewman lost it sometime after that. The vision suddenly came into my mind, and I was transported back to the deck of the Revenant. I was below looking for it at the time, then a former crewman of mine informed me of the rumour.

"Fletch lost a wager to Randy recently, apparently he bet a pistol instead of money," said the crewman.

"Speaking of pistols have you seen mine? I swore I had it down here."

"What did it look like?"

"Leathery brown, with a bit of gold on the mechanism."

"Uh... well, that might be a problem."

"Why?"

The crewman looked at me awkwardly, and my face quickly distorted in fury. I stormed towards the quarter deck and searched for Fletch, then I located him and furiously marched towards him. Captain Maroo was on deck as well, and he saw me move in on an unaware Fletch.

"Casper!" said Maroo.

I stopped moving, and Fletch turned around after the captain's call.

"What seems to be the problem lad?"

"My pistol is missing, a crewman below informed me that Fletch might be responsible."

"Is this true Fletch? Have you misplaced Casper's pistol?"

"I swear to you captain, I didn't know it was his," said Fletch.

I unsheathed my dagger and aimed it at him, and the captain intervened and placed himself between us.

"Easy Nait! You're the one that convinced me to take him on remember?"

"Maybe I was wrong about that."

"I was sure that I'd win the wager, and I was desperate to compete so I used the pistol as my own, I'm sorry Casper."

"Where is it!? That was a special pistol from the navy, despite not being a part of it anymore it still held value to me."

"Apparently it's been lost, the crewman that won it from me lost it recently."

"You brat! We should've left you back in Nassau!!"

"ENOUGH! My cabin, the both of you, now!" said Maroo.

He made an absolute mess of things because of this, and after that I hoped that he never gambled again. The memory faded, and instead I pondered on the things I'd miss if I died out here. The tavern girls, the rum, the gambling, and of course, the old shanties. Moments passed then my thoughts returned to Fletch, and I pictured his home in Nassau, and the day that we first met.

It was three days after I'd joined up with Maroo, and he had concocted a plan to raid Nassau and other nearby towns. The town put up a decent fight with its fort and small fleet, but Maroo was at his strongest then, so nothing could defy him. Many of the town's folk spited us, but once Nassau was ours they soon quickly bowed instead. Fletch was the first to approach us, and he barely hesitated in doing so.

"Captain Maroo, I'd like to offer you my services in exchange for my life, I was once a firearms apprentice, so I could help you if you'll let me."

"Your quite young to be aboard a pirate ship, I don't think your services will be required young man," said Maroo.

"What if we give him a chance? You've lost some men here recently captain, so maybe recruitment is a good idea."

"Already questioning me Mr Nait? Very brave, but also dangerous. I've risked a lot by taking you on, but unlike freckles here, I see potential in you."

A few hours later an English schooner arrived in Nassau, and against captain Maroo's wishes, Fletch fought them off alongside him. Fletch outshot all of the captains men including me, and despite not being a swordsman, his gun craft was most impressive. Maroo reluctantly took him on after, but he wasn't trusted or regarded by him for a while.

A few nights later I caught him near our cannons, cleaning and admiring them up close.

"One day this is where I'll be, operating a cannon aboard a ship, instead of a firearm inside of a room."

"I wouldn't get too excited, the captain is… picky about who gets what."

"What about when it comes to you? You seem to be one of his favourites, a man who's far younger than his comrades."

"I can't answer that, but I did stand up for him when it mattered, so maybe that was enough."

"Why did you join him? Did he force you? That's how it is with pirates isn't it? You serve them or you die."

"He didn't force me, I joined him because I was lost, lost and angry at what I used to serve. And when you feel like that, you just try and go with what feels right. Feelings can blind you but they can also lead you towards something greater."

"I joined because I lost my way of life, I was close to becoming a gunsmith specialist, and your raid ended that."

"I lost my way of life too, but sometimes… you get one back."

Fletch's time aboard The Revenant was the most fascinating out of all of us, except for maybe the captain. I never learned about Alva Maroo's humble beginnings, but I guess I didn't need to. Maroo was very private with his life, all though learning that he may have loved Commodore Weiss was still a shock to me. Romance never seemed to be a thing that he'd bother with, but it does explain some of his strange absences during my year with him. I wish I knew how he did it, how he kept our way alive, but I guess it didn't matter anymore, because it was all up to me now.

White sails appeared off in the distance, and my memory and thoughts dissolved. The ship was at least an hour or so away, but it was there, and it was seemingly heading in my direction. All I could do was stay on course, and make sure that they could see me when the time came. I closed my eyes and tried resting again, then I hoped and waited for the tide to keep me in sight.

The storm seemed to be almost upon me, and the sky was dark and grumpy above me. While I rested the ship drew nearer, and hope began to return to me, I opened one eye and raised one hand, and the Spanish schooner suddenly arrived. I don't know if it was the one that appeared earlier or not, but I didn't care, so long as they took me with them.

The storm started and the sea quickly grew rough, then the wind and the waves pushed me away from them. The crewmen panicked as the weather suddenly turned wild, and the barrels swayed violently, making it hard to stay balanced. A few minutes passed then the wind picked up again, and the barrels continued swaying from side to side. During my years at sea I'd never gotten sea sick, but if this kept going then perhaps today would be the day. I'd never been in a ship killing storm either, but I'd heard of them, and perhaps dodged a few in the past. The waves knocked the Spanish schooner violently, moving it around and pushing it forcefully into precarious angles. Somehow I'd never imagined a scenario like this, where everything went bad after I left the island. If or after I got off I always thought everything would get easier, and if it didn't, well… then I'd just admit defeat; it was always one or the other.

A rogue wave suddenly hit me full force, and before I knew it, I was pushed into the sea below. I was shell shocked, then I quickly swam up for air. Upon resurfacing a large portion of wreckage appeared nearby, and I guess I didn't have to worry about Spain anymore, since there schooner was probably long gone by now. The cold and the tide quickly sapped me of my strength, and I struggled against the current, so I swam towards the debris nearby. Portions of the ship remained afloat, but they quickly floated away, as would I soon, out in this deep, everlasting; blue nightmare.

3 days later

CHAPTER 25

Captivity

It is day three of drifting across the sea, and most of the ships wreckage had floated away by now. I'm lying on top of the few pieces that remained, and I had to wait until the storm was over to climb onto something better. Food and water is all I can think of, and rest is in short supply, when two of the last three days had been raining constantly. Necessities were like the lover or lovers that you always took for granted, when they were around you never cared for them enough, or showed them much appreciation, and when they weren't you practically begged for them to come back. That was an accurate description of what I was feeling right now, and there was nothing that I could do about it.

I'd looked for signs of nearby land, but there were no birds, no ships, and at this point, no hope. All I had left was my clothes and my sword, the one that I'd taken from Daze before all of this happened. All thoughts of vengeance were long gone, and even if I survived I had no idea where I would go next. I'd become too weak to move around, and it wouldn't be long before I diminished completely. White sails suddenly appeared further away, and by some miracle they didn't seem to be fake. A small ship inched closer, but it was a ship nonetheless and I just hoped that it was coming my way. A while passed then the ships shadow enveloped me, and I raised my hand and moved about weakly to show that I was alive.

Minutes passed then I was dragged off the debris into the water, and I was submerged for several seconds until I resurfaced. I was blindfolded by my rescuers and they spoke in a native tongue, one that was unfamiliar to me. They helped me onto the deck then sat me down.

"Stay put," said a man's voice.

Several minutes passed then I was offered food and water to help restore my strength, and when I'd finished I wanted to learn more.

"Why am I blindfolded?"

No one replied.

I lay against the ships railing, trying to stay awake while listening to any sounds or noises that could help me make sense of things.

The ship moved and foreign orders were given to whoever was crewing it. It seemed like no one was paying attention to me, but why would they since I was withered castaway. My thoughts drifted to the future while I fought off sleep, and for the first time I had no idea what my future would hold. I didn't have anyone to help me shape it, and right now it seemed formless and non-existent. I'd been a colonial, a pirate, a castaway, and a prisoner, how could I use any of that? Just thinking about it made my head hurt. Moments passed then I succumbed to my fatigue, and I gave up fighting my drowsiness.

A crewman awoke me however long after, and helped me to my feet.

"Walk," said a man's voice.

A ramp was placed underneath my feet, and I walked across it until I touched sand. Was I on another island? I wish I knew because I was sick of them. Heat and light blazed upon me, and wherever I was it was too much for my liking. Birds and dogs chirped and barked in the distance, so at least there was wildlife while I walked along the sand. I transitioned onto grass and there were murmurs of people nearby, they spoke in the same tongue as those on the ship, and therefore none of it was translatable. A few minutes passed then I was grabbed and led towards another location, and I was escorted into some kind of enclosure. It was a broad guess, but they tied me to something so I assumed that it was.

They took my sword then left me, and when I suspected they were gone I tested out my new restraints. I moved three steps and I was pulled back, and I wanted to remove my blindfold but I was concerned about the consequences. Moments later footsteps approached the enclosure, then after some native tongue an elderly woman approached and entered my vicinity.

"Why am I here? Who are you people and why have you blindfolded me? If you don't want me to see anything then you should've just left me where I was."

"Your questions will be answered once ours have been, my men took a chance fishing you out of the sea, but they are curious as well as cautious ; so if you cooperate then this will be over soon," said the elderly woman.

"So I'm a prisoner? Great... I go from being stuck at sea to being stuck on an island, or whatever this is."

"I can't help you with your past but I can help you with your future, I just need to know that I and the people that I live with can trust you."

"So you want to know why I was out their? Where I come from? And what my plans are, or were? Very well, I'll tell you."

"You look like a sailor, merchant? Or something else."

"No I'm not a merchant sailor, just a regular one. I was trying to escape the storm."

"Where were you going? Before the storm interrupted your voyage?"

"I don't know exactly, I was just trying to survive and reach land."

"A sailor who doesn't know where he's going? That seems odd."

"I was a castaway all right! So was my friend, but he's dead now, as would I be if not for your crew."

"How unfortunate, I would've liked to have heard your friend's side of the story."

She stayed quiet and her silence unnerved me.

"Where are you from?" She asked.

"Kingston, but in recent times I'm not from anywhere, because like I said before, I was stranded."

"Very well, where you're from doesn't really matter, all that matters is what you are, and who."

She turned to leave and I called out to her.

"I told you what you wanted to know, can you answer some of my questions now? Please, I need to know more."

"All you need to know is that your freedom depends upon your actions, speak your truth and you shall have little to fear from us."

She left then spoke some commands to whoever was nearby.

I was annoyed, but it could've been worse so I had to count myself lucky.

I listened in on the sounds nearby, and it seemed like I was in some kind of shelter or hut. The natives continued talking in their native dialect, and dogs barked frequently, making me think that I was in a village of some kind. I wasn't sure if the lady believed me or not, but I hoped that she didn't suspect that I was hiding something. Apathy and hopelessness swirled within me, yet I didn't feel like I was in danger, all though I didn't suspect that I'd be leaving soon either. I lied down and let my thoughts scatter around inside me, I didn't have much time to think about them, since I just wanted to get through the day as quickly as possible.

A while later someone approached the shelter, and multiple footsteps moved towards me. I stayed where I was while they came in, and I pretended to sleep in the hope that the encounter would be swift and effortless. A bowl was placed alongside me, along with something else that I couldn't distinguish. A hand touched my shoulder and shook me, and a sharp pain within it caused me to groan.

"I've brought you food and water sailor, the madam wants me to tend to you," said a young woman's voice.

"What does the other one want? To ensure that I'm cooperative? Kind of hard to be if I can't look or talk to you about anything."

"There are two ways this can go, the madam has selected us to execute either of these two ways; she is a fair leader, but also very firm. I represent her fairness, while my colleague represents her firmness."

"So food and water is supposed to represent fairness? Wow, what a cold outlook you have on foreigners."

"The food and water is not what I'm here for, the madam has instructed that information be rewarded with comfort, and misinformation be rewarded with discomfort."

"Ok… I'm not going to comment on that, am I allowed to eat and drink first? Because my hydration is really bad right now."

"First tell me your name, then tell me your origin, then tell me why you've chosen to live this way."

I sighed, I guess I'm not getting that drink anytime soon. The colleague shuffled their feet, as if they were waiting for a specific order to be given.

"My name is Casper Nait, and I was once part of the colonial navy in Kingston. I haven't been for almost two years, but I chose that life because I thought that I could help the men there."

"The madam suspected as much, but you don't look like a naval man, you claim to be a simple sailor yet your armed, explain that."

"I had brief troubles at sea, my friend and I were armed because of this, but it didn't matter in the end."

"It's a shame we couldn't meet this friend of yours, it would've been interesting to hear what he had to say," said another woman's voice.

"Tell me Casper, since you were a colonial were you involved in any way with slaves? Did you see or hear of any?" asked the woman.

"No, but I knew it was around, and I made it very clear that I didn't want anything to do with it."

"How were you able to make such demands? Surely your superiors decided what you did or didn't do."

"Most superiors were like that, but I was fortunate to have an understanding one, it was there superior that was the problem, there superior was the reason I was forced to leave."

"Why do you oppose slavery? Isn't it good for business in England?"

"I don't believe in orders unless it's for their own good, and slavery is never for anyone's own good."

"I see, well thank you for answering so diligently."

She paused then knelt beside me.

"Open your mouth."

I complied and she poured water inside it. Relief reached my throat while the water dripped down, then she poured it in too quickly and I almost choked. She stopped, and stood upright.

"I will now answer some questions you may have, after that you will be temporarily released for your own comfort, but if you try anything, my accomplice will stop you," warned the young woman.

Moments passed while I recovered from the swift drinking, then I nodded in understanding.

"Good, then release him and leave us alone."

Her accomplice loosened and removed my bonds, and I thought carefully about what my first question would be.

"We're in a village aren't we? A slave or former slave village, where you've all managed to escape from colonial rule."

"You are in a village, but none of us have escaped colonial rule, no one ever truly does."

"We've just managed to put some distance between us and them," added the young woman.

The bounds came off and the other woman stood up and muttered some dialect to my caretaker, then she left.

"Now that your arms are free take off your clothes, they need to be replaced with new ones."

I did as she asked and she gave me non-verbal permission for me to remove my blindfold, so long as I faced the shelter wall while doing so. I undressed myself until I was nude, then she took the clothes off me and reinstated my blindfold.

"Lie down Casper, and stay as you are for the remainder of the night, if you don't, trust that I will know, or my accomplice will."

She quickly left, and I grew concerned about the cold and the discomfort that was to come.

CHAPTER 26

Truth

It's morning, and my naked body is sore, dirty, and shivering all over. Sleep was hard to come by last night, and the breeze continued affecting me even now. My blindfold is still on, and I moved around to try and find my clothes. I wouldn't be able to put them on yet, because I was too cold and sore to fit into them. I didn't understand the methods of these people, the blindfold, the hospitality, the nude sleep, I couldn't fathom whether I was being punished or not. It was better than the commodore's hospitality, but only because being caught by them was demoralizing, and worse yet, they probably knew that. My arms and legs hurt the most, but my shoulders seemed ok, at least compared with the rest of my body.

I wondered what Kaleen was doing, and whether she'd parted ways with Daze and Leri by now. Would she pursue the commodore like she said she would? If she does she'll die in the attempt, like the fool she is. I wish she'd stayed with me, because if the word on her is true then I'm sure the both of us could've got what we wanted. My thoughts also drifted to Zaria, and I wondered if she was even alive at this point.

Even if she was slavery wouldn't be much better for her, so a part of me didn't know what to cling to. Approaching footsteps suddenly interrupted my thoughts, and a figure entered.

"Take off the blindfold and put on your clothes, the madam will be here shortly," ordered a woman's voice.

I removed my blindfold and a bulked up maroon woman stood before me, she had two dark ponytails and a large sheathed knife resting on her hip.

"You've been given the gift of sight sailor, continue to cooperate and you will be given other comforts as well; but if you ruin them, then they will be taken away!"

"I understand, so this was intentional then? This was all a fear tactic from the start, very impressive."

"Be quiet sailor! Our methods are none of your business, all you have to do is obey them."

I nodded quickly then remained quiet. The maroon remained where she was so I assumed that she'd be present for the meeting. If the madam was the elder then this must be her protector, or perhaps some kind of warrior for the village. Several minutes passed then footsteps finally approached the shelter, and the madam walked in at last.

"Thank you Serena, please wait outside while I speak with Casper alone," said the madam.

Serena bowed in response then left immediately, and she scowled at me while doing so.

"Serena has probably explained this, but thanks to your cooperation your sight has been restored. Depending on how this next conversation goes, maybe your mobility will be next."

"But not my freedom? I'm just one man, I'm not a threat to an entire village."

"That might be true but freedom must be earned, so for now you will stay in this shelter, whether it be in restraints or not."

"I've told you everything! My origin, my name, why I chose to live that way, what more could you want to know? You already have everything that you need."

"Just one last thing Casper, have you ever encountered pirates? Whether it was as a naval man or a simple sailor; remember to speak your truth."

I paused, as much as I wanted to lie I couldn't, and if I did I'd only make things worse.

"Yes I have, when I left the navy I encountered them."

"Did you help them?"

"Yes, I helped them seize a ship alongside their crew."

"Why did you do it? For revenge? For spoils? What was the motive?"

"I did it because I was desperate, desperate to feel alive and free again, I had nothing at the time yet they threw me a lifeline anyway, they gave me a second chance, a second soul."

"So you became one of them'? You not only encountered and helped them but you actually became one of them?"

"Does this disgust you madam? Do you still foolishly believe in the lies that England and Spain spread about us? Along with everyone else, because we dared to live outside their laws and rules."

"Pirates have done a lot of harm to the seas, and they've been especially harmful to the maroons here; so yes, I still believe in the stories they've spun about you."

The madam turned to leave and I grabbed her before she could, and she eyed me scornfully.

"I've known maroons who once believed in the pirate way, and we're not all the same despite what you may say about us: remember that before you condemn me to death."

"Release me Casper, or Serena will do it for you."

I obeyed and let go of her arm, then she nurtured it briefly.

"I will consult with the other maroons, and you may be right about us, but the maroons that sided with piracy generally regretted it."

I paused, then she left before I could reply. Serena walked back into the shelter after, and she eyed me cautiously, then beckoned for me to sit down.

"It's not looking good for you sailor, or should I say pirate? Who would've thought."

"I was told to speak my truth and I did, but if she dislikes pirates so much then why doesn't she just execute me? I don't understand her."

"Only a few of us do, but perhaps there is a small part of her that sympathizes with your kind; after all, we're not all the same."

"Did you just quote me? A pirate, how sinful of you."

"Tell anyone and I'll cut your face', said Serena, who tried hiding a smirk afterwards.

"Were you aligned with pirates once?"

"No, but I helped one once, even though the others wanted him dead."

"Who was he?"

"I don't know, but he had a shaved head, brown eyes, and red spots across his forehead: he also said he was alone, and that he was driven out of his manor in Kingston."

Bonnet, this woman had met Bonnet, it had to be, but if so where was he? Unfortunately, I was too afraid to ask.

"I didn't know that he was a pirate, I only found out with the others when our ambassador came, apparently he was friends with Alva Maroo; and if they got to him then piracy would be over."

Serena got up and kicked dirt in my face, then she returned to her post.

"Don't think I'm going soft pirate, only one white man has accomplished that."

She left and I moved around the shelter, because if I tried to leave then I'm sure she'd plunge that dagger straight into my neck. I lied down and rested, then I closed my eyes and lulled myself to sleep.

Another maroon awoke me later on, a petite woman with long free flowing dark hair. She was slender and curvy, and I had to admit, she was attractive.

"My name is Sandy, I was here with you last night, but now I've been asked to take you on a tour of the village. Serena will escort us as well, in order to ensure everyone's safety."

I was still wrapping my head around her name, which I didn't even know was a name, but finding out that she was the one that asked me to sleep naked last night soured things; because her potent attractiveness complicated the matter.

"I thought I was supposed to stay in this shelter? Has the madam changed her tune? If so everything that's happened feels unnecessary now."

"Don't question our methods, do you want to leave this shelter or not? this may be your only chance to do so."

"Fine, of course I want to leave, I'm just trying to make sense of things."

"Well maybe you should stop that, you might hurt that primitive brain of yours."

Serena approached and I bit back a reply, and she immediately moved towards me. She bound my hands and Sandy took frontal position while Serena took the back, probably so that she could backstab me if I fell out of line. We left the shelter and the sun blinded me immediately, and when I could see again the scenery returned to me. The village comprised of small tents and shelters, and there was another wooden enclosure which I couldn't distinguish from where I was standing. Green appeared everywhere you looked, along with patches of dirt and sand mixed into it. The three of us continued walking, then Sandy explained some of the maroon's past to me.

"After 1720 the maroons were forced into a treaty with England, those of us here got off easy, but others on plantations weren't so lucky," said Sandy.

"Once a month we receive a visit from a colonial ambassador, one who ensures our word is honoured; in exchange for our independence we must relinquish a certain amount of maroons each month, maroons who work for them as workers," said Serena begrudgingly.

"That's terrible, but why are you telling me this? This has nothing to do with me."

"Actually it does, because the colonials are aware that various maroons here once joined up with pirates, and as a penalty for that affront, we've had to comply with their rules ever since," said Sandy.

"Unless they were forced I don't think you can blame pirates for this."

"The madam would disagree with you, since she blames piracy for the disappearance of her daughter. It's been almost a year since she's seen her," said Serena.

Later I was led towards a small hut, and both women forced me to enter it. I opened the door and a large group of maroons were inside, and I was confused by this, then I was quickly untied and pushed inside. They locked the door behind me, and I was left alone to face the eight angry looking maroons close by. Most of them were men, but there were a couple of women as well. I didn't know what to do, and one of them suddenly rushed in and attacked me.

"Sandy! Serena!" No one replied, and instead the rest of them rushed towards me.

There was no way that I could fight them all, but even then what choice did I have? Other than being pummelled into oblivion. The first attacker hit me with a bone crunching tackle, and I wasn't even close to fully recovered. The impact hurt like a bow swain's lash, and I fell to ground groaning and clutching my insides. I didn't even get the luxury of reacting to the fact that I'd been deceived, sure I got to see some of the village, but it was a far cry from an actual tour. The fight was a blur of punches and kicks after the tackle, and I was rag dolled from one wall to the other, preventing me from getting even a single hit in on any of my aggressors. After this I probably wouldn't live to see a real tour, especially with my face getting the worst of it. Blood and bruising covered my chest and ribs, and my face was so sore that I could still feel the blood forming upon it. I'd probably have to hide it afterwards, sure it was charred already, but now it would look even worse.

Only two or three people attacked me, but they were all fit burly men, and every blow they dealt found its mark. I didn't know if Sandy or Serena were watching this, but maybe they'd been covering up there disgust for me all this time? Or perhaps they were just following orders? Maybe before I died they'd have the decency to tell me which it was.

"That's enough!" shouted Serena.

She moved towards me while I lost consciousness, and when she arrived my eyes blacked out before I could look into hers.

I awoke after being dropped insensitively onto the ground, and I was returned to my shelter while life slowly returned to me. I couldn't move or react, the only thing I could do was groan or cry. Blood continued streaking down my face, and my sores and scabs ached constantly.

There stinging was the worst part, worse than any tavern brawl or school fight I'd ever been in. It was like a part of my soul had been taken from me, but after everything that I'd been through, it didn't feel like there was much of a soul left. Footsteps approached me and I prayed that it was someone who'd come to finish me off. A bowl of water was placed beside me, along with multiple cloths and bandages, Damn it!! I was going to live.

"You need to relax Casper, this is going to hurt," said a girls voice.

I screamed while she washed at my scabs and sores, and the cold water shocked and amplified the stinging sensation from before. I struggled to stay awake while she cleaned them, then she finished and moved on to bandaging me. I didn't want her to, but the agony finally ceased while she did. Lifting my head was too difficult, so I had no idea who was treating me, but they sounded familiar, however I couldn't pinpoint a name.

CHAPTER 27

Recovery

Two weeks passed while I rested and recovered, then at long last, I was able to stand and walk again. My face, ribs, and chest had been covered in bandages, and they hadn't been changed since the day they were first applied. I was given food and water throughout the weeks, but it was always difficult to reach when it arrived. New clothes were laid out for me, and I was unable to wear them, because the effort was too great to do so. Footsteps approached the shelter and a new maroon woman walked in. she was armed with a sword and a dagger, and she held the dagger close while she approached me. She helped me dress into my new clothes, and remained quiet while doing so. I hadn't seen anyone since my beating, but perhaps everyone was under orders not to since the madam wanted to punish me.

She finished dressing me and moved away, then she left but paused at the entrance.

"We'll be getting a visit from a colonial ambassador soon, and I suspect after that you will have your chance to leave."

"So my advice to you is to wait," she added.

She quickly left then I inspected my clothes. I was dressed in almost the same apparel as I usually was. I had navy blue pants, a black shirt, a brown coat, and even black boots. Despite her advice I had no intention of waiting, I'd already been here for long enough, and I wanted to leave pronto. I'd spent the past two days testing out my mobility, and it wasn't very good, but if I could sneak out after dark then maybe it wouldn't have to be. The first week of my recovery was the darkest point of my life, a point where only bitterness and hatred existed. On the inside I was hollow, hollow and numb like a ghost wandering the sea.

Maybe the commodore was right, perhaps after all that has happened I was just a thing to be concealed from the world; a terrible phantasm that would wander endlessly across the biomes of the world. But like any former spirits, I would not pass until my task is complete, I would not rest until our business is concluded. During piracy she was my spectre, but now, I would become hers.

I was no longer restrained so I assumed that there was no one outside. I'm sure there were patrols, but I doubted that anyone would suspect a potential escape. If I was successful I could prepare for the ambassadors visit beforehand, and I so hoped that it was my dear Governor Manson, so that the grubby worm could lead me back to Weiss. The beating had done one good thing for me at least, it had made me realise just how alone I was. I'd spent so much time trying to make allies, whether it was with sailors, maroons, or anyone else that came by; but no, I knew better now, this was something that I had to do alone. With Fletch gone I was the last of the Revenants crew, but despite this, I would show the world just how much damage one pirate can do.

I had to wait until nightfall, so I prepared myself for meditation, in order to bide my time. I closed my eyes and concentrated, though my mind struggled to settle. No memories formed within me, and my damaged mentality fractured my focus. A while later I finished, then I peeked outside the shelter. There was no one nearby, so I exited carefully while creeping. I headed left and hoped that it was the right choice, and various torches burned around the village. They helped me see where I was going, but every time I moved my body ached. As long as I stayed at my current pace the aching wouldn't turn into agony, but it was something that I'd have to live with. A path appeared up ahead which looked to lead away from the village, and nowhere else seemed to appeal to me, so I moved towards it without much deliberation.

Maroons talked nearby so I stopped, and a minute or two passed and they moved along. I continued walking until an awful realisation came to me, there were shrubs and bushes nearby, but there was no cover and therefore nowhere for me to hide if I was spotted. I stayed low and continued advancing, and there were more torches up ahead, but this time they were moving. They moved towards me and I stayed still, then they passed me and none of them seemed to illuminate my presence. Things were going well so far, but I didn't know if I was heading in the right direction or not. More torches appeared up ahead, and these ones weren't moving. I observed them for the time being, expecting them to break from their position at any moment. A few moments passed and they didn't, so I had to assume they were guards.

I brooded on how to get past them, then a light suddenly shined upon me, and I quickly cursed myself for not watching my back.

"Casper!" shouted a woman's voice.

The voices identity echoed through my mind, and its familiarity returned to me, it was Sandy's voice. How did she know that I'd left!? The damn girl would ruin everything if she didn't stop.

"Casper!" shouted another woman's voice.

Serena, but how? how did they both know that I was gone? Why of all days did they decide to check on me now? The shouts attracted the interest of the guards, and they quickly moved towards my position. If I was careful then they might move right past me, but they'd probably linger due to the women's efforts. They moved towards me and I lied on my stomach, and I remained still and a few moments passed while they ran past me. When they were gone I crawled towards there last position.

I continued crawling until a fence appeared up ahead, and it looked like a way out. Voices came from the village and it seemed that they were now aware of my absence. I reached the fence then moved towards the exit, however a veiled figure lingered nearby.

"If you leave you will put us all in danger, the ambassador will arrive in a few days; you must stay so that you are not noticed by them," said a soft female voice.

She sounded like the girl who'd cared for me after my beating, but her concerns were of little interest to me.

"If you're going to stop me then now is the time to do it, otherwise you'll let me go if you have any regard for me."

The veiled figure drew closer and removed her veil. She looked a lot like Zaria, except she was thinner and shorter, and her hair was braided. She carried no weapons, and it seemed that she was of no threat to me.

"I'm not here to stop you, I'm here to warn you that your departure may have unintended consequences; besides, you're still weak from your injuries."

"I'm aware of that, but I have to learn who this ambassador is, then I'll work out what to do next."

"You're going to fight them aren't you? But you'll die, especially if you attack this ambassador."

"I didn't say I was going to attack them, now if you'll excuse me I was just leaving."

"It's a commodore! Or sometimes there representatives, they will be well protected."

"I'm sure they will, colonials always are."

I left and looked back to see the maroon girl still watching me, who was she? And why did she help me? I did not know. Darkness shrouded the view beyond the village, and I would have to follow blindly for tonight. With nothing on me I was once again at the mercy of Mother Nature, I just hoped that she would be more merciful this time around. A few minutes passed while I wandered, then I tripped and fell into the ground. Wherever I was would have to be good enough, because I had enough injuries to worry about without adding a new one. I groaned in pain then readjusted my position, and I nursed my foot while staring blindly into the dark. The night was humid but come morning I'd be in for another cold chill. I gazed up at the stars and my eyes drooped, then a few moments later, a worry free sleep came over me.

CHAPTER 28

Survivors Curse

I awoke the next morning to the presence of someone nearby. I moved myself upright and a blade was quickly pressed against my neck. A maroon man resided nearby, and he sat and cooked at a small fire. An animal was skewered across his fireplace, and it looked like a bird but I couldn't tell for certain.

"You thought you could sneak out last night and we wouldn't find you, your quite the fool aren't you pirate?"

"I'm not staying there anymore, and if you intend to take me back you'll have to kill me first."

The maroon grinned then turned over his food, and he ensured that his blade stayed pressed against my neck.

"The madam wants you for a trade, there's no use for you so she wants to hand you over to the ambassador when they arrive."

"You can't bargain with England, not without losing your soul in the process."

"Perhaps, but it's not my call; so once this food is cooked and eaten, both of us are heading back."

I pushed his blade away from my neck and the metal cut into it while I fled. I ran towards the nearby rocks and I could use them to disarm him. I was a former naval man so I wasn't afraid of being unarmed, and this wasn't the first time that I'd had to disarm thugs like this. The maroon advanced on me and I looked at his sword, and the mutt was using my own.

"You're going to kill a pirate with his own weapon!? You soulless cretin, have you no heart?"

The maroon ignored me then slashed towards my gut, and I avoided it then grabbed a nearby rock.

"Your weak and injured pirate, make this easy on yourself and surrender."

"I can't, and I won't! I didn't give England that satisfaction, and I won't be giving it to you either."

The maroon thrusted his sword towards me and I threw a rock towards his chin. The rock stunned and injured his face, and he grunted in pain while I moved towards him.

I pinned his sword arm in an arm lock, then tried forcing him to release the weapon. The maroon resisted and I released him then kneed him in the face, then while he squirmed in pain I reapplied his arm lock.

"Give me the sword and walk away, if you don't I'll break it."

"Go ahead, if you do the others will hear me," taunted the maroon.

I increased the pressure and he squirmed, then he held on so I contemplated my options.

I released his arm lock and punched him in the chin, and he cursed violently, then while he recovered I reached for the rock. I grabbed it and violently smashed it into his knee, and he whimpered into the ground helplessly. I moved behind him and he rose to one knee, then I held the rock against his face.

"You're injured and weak maroon, make this easy on yourself and surrender."

The maroon dropped the sword immediately, then out of malice, I scraped the rock against his face. He cried as the stone cut into his flesh, and a few moments passed while I thought about all the things that these people have done to me. I figured a bit of torture wouldn't hurt, and this maggot would remember it for a while. I released him then pushed him away, then as a precaution I whacked him with the rock and he collapsed back into the ground.

I reclaimed my sword after knocking him out, then went to check on his would be meal. His food was cooked so I was happy to devour it, and I didn't know what it was, but I didn't feel sick upon eating it. After I finished I assessed my wounds, including the fresh cut on my neck. I had nothing to clean or bandage them with, so I'd have to deal with the trickling blood for now. I was back to being a stranded survivor, and I'd have to seek out a new place for the night; if one maroon could find me then I'm sure the others could as well. My mobility was better than it was yesterday, and I hoped that it continued to improve. I had to avoid fights for the time being, since I was in no shape for a battle. I couldn't run either, so if there was a pursuit then I'd be in trouble.

I wandered the tropics armed with my sword and rock, and a black goanna suddenly appeared to meet me. A minute or so passed while it followed me, and its tongue flickered while it trailed behind me. A lone jackal also appeared, and it snarled at me while I continued walking. It moved towards me and I stood my ground, then it fled towards better prospects. Moments passed then a fox appeared also, and it kept its distance upon seeing me. Sand appeared while I continued trekking, and this attracted my attention as I wondered if I was close to the beach. I continued walking until the sands and the sea came into view, then I rested and explored my surroundings.

To my horror an English encampment came into view, it was several hundred yards away, yet there was a large ship anchored towards the shoreline. Any attempt I made to get off this island would be infinitely harder if that ship or encampment spotted me, and it seemed that I'd have to find another place to depart from. I observed the encampment and a minute or so passed while I squinted, then a single colonial came into view. There was little chance of him spotting me, but I got up and left anyway.

Seagulls and herons squawked nearby, and I headed further into the tropics, while checking to make sure that I wasn't being followed. I continued journeying until I came across a small stream of water, I didn't have a bottle or a fire, so I couldn't drink from it yet. I moved on and came across a large clearing, then after passing through it an abandoned stick shelter came into view. It was big enough to stay in, but I would need something to cover it with, considering the rain was always a factor here. With the shelter seemingly sorted I now needed a fire, but I had no ideas on how I would start one. I sat down inside the shelter, brooding on what I should do next. I was scared on the inside, scared that this would be it. Last time I was prepared for a life on an island, but this time I wasn't, and this time I was alone. A few minutes passed then I got up and left the shelter,

I estimated that I had several hours until dusk, and I needed timber and food, so I had to use that time wisely.

I left the rock in the shelter then headed back towards the stream, I knew where it was so I figured that it was best to scout that area first. I wanted to remain close to the shelter, and it seemed like a good starting point for me.

I located the stream then quickly scanned the surrounding area. Various sticks were bundled up along the ground, but apart from that, there was nothing that appealed to me. I collected them then moved on, and a bush appeared up ahead, one with orange fruits attached to it. I tasted them and concluded that they were edible, then picked as many as I could until my hands were full. I placed my sword in my pants then headed back, and it wasn't comfortable, but it was the only way that I could carry it along with my findings. I made it back then placed the sticks and the fruits next to the rock, I'd just eaten so I figured it was smarter to save the fruits for tonight. The only dilemma left was water, and how I would collect it from the stream. Another dilemma suddenly hit me, I'd have to hand drill a fire without my dagger, and it would be much more inconvenient without it. I groaned and carefully pulled my sword out of my pants, then I left again, to explore the clearing around me.

I collected extra sticks while I walked, and various flowers sprouted from the grass and bushes around me. I continued walking and a dead fox appeared up ahead, it appeared fresh, and I didn't want to encounter any more jackals. I quickly left the area then continued exploring, and I tried thinking about how I could collect the water from the stream. My thoughts turned to a log, or perhaps a leaf, but where would I find them? I was stumped by this dilemma. I collected some extra sticks then headed back to the shelter, and when I returned I quickly got to work on hand drilling my fire. I had no dagger so I was already frustrated, and I started drilling and hoped for the best. I rubbed and rubbed, and no spark ignited, then I tried again, and still no spark emerged. I tried a fourth time and lost my temper, then a few moments passed, and when I was calmer I tried once more. I rubbed vigorously and a spark finally sizzled, then I surveyed every direction around me, and suddenly, a thought hit me.

Shells, the shells at the beach might be able to help me carry water back to the shelter, but could I find any that were big enough? That was the golden question. I would have to go to the beach before nightfall, and if there were large or medium sized shells there, then perhaps my water problem could be solved.

I would have to be vigilant if I went there, but I was confident that I could search the beach and return without worry. I grabbed an orange fruit and placed it in my pants pocket, then I looked over my supply stash, and walked off towards the beach.

Several minutes passed then the sand trails appeared again, and upon arriving at the beach I walked in the opposite direction of the English encampment. The single colonial remained there, until he faded from view and no longer mattered anymore. The beach didn't have any rock formations, so finding bigger shells might be more challenging then I hoped. Small white crabs scurried across the sands while I surveyed them, and none of them were big enough to eat but they reminded me of Twin-Reef Island. Potential shells came into view, and they were big enough to drink from but it would take a lot of sips for me to hydrate myself with. I continued searching and only miniature ones came into view, then I started thinking that this shell idea was futile. I gave up and stopped searching, then I sat on the beach and brooded while looking out onto the horizon.

Injured turtles lay stranded along the shoreline, and I sympathised with them, since they must've felt just as hopeless as I was. A dark thought suddenly entered my mind, and I stared at the injured creatures, then looked away out of shame. If I was desperate enough I could kill one of them for their shell, but I hated the idea, and I didn't want to resort to it. The beach was quiet and there were no birds in sight, it was just the waves and I, alone again. I got up and continued walking, then I begrudgingly looked across the area.

I turned to leave until a glint caught my eye, then I moved towards the shallows in order to investigate it. I drew closer and a single bottle floated in the waves in front of me, my prayers seemed to be answered, and I couldn't believe my eyes. I picked it up and a parchment and a coin lay inside it, but I didn't care about that, I was just relieved to have a bottle. I relieved myself of the shells then carefully placed the bottle inside my pocket. I put the bottles contents in my other pocket, then smiled as my day had been salvaged.

I headed back to collect my water, then after that was done, I could spend the next couple of hours resting with my supplies.

CHAPTER 29

Last Plea

The evening arrived and I organised my fire and water for the night. I gathered my collected fruits after, then started eating them while I prepared myself for sleep. While I ate I thought about tomorrow, and all the days that would follow; I wasn't sure where I was going, and no part of me told me what I should do. As a pirate I wanted independence, as a castaway I wanted revenge, and as a naval man, I wanted belonging. Nothing stood out, I still wanted revenge, I still wanted independence, but they were like clouds; clouds that I kept running towards but could never reach. In these last few weeks I've learned that you're never in control, you're just tricked into believing you are. If that was the only lesson I took out of this life, at least it was a lesson that I'd never forget.

I finished my fruits then my curiosity peaked, and I pulled out the parchment from the bottle and gently unfolded it. I laid it down on my side and skimmed over it, it was a farewell letter, from a man who'd given up hope.

Dear Crewmen

I know you'll never receive this but I wanted to record my last thoughts while I can. I've been away for four months now, and only three of them were for unavoidable reasons. I've been stranded here for those remaining months, and after trying everything I could to come back, I've finally lost hope. Our time together was short but it was some of the best times of my life, and I'm sorry that I've abandoned you, but I had to get away for the sake of our cause. I did the best I could with the time I had left, and so with that said, I have little to regret. I don't know what will happen to you, but I trust in our partners plan. We've been sabotaged, we've been hunted, we've been denounced, and yet still we live. The spirit of free men lives in on those who follow the black, and as long as one of you lives, then free men shall live again.

Yours Sincerely
Neagan

Neagan, this is Bonnets letter! He's still alive! Or is he? I don't know but I was getting closer. It didn't mention what he was up to, or what the fate of his crew was, but the letters existence gave me something to cling to.

His wording was inspiring, it was organic and almost posh, as if the man had had experience in wooing people. Perhaps it was just men though, since the women I know seem to hate him. Squawking birds suddenly interrupted my thoughts, and my peace of mind vanished. The sounds stopped and I cursed at them, then I closed my eyes and hoped for a good night's sleep.

I awoke the next morning and immediately removed my old bandages. Blood and bruising still remained, yet I was feeling better than before. Pain was becoming less and less frequent, and I was feeling confident again. Fear and doubt shrunk inside me, to a point where I could almost hope again, or feel hope again. After taking off the bandages I headed towards the stream, with the intention of washing this smelly body of mine. I didn't know for sure if it was smelly or not, but when it came to this subject I had a special sense for it. The maroons hadn't shown me the kindness of a bath or a shower, but then again who knew if they did that sort of thing. A few minutes passed while I walked towards the stream, and upon arrival I searched for a good spot to clean myself in. I located one then quickly removed my clothes, and when I finished undressing, a shot suddenly went off. A loud scream quickly followed, and I paused hesitantly upon hearing it.

I remained still and there were no signs of activity, then I put my clothes back on and settled for a face wash instead. I tried distinguishing which direction the shot came from, but I couldn't tell. I didn't want to wander too far away, because the further away I went the more chance I'd have of being recaptured. A few minutes passed while I scouted the area, then I gave up and headed back to the stream. I undressed again and entered into the streams waters, and the coolness was cleansing, and it helped soothe all my aches and pains. Moments later stinging erupted from my sores, and I grimaced terribly but remained inside the stream. Cleanliness and coldness engulfed my body, and several minutes passed while I soaked in it.

I exited then dried myself off with my coat, then I laid on it and rested. A few moments passed then I changed back into my clothes, then I searched for firewood, and there was none around.

I searched until I located some, then I bundled it up and headed back to the shelter. Faint footsteps approached me while I walked, and I tried ignoring them yet they kept coming. I dropped the firewood and drew my sword, and I stayed still while I waited for them to find me. A while passed and they got closer, then closer, until a figure approached. A dark skinned girl with a black ponytail drew near, and she appeared injured, and worse yet... she appeared to be Zaria. She bled badly, and she seemed to be getting weaker by the minute.

"Zaria? What happened to you?"

She collapsed upon reaching me, and I caught her before she hit the ground. Her brown eyes struggled to stay open, and I searched for her wound and blood quickly moistened my hand. Dread enveloped me, then my hand touched her wound. She'd been shot in the back with a firearm, and I tried stabilizing her until voices suddenly approached us. I placed her on my back then moved, and while I moved the voices drew nearer. I quickly jogged and prayed for an escape, and I continued jogging until I reached the shelter. I leaped inside it and carefully laid Zaria down, then I spied outside the shelter. A minute or so passed then a skinny redcoat man appeared nearby.

He lingered and I grew concerned that he wouldn't leave.

"She's not here lieutenant!"

He moved on and I sighed in relief.

When he was gone I immediately returned to Zaria, and she was fading quickly, and I had little to treat her with. I looked around to see what I could do, then Zaria moaned and I turned to her.

"Don't bother, the wound is too great and I'm already dying. There's only one thing you can do for me now."

"What is it? Tell me."

"Take my body back to the maroons, they'll mistrust you at first, but they will repay you in time."

"No, I can't, they'll kill me! Or lock me up, I can't do this."

"My family is there Casper, please, please take me back to them, I know it'll be hard but they'll be grateful if you do."

I sighed in resistance, and Zaria's grip weakened, I had to fulfil her wish, even if I suffered for it.

"All right, I'll do it, I'll take you back."

Zaria relaxed then sighed happily, and I tried calming myself in the meantime.

"She's here Casper, the commodore is here and she's looking for you, she's scared, scared that she won't find you. Help my people, help them and they will help you fight her; please help them, you're the only one who can."

Zaria's hand went limp, and her eyes closed leaving me miserable and distraught. My heart knotted and contorted restlessly, but I would honour my promise to her, she deserved that. I sat motionless while Zaria's body remained in my arms, I couldn't move, and I could hardly think.

I searched her body while I recovered from her passing, and she had nothing on her, not surprising since she was still a captive of the commodore's. I dreaded returning back to the maroon village, but there was no way around it now, still, I needed supplies first. I had to go back and retrieve my firewood, and I'd need food and water before I set off towards the maroon village. I'd have to keep a lookout for any redcoat patrols, which I'm sure were still around all though I prayed that they'd gone back to their encampment. I said some final words to Zaria, then left and searched for supplies. I walked north since I was unfamiliar with it, and I scouted the surroundings for any fruit trees. I carried my bottle in my pocket and kept my sword close by, then while I walked nuts appeared on the ground nearby.

I collected them then continued searching, and I exited the clearing and more shrubs appeared just past it.

I continued walking and a coconut lay on the ground, and I collected it then continued on, and more nuts appeared while I trekked. No fruits were in sight, so I gave up the search and headed back. What I had now would have to suffice, and I needed water and firewood next.

I returned to the shelter and dropped off the food that I'd collected, then I headed back towards the stream. The temperature rose from place to place, and I suspected that the morning was over, since the humidity started to rise.

I reached the stream then washed myself in it, and I drank whatever was left in my bottle. I refilled it then I pondered. My thoughts turned to Zaria and the stream's trickling water echoed inside my mind, I couldn't get her voice out of my head. Her death replayed itself in my mind multiple times, and it haunted me, because I was supposed to help her. She'd helped Fletch when he was his at his worst, yet I couldn't help her in kind, it was wrong, and it was ruining me. I set off to reclaim my firewood, then a minute or so passed and I arrived back at the scene. It was scattered all over the place, and a minute or so passed while I reorganised it. I carried it back with me, and a few minutes later I returned to the shelter. I dropped the firewood off, then paused. A part of me wanted to investigate the English encampment, to see if the commodore was inside, but that would have to wait, Zaria's plea was more important.

I cracked open the coconut and shuddered while drinking its contents. I then ate what was inside, and it was something edible, so I couldn't complain. I ate a handful of nuts after and all though it didn't fill me up it would suffice for now. I gazed at Zaria's body, then gently moved it out of the enclosure. I wish I had something to cover it with, but I didn't want to waste time with that. I lifted Zaria onto my back then set off towards the maroon village. I said a quick thank you to the shelter, then farewelled it because I'd probably never see it again.

CHAPTER 30

Return to Me

The maroon village appeared up ahead, and I placed Zaria on the ground upon seeing it. I rested, trying to recover from the extra load that had worn me out. I'd spent countless minutes walking here, and I wasn't sure if that was natural or not. I drank from my bottle of water, and when I finished some colonial voices suddenly came to life. They must be sentries, which meant that the ambassador would be arriving today. Dropping off Zaria at the village would be more difficult if that was right, but it was too late to turn back now. I crept into a low stance and walked towards the voices, then while I moved the voices grew louder.

"The exchange is on today men, keep alert in case there's any interference," said a colonial.

"Yes lieutenant!" shouted another colonial.

I continued moving and the sentries came into view, and I quickly darted behind a tree upon seeing them. Two soldiers faced each other, and I seemed unnoticed for now.

I watched them and a few moments passed while they remained still, then I left and scoped out another route. From this point on I had no idea where I was going, so I had to hope that something would present itself. I continued venturing forward and three more sentries appeared, and this time they were patrolling, which meant that there was a chance that I could sneak past them. I drew a mark in the ground with a stick to remember this route, then I continued moving in order to scope out other points of entry. Several minutes passed and I surmised that I'd scoped out all of the village's surroundings, and sneaking past the patrol seemed like the best option. I quickly returned to where Zaria was left, then I breathed deeply before lifting her up. I stayed low and walked slower, then I moved towards where the patrol was located. I arrived then watched them again, and a few moments passed while I tried estimating when I should sneak past them.

Carrying Zaria with me meant that I had to give myself some extra time, but despite this, I continued watching them. I grew confident with my estimates, then I moved towards the opening while the patrol walked out of sight.

I creeped across and reached the village entrance, and everything seemed to be ok.

"Halt!!"

I stopped and lowered Zaria to the ground, then I dashed towards the tall grass nearby. The guard approached and spotted Zaria's body, then he looked in my direction.

"This is her! She must've backtracked and bled out here, the commodore will be relieved."

"Should we take the body back then? For proof or reassurance of our claims," said a second guard.

"Not yet, we were asked to patrol the area so we'll stay here for now. But once our shift is over, we'll take the body back."

The guard left and returned to his normal sweep, and when he was out of sight I emerged from the grass. I scanned the area to make sure I was clear, then I lifted Zaria again. I reverted back into a low creep, and cautiously moved towards the maroon village.

While I entered the atmosphere was unusually quiet, I suppose the exchange was the reason for this, but I suspected there was more to it. I continued moving and scanned the huts nearby, but in my mind I kept wondering, how do I do this without being caught? And how am I supposed to find a family that I've never met before? This was more challenging than I thought. A part of me wanted to leave the body here and now, but if it was me then I suppose I'd want better treatment than that. I continued walking and entered into a hut, and a knife rested on the ground which I was tempted to pinch. I entered into another hut and a wooden stand stood inside it, along with half a dozen books resting atop it. Another item attracted my interest though, a flute along with a wooden statue depicting a fish.

I exited then entered into a third hut, and a lone pistol rested inside it. I inspected it and wasn't sure if it was loaded or not, but there wasn't any additional shot or powder nearby. Voices suddenly startled me, and I moved towards them in order to learn who they belonged too. A private conversation came into view while I walked, and I crept closer and laid Zaria on the ground. I continued moving and the voices grew louder, then Commodore Weiss and the maroon leader appeared up ahead. They conversed among themselves, and the commodore's composure seemed fidgety.

"A maroon was found wandering Kingston Shauna, alone! I hope it wasn't one from here, because that would be very unfortunate."

"It can't be from here, everyone is accounted for; whoever you saw must be from somewhere else."

"Don't take me for a fool, I know your family has past ties to piracy, perhaps there's something that you'd like to confess?"

"My daughter's been gone for a long time, so if you're suggesting that it's her," she paused, then stopped to recollect herself.

"Your right it could be anyone, but she was unaccounted for so I have to speculate regardless."

"Is there anything else that you would like to consult with me about?"

"Neagan, I assume he's been dealt with by now, you said last time you were having trouble finding him."

"Yes we were, but he's dead now, so he's not a threat to you anymore. I still think you should pass on his last words to his crew, they would like that if you did."

"For twenty workers I'll pass on the message, if there still alive… besides, your last batch of workers weren't up to scratch."

"The agreement was ten workers a month, and there long months from what I've heard."

"Take it or leave it, I'm trying to put piracy behind me, even if one of them was useful to us."

"I'll leave it, you have what you want so there's no reason for you to linger."

"I have one more reason, I want to know if you'd had any strangers here recently?"

"Not recently, why?"

"I received word that a potential pirate was seen near this area, so I was wondering if they'd shown up here."

"Well if they do they won't last long, you know how I feel about them."

"Yes I do, but I have to wonder regardless. Good day madam, I'll be leaving now."

The commodore left and the madam stayed, quietly contemplating her discussion I assume. Since she was alone I could use this chance to confront her, and make her tell me where Zaria's family is; and if she resisted, then I could hurt her in clear conscious. Either way I needed her to talk, willingly, or unwillingly.

I contemplated my approach, and weighed up whether it should be peaceful or aggressive. I wanted to incorporate both, but that sounded impossible. I lifted Zaria onto my shoulder, then adjusted her body weight slightly. I reached for my sword and Zaria shifted, I couldn't draw it, not without dropping her. I moved towards her with Zaria in tow, and the madam frowned upon seeing me. She noticed the body and her frown changed into confusion, though she remained where she was.

"Who is that? Have you brought a body to threaten me with?"

"Her name is Zaria, I'm trying to find her family: after that I'll be leaving."

"Zaria? No… it can't be, your lying!"

I gently lowered Zaria to the ground, and drew my sword as a precaution, in case she retaliated in kind. The madam approached me, seemingly conflicted about whether to attack or to mourn, then she looked at the body, and saw that I was right. She knelt down and cradled the body in her arms, and she mourned terribly, and I looked away out of guilt.

"My task is done then, so I'll leave."

I moved back towards where I'd come from, and the maroons intercepted me. From there expressions it seemed like they'd overheard our conversation. I kept my sword ready as a deterrent, then I walked by them again and I couldn't get through.

"You carried her all this way even though you didn't need to, and you knew that we mistreated you and yet you returned anyway; it seems I was wrong about you, and because of that I am in your debt," said the madam.

"I didn't do it for you I did it for her, she helped me in a time of need, but I wasn't able to do the same; so whether I liked it or not, this was all I could do for her."

"Then stay with us tonight, with the colonials gone it will be easier for us to convene."

"I'll take my chances elsewhere, I'm not staying with those who beat and broke me for self-gratification."

"I know what I did was wrong, many people in this village agree on that; but you have to know that for so long I've wanted to find the crew that took my daughter away from me; I never could of course, so instead I punished you. It doesn't make it any better, but I just wanted to explain why it happened."

"YOU CHOSE THE EASY WAY OUT!! Like so many others do, you're just like the colonial leaders, you abuse your power; so sure I understand, but I do not forgive, so don't try and ask me to."

I put my sword away and left, otherwise I'd use it and make things worse.

"What did they do to you Casper? What did England do to spark such hatred within you?"

"What does it matter? Like you I'll never be able to inflict my deepest and darkest desires upon them."

"You're giving up? After surviving this long? Why would you do that?"

"Because I'm not strong enough! Because everywhere I go I'm treated as the enemy; and because of you I can't even fight back!! Your villagers made sure of that."

The crowd fell silent after my outburst, clearly shocked by my aggression. I was surrounded by potential enemies, yet here I stood, like the wounded dog fighting his own pack. I walked off before things got worse, and my shoulder ached while I left, and I tried nursing it along the way. I exited the village and drank from my bottle of water, and I emptied it then started walking back towards the shelter.

My stomach growled while I walked, letting me know that it would be the first thing to tend to upon return. I'd have to refill my water as well, especially before nightfall. Footsteps moved towards me while I walked, and I turned to see maroons following me. I immediately stopped and turned to face them, then Serena approached and it appeared that she was leading them.

"Madam Shauna wants to help you, if you meet with her tonight then she'll help you depart the island."

"Is that so? I thought the maroons signed a treaty, if you do this then you'll be breaking it."

"She can't help you on the battlefield but she can help you get to it, you just have to meet with her, along with myself and Sandy."

"I don't trust her or you, so I'll find my own way off this island thanks."

"That's unlikely, another pirate already tried and failed at that. Madam Shauna believes that you're the pirate the commodore is looking for, and she believes that she's afraid of you."

"Why would she be afraid of me? She's only afraid that I might tarnish her reputation."

"That still means she's afraid of you, a free, uncontained, and uncontrollable you; we've never seen the commodore like this, so you have to seize this while you still can."

"So what are you suggesting? That I torment her? That's impossible."

"Killing her is impossible... perhaps, but no you should show her what you're capable of; bring her worst fears to life, then live long enough to see them through."

"But what about my crew? Or my captain? If I can't kill her then she gets away with that."

"Sure she gets away with that, but if you do this, then she may regret getting away with that; don't avenge them by killing her... avenge them by surviving her."

"It doesn't sound as satisfying, but I see your point, perhaps you have experience with this sort of thing? Or did you just make it all up?"

"The tribe may have surrendered to the colonials, but some of us still imagine what it would be like if we didn't; I was one of those people, and I had my wishes for what I would do to them should we have prevailed."

I nodded in understanding, then farewelled her.

"You can spend weeks trying to survive here, trying to escape this lonely island, but if you die in the attempt; then what we saw today will have gone to waste; and if we're honest with ourselves, none of us want that."

CHAPTER 31

One Man Crew

The sunset arrived and I went looking for the maroons. Minutes later they found me, and they escorted me towards Madam Shauna. I didn't give Serena an answer when we spoke, but I thought on it during the afternoon and sought out the maroon foragers to deliver it to them. The foragers also helped me find fruit, which I appreciated because I was craving them. I returned to the stream after I'd gotten fruits, then I bathed in it and explored the island after. When I was finished I headed back and sought out the maroon escorts, who currently walked with me while I moved towards the beach. Several minutes later the sand trails appeared, and a few minutes passed then Madam Shauna stood along the beach waiting for us. Sandy and Serena were with her also, and upon reaching them the escorts quickly moved to stand alongside the madam.

"Everyone here is tasked with assisting you on your journey, so allow me to be the first," said Serena.

Serena revealed a sword from behind her back, and bowed slightly before presenting it to me. A sheathed cutlass rested on her hands, one similar to my own except for one slight detail.

The handguard was gold and the blade was dark grey, making it different from my silver bladed one.

"It belonged to the pirate that once resided here, I kept it hidden after his death, and now I want you to have it; you may need it where you're going."

"Thank you, I promise I will use it well."

Serena moved away and Sandy moved in instead.

"In this sack you shall have everything that you need, fruit, medicine, and navigational tools: keep it safe, and it shall keep you alive."

I nodded and smiled gratefully.

Sandy moved away then the madam approached me, all though she had no apparent gifts to give.

"I don't know what you're hoping to find in Kingston, but I implore you to remember that it will no longer be the place that you remember. You must always be cautious once there, if you're not then you're already in danger."

"I know it'll be different, but I also know that it's where I'm meant to be. I just don't know what I'm supposed to do once I'm there, the answer isn't so clear anymore."

"Trust in yourself and you will find your answer, nobody ever knows what their truly capable of until the moment arrives, but this is your chance to find out; after that, the rest is up to you."

"Understood."

The maroons and I waded ourselves towards the sloop, then I waved to the women and boarded it. I slid my new cutlass into my belt upon boarding, and smiled at its glistening appearance. I helped the maroons disembark after they boarded, and when we were finished, I happily looked back while our ship departed.

Maybe now things would finally come to an end, maybe now I could finally put this endeavour to rest, once, and for all.

The journey would be long and the maroons didn't need me, so I went below and searched for the nearest hammock to lie in. I still didn't know what my plan was once I reached Kingston, and it's been almost a year since I've been there, so finding my way around might be tricky. All my former allies came to mind since I might see them again, and some of them were even friends at some point; but would they understand? Probably not. I was there monster now, and therefore I would kill them if I had to. In the end anyone that defends her from me will die, whether it's a man, woman, or child, no one will be safe if they try and protect her from me. The maroon's think that I will have to choose between survival and revenge, but for me, revenge was survival. It is the survival of my soul, and without it, I might as well die here and now. I've survived marooning, storms, pirate hunters, and insurgents; right now I couldn't envision a reality where everything that I've fought for died in Kingston. That was not acceptable to me.

I reflected on what my crewmates would do if they were here, what if instead of me it was them? Would they give up? Walk away? Seek out an ordinary life? I didn't know, but I also didn't know how someone could live with that, how could they live knowing that what they've lost is far greater than what they've found, or what they've recovered, to me, that sounded like hell.

If there's one thing the colonials taught me, it was grit, to not give up on your men even if your elders do; because despite their struggles, some of them were worth going the extra knot for; even if they hated you for it.

I worked so hard to build something there, and I worked even harder to build something with Maroo. I can't let go of that, I won't! not without a fight! And they will get one, and I will not let go until it's over, over for them, or over for me. Piracy taught me true acceptance, and when you belong to that you become more powerful than anyone could imagine, and with grit and acceptance, you become damn well near indestructible. With those two a perfect world is almost achievable, something that I'd always dreamed of, but was always sceptical to as well. If I succeeded I don't know what will happen next, I just know that I will have the peace of mind to figure it out; then the balance will take care of the rest. The goal of revenge might be an impossibility, but like I've said before, if I can't have her life, then I'll take her child's instead; then like me, she will be alone in this world forever.

But before any of that could happen, Kingston had to learn that piracy is not so dead after all. I will attack them, I will pirate them, and then I will escape them... for now. The rage inside me wore me out, and moments later I nodded off to sleep.

I awoke to a mist of darkness, and I carefully exited my hammock in order to make my way towards the deck. I emerged and the stars shined upon me, and combined with the calm sea, it made for a beautiful night ahead. The stars glimmered and glowed in synchronization, and the waves moved pleasantly to fill in the quietness around me. A few maroons played with dice nearby, and it seemed like a good past time but I was more interested in the scenery. I walked towards the bowsprit and leaned against the ships railing, then I scoured the darkening sea. This was a peace that I had missed for so long, and because of that, I would never take it for granted again. I closed my eyes and tried to meditate, but I struggled, and a few minutes passed then I stopped. I sat down against the ships railing, and the peaceful atmosphere lulled me into a daze. I dozed off after, while the sea carried us along the waves.

I awoke and looked through my satchel, and a small spyglass was inside. A compass was in there as well, along with a few other sailing tools. I'd have to swim for Kingston's shore tomorrow, and I'd have to make sure that this satchel was secure.

The maroons went to sleep and I took first watch, then an hour or so passed and my watch ended and I swapped with another crewman.

I awoke to a brisk and windy morning, and I pulled out the spyglass and located Kingston off in the distance. I was so close now, and in mere hours I'd be able to graze its streets again, and I'd be in the presence of civilization once more. I started eating all of the food that Sandy had given me, because it'd be no good to me after my swim. I also used the medicine that she gave me to treat my bruising, which was swelling across my face and chest. The paste was effective so far, but the bruising would remain for weeks to come. I drank some water and quenched my overnight thirst, and any that I didn't need I poured onto my body to wake myself up. The maroons saw Kingston in their sights, and they began their stealthily approach towards its waters. There were no longboats on this vessel, so this was the best that they could do without being exposed. I'd told them I was a capable swimmer, but a head start would be nice since anything could happen while you're at the mercy of the sea. My eyes remained fixed upon Kingston while we approached, and as we moved closer I prepared myself for the task ahead.

An hour or so passed and the docks appeared and came into view, it wouldn't be long now until I was asked to swim for shore. I figured that I had a five hundred yard swim ahead of me, but as long as the sea stayed the way it was then that shouldn't be a problem. With everything that I was carrying I would be tired by the time I got there, but I'd make it, I had to. I waited patiently while we edged closer and closer to where the maroons wanted to stop, and I was ready for their call, whenever they decided to make it. Two fishing ships appeared nearby, and they were the only ships in sight so there wasn't much to worry about at the moment. But I understood and respected there caution, and I didn't press them into sailing closer.

We reached the drop off point and I quickly farewelled and thanked the four maroons, then I dived into the sea. It was colder and rougher than I expected, but my body still had some resistance to its temperature. My two swords weighed me down, and the current pushed against me. I power swam to avoid early fatigue, and I put my satchel in my pants to ensure that it didn't float away. It wasn't a comfortable feeling, but I had little choice, since I would need it later on.

I turned around and the maroons were already leaving, apparently they weren't interested in seeing if I could make the journey or not. I focused on other things and continued swimming, and I pictured Twin-Reef islands sands, along with its trees and wildlife. I pictured my former crewmen as well, to help spur me on towards shore. I pictured the crabs and fish, and I imagined myself eating them if I ever returned. A few moments passed while I rested, then some fishermen looked at me quizzically, and they shook their heads in disbelief. I continued swimming and gritted myself through the current, and the water grew less and less rough, all though I continued readjusting myself to stay on course.

My arms and legs burned from the effort, but that only meant that if I stopped then I wouldn't be able to start back up again. I pressed and pressed until I touched sand, then I waded myself towards the Kingston shore. It was less than a hundred yards away and I crawled towards it, digging in deeper than I'd ever known before. Closer and closer I crawled, then finally... I pulled myself out of the oceans reach. I had nothing left, though I smiled as I rolled onto my back, and I gazed up at the glistening sky above me. I was home.

CHAPTER 32

Fallen Men

Several minutes passed while I caught my breath, then I dried myself off on the beach. My eyes turned to a watch tower nearby, and a colonial soldier was perched atop it; with his musket at the ready. I walked towards the markets and bypassed them to enter the city's centre. Everything seemed to be the same here, but the mood was different, like it was angrier or scarier than before. Kingston's white timbered buildings were the same, and I assumed that its manor was as well, with its sandstone like exterior. I headed towards the chapel up the street, and I figured that I could use some divine company right about now. I arrived and sat at its entrance, and I brooded on what my next move was. I had anonymity so I had to make use of it, but I didn't know how. When I was on Twin-Reef Island I could always picture how my revenge was going to go, but now that I was here, I couldn't do that anymore. My dreams had finally caught up with my reality, and now I didn't know how to move on.

A growing crowd distracted me from my brooding, and an old speaker ushered them in, a wig wearing klutz who looked like a street urchin that just drank one too many bottles of grog.

"Citizens of Kingston! A fiendish wench has infiltrated our wonderful city, one who comes from the east!! Two days ago she attacked our soldiers here, but now she has vanished… like a demon from the abyss!"

A fiendish wench from the east? That's a vague description. There were no leads it seemed, all though… there was one possible culprit.

"This woman is foreign and grotesque, and she must be found before she strikes again! If anyone has any information on her whereabouts, please come forward, so that we can end this treachery."

The crowd remained silent, but they were entertained by the coot's efforts. The speaker continued his rant and I left, and I wanted to figure out my plan elsewhere. I needed to explore Kingston before I did anything rash, and I needed to find a ship, but I had no ideas on how I would get one. Pirating ships used to be an easier line of work, but now it seemed almost insane, especially if you were alone.

"Casper!" said a man's voice.

I ignored it and continued walking.

"Casper!"

I turned around and a young colonial boy approached me, and he recoiled upon seeing my face. He looked the same age as I was when I first joined up with them, and he was tall and lean, but chunkier than I was. He had shaggy brown hair and woody eyes, and his skin was milky white, which put me off and made me slightly jealous.

"Casper? It really is you after all these months, it's good to see you again."

"I'm sorry I don't recall your name."

"Michael, I was one of the recruits you trained two years ago; I'm sorry to hear what happened, the governor shouldn't have gotten involved in naval business."

"It's the commodore's fault not the governors, the former one, there the one that chose ambition over loyalty."

"Perhaps, but I suppose it doesn't matter anymore, what matters is your back! The word was that you'd left Kingston for good."

"I didn't leave by choice, I just had to get away from it for a time, you know… to clear my head and rethink things. It was tough, but I think I've achieved that."

"Well that's good to hear, the former recruits wanted to protest, but we were just recruits, so I'm sorry that we couldn't do more."

"Well… I've learned from it, so it's all right."

"So… after all this time what's brought you back now? I take it this isn't a social visit, it rarely is with you."

"I'm looking for someone, I saw them not long ago but I wasn't able to catch them in time; so I'm hoping that they've stopped by here."

"Well we've only had a few visitors recently so the odds are against you, who are you looking for?"

"Commodore Weiss, she and I have some business to settle, so I was wondering if she'd returned here."

"Well she did arrive with her fleet a few days ago, but no one has seen her since; I could take you to the manor if you want? If she's still here then that's where she'd be."

"I'd appreciate that, but will they let me in? A former naval instructor."

"Well we can try, maybe some of the other fella's are on duty; if they are then they'll let you in."

My mind laughed while he spoke, a colonial soldier was gonna escort me to a place that I intended to attack anyway, but regardless, I had to use this moment wisely. We walked towards our destination, and several townsfolk passed us by. Some of them seemed to recognise me, even with my new look. A while passed then the bell tower came into view, which indicated that the manors gates were nearby. The plantation fields also came into view, and they reminded me about what the maroons said about their treaty.

Several minutes passed then we reached the gates, and Michael left to go and talk to the two guards. They shook their heads at Michael's suggestion, and I approached them for a chat and they brandished their swords at me.

"The commodore isn't interested in talking with anyone right now, so whatever business you have with her will have to wait," said the first guard.

"But this is a naval instructor, he trained me and several others in Kingston, surely she can find time for him," said Michael.

"I have my orders, and I'm sorry but no one is allowed in at this moment; especially with a wanted fugitive in town," said the second guard.

Michael and I quietly walked away, and we continued moving until we were out of there hearing range.

"I'm sorry I couldn't get you in, some of these old toads just couldn't give a toss these days."

"I appreciate your efforts regardless, but I'll come back another time, you should probably get back to your post."

"Yeah you're right, not that it's much of a post today; still it was good to see you, stay safe Casper."

I smiled and nodded, and he ran off back to his post.

When he was gone I surveyed the manor again, trying to find any alternate ways to get inside. The only alternative way to get in was to climb, and I'd have to scale the fence in order to learn if the commodore was inside. To the far right there was an enclosed deck which would give me cover if I climbed the fence, but that would have to wait until nightfall, as would the attack itself. I headed towards the bell tower because it was a marvellous piece of work to look at, and even though it barely rang, I'm sure the views from above it would make even the sentries atop their towers jealous. I arrived at the tower and a hangman's stand captured my attention. With its presence, I forgot all about the tower. The nooses were empty, but the stench of death still emanated from them, as did the voices if I imagined them. A crowd and a host appeared in my mind, and the ugly affair played out in front of me. It was a side to civilization that was always ignored and supressed, and instead they tried to tell you that men like me were far more different to men like them, but the truth is… they weren't.

I left the stand behind and moved towards another watch tower, and the sentries eyes locked with mine. I passed him and encountered the markets, then instead of going to them I moved towards the beach instead.

I moved hastily and three large stones came into view, they were standing together, yet it was a sight that I didn't recall in Kingston.

The unfamiliar attraction interested me, and I bent down and touched the sand beneath it, and its softness also piqued my interest. The sand was softer than even the special sand on Twin-Reef Island, and feeling it reminded me of touching grain, all though it was like your first time feeling it all over again. I moved towards the rocks and a loud moan came from nearby, and it seemed like someone was hurt. I navigated my way around the stones, and I reached the end and someone attacked me.

A figure slashed towards me and I dodged the assault, then I eyed my attacker and a young woman looked back at me, a young woman named Kaleen. She was gravely wounded but she noticed that it was me, though she was in too much pain to respond. She held her waist, but I couldn't tell if she was bleeding or not.

"So it is you then, you're the one who's been terrorising Kingston, I should've known, you're the only one who could."

"I'm only terrorising the commodore, but as you can see I've failed in that."

"If you hadn't deserted me I could've helped you, we could've been allies instead of what we are now."

"I wouldn't have been able to justify anything if I'd taken you with me, if I did I would've lost all hope of keeping the others with me."

"Well it looks like that happened anyway, so that's another failure for you to live with."

"I'm not gonna apologise, so if you're here to kill me then go ahead, if you don't then my wounds will."

"You saved my life so I can't kill you in kind, but since you almost ended it that leaves us at an impasse."

"What does that mean?"

"It means we need each other, you need my help to live, and I need your help to leave; but first I need to know where your ship is."

"I'm not gonna tell you that, how stupid do you think I am!?"

"Very stupid if you don't cooperate, so you can either tell me where it is… or I'll make you tell me."

"Figures that a pirate would threaten a weaker opponent, since there weak themselves."

"Not by choice, we just do whatever is necessary."

"Fine… I'll tell you where it is, but you have to take me with you, please; I've been stuck here for days."

"I can't trust you Kaleen, but I'm willing to trust your ship; therefore there's no reason for me to help you, and there's no reason for me not to hurt you."

"So you'll sail away and leave me here? Just like I did to you? Even though I'm the only one who shares your conviction for revenge."

"I live in a post pirate world Kaleen, I have no allies anymore, only enemies."

CHAPTER 33

Blood for Blood

Kaleen fell unconscious after defying me, but I got what I wanted from her. My hands were covered in her blood, and her wound bled and drained her of life. I couldn't walk away though, it didn't feel right, even though it made me feel good. I tore off some of her tattered clothes and rinsed it in the sea, then I bound her waist tightly, and applied some of the paste that the maroons had given me. I didn't know if it would help, but it was all I had, and attempting to save her was better than not attempting. My conscious was a curse sometimes, but I had to try and ease the differences between us. She'd be sore when she awoke, but she'd be alive as well, at least I hoped. I was disappointed that I'd resorted to torture, but I've learned recently that I have to do this alone; piracy was gone for now perhaps, but maybe one day it could return, and if it did then I'd be there. Kaleen confessed that her ship was anchored close to Kingston's manor, but I would have to swim to reach it.

I left her and headed further inland to where nature was still untouched. I ventured towards the hills and the woodland, and several townsfolk appeared nearby. Most of them were hunters, but a few of them were wood workers as well, along with a few colonial patrols. A few minutes passed then the waterfront appeared, and the sea was much rougher than before.

I waded towards the sea and when I was deep enough the current quickly pulled me in. Kaleen's sloop appeared close by, but reaching it in this current would be difficult. I started swimming and my hunger and thirst hit me, and if there was no food or water on board then I'd be in trouble. Several minutes passed then I reached the sloop, and I slowly clawed myself onto its deck. I clutched my aching stomach upon boarding, and I tried easing my throat which was also causing me grief. I couldn't focus on anything, and I waited for my strength to come back. Moments later I recovered and moved towards the cabin, and I hoped that something was there that could treat my afflictions. A half-filled bottle of water appeared which I drank upon sight, along with fruits and breads which I also consumed.

It appeared that Kaleen had a decent food supply, and her water was sound but she didn't have much else. Her cabin seemed to be lacking, and I investigated it.

I opened a wooden draw and a small deposit of coins were inside it, along with the playing cards that belonged to her mother. No sailing equipment appeared in sight, but a single map lay on her table. Various scribbles covered parts of it, and they were all names for the various tropical islands that she'd picked out; like Twin-Reef, Salt Shore, and Riptide.

She must've gotten this when she was in Havana, unless it's been hidden for all this time. I didn't have a map to compare it too, but there was nothing on it that could help me. Since the ship was mine I needed to move it closer towards the mainland, but I had to be mindful of the fort as well. If I could dock under its sands then I'd be safe for the time being, but once I departed I'd be fair game once more. I moved towards the helm and hoisted the anchor from below, then once it was recovered I took the wheel and the ship glided across the sea. I smiled while I sailed, but I still needed to figure out how to get into Kingston's manor. I had to do that by tonight, because I didn't want to risk the fleet leaving come tomorrow. I recalled vague memories of what the manor looked like on the inside, but finding the commodore would still be challenging. I'd have to be patient, because I'd only get one shot at her, and if I failed, then I'd be finished.

A while passed then the landmass under the fort came into view, and I quickly steered the ship towards it. A few sloops were docked there already, so it wouldn't stand out any more than they did. I arrived and surveyed the fort, and I marvelled at it, a towering and formidable structure of earthly power. The walls of the fort were painted with a bark like brown, and atop it, its roofs were painted green, giving it a nature like appearance. Twelve black guns occupied the forts defences, and only four of them were in sight. The fort may have been made of stone, but it was built like a structure of nature. Kaleen's coins were with me, and I was tempted to go and spend them. Rum was something that I'd like to buy, but it wasn't what I needed right now. I pondered on what I needed most, and a few moments passed then an answer came to mind. To scale the manors fence I would need a grappling hook, and if I had one, I could maybe even scale the manor itself. I'd never used it for that purpose, but nevertheless if I got stuck then maybe it could help me. I'd have to ask the harbourmaster, and hope that he had what I needed. I needed some rope and a hook, and if he didn't have it then I'd ask the fishermen instead.

Other items I could use were blankets or a hat, but I'd have to see what else was around before settling on those trinkets. I headed towards the ships railing and jumped off into the sea, then I started swimming towards the mainland. My body was so tired of swimming, but at least this swim would be shorter than the last. A while passed then I reached land, and I slowly crawled towards shore. My legs were unsteady, and I rested while they wobbled from fatigue. My arms were stiff as well, and I lied on the sand for the meantime.

A few minutes passed then I carried on, and after I'd done this I'd have to rest on the sloop until nightfall. If I didn't do this I'd die in the manor tonight, and my mind already told me to stop, but I ignored it and willed myself forward. My eyes blacked out then returned to normal, and I'd have to deal with it for the moment. I moved towards the small markets, and they only had fish or crabs on their stands.

"Where's the harbourmaster?" I asked.

A fisherman pointed me towards him and I approached his stand. A burly dark skinned man greeted me, though he grimaced upon seeing my deformity.

"Do you have any rope or hooks for sale?"

"I have rope but not hooks, are you going fishing friend?" asked the harbourmaster.

"No I just wanted a grappling hook, just for a bit of fun you know."

"Well there a rare find but if you can make one yourself then I'm happy to sell you the rope for it."

"How much?"

"Four shillings, just went on special this."

"Lucky me, all right I'll take it."

We did our exchange then I farewelled the man.

"One more thing, ask the fishermen nearby for a hook, one of them should have one."

I spoke with five different fishermen, and only the last one had what I wanted.

"Aye I have a hook for you, but if ye want it you'll have to help me unload my latest haul first," said the fisherman.

After that laborious task he attached my rope and his hook together to craft what I wanted, and relief fell over me after it was complete.

"Thank you fisherman, you've helped me a lot."

Now I just needed supplies, for me and the ship. To get these supplies I'd probably need more coin first, and how does a humble pirate accomplish this? Simple… he swindles it from the tavern folk. It's the one place where people don't care if you trick or beat them, unless that's changed recently. But before I could go there I needed to rest, so I headed back to my ship immediately. I moved towards the sea and swam back towards the sloop, and a few minutes passed then I returned and boarded it. I moved towards the cabin and stripped off my damp clothes, then I laid on the bunk and quickly fell asleep from exhaustion.

A dream suddenly ensnared me, and an image of Fletch appeared in my mind. The two of us were in a town, all though I wasn't sure which one.

"We're free Casper, we've got all we need and we're free, it's hard to believe isn't it?" asked Fletch.

We were on a day out together, which never happened in reality but I guess this was something that I did want to happen. Suddenly Fletch disappeared, and I was left to try and find out why.

An image of us drinking together came into view, then we strolled through town and mucked around like little boys at school. The image lingered, then suddenly… it too vanished. The dream seemed like a farewell, and it was the first dream that I'd had in weeks. It was vague and unclear, just like my life at the moment. You can only dream what you can imagine, and right now, I couldn't imagine much. I awoke and still seemed tired which was frustrating. I lied on the bunk and my thoughts dwelled then dwindled, it bothered me that there was so much unresolved emotion inside of me. This just reinforced my current belief: that you were never in charge of anything, not now, not ever. I got off my bunk and started eating bread and fruit to regain my strength, then after I'd finished, I drank some water as well. I exited the cabin and observed the ongoing sunset, there was still some time to kill, so I weighed anchor and sailed towards the docks.

This was a risky move, but since it was nightfall I hoped that the darkness would help me. A short while passed and I arrived at the docks, then I washed my face with water and quickly redressed myself. My first stop would be the tavern, because if I failed at the manor I'd never see the tavern again. It's been a year since I've been to it, so it'll be interesting to see if it's still the same. After my job loss with the navy I spent a lot of time there, and I tried to gamble what I'd lost in income. I hope I did better this time, otherwise I'd be forced into more unpleasant methods. I started the short walk towards the tavern, and quiet dim lit streets awaited me. A humid breeze also blew in the air, making the night seem calm even though it wouldn't be. While I walked the quietness quickly changed into laughter, and numerous shouts came from the taverns walls. A few minutes passed then I reached the door, and I entered inside and it was quiet compared to its usual bustle.

A few men played slapjack nearby, and there game interested me more than the others did. I'd played it here before, but I was surprised that it was still going. Another table was playing blackjack, and that was the norm for gambling in Kingston. There were two options for me tonight, unless I took option three which was to have a drink, but that would be unwise.

"Put me in the next game boys, I've got shillings to spend."

The two men nodded then continued with their game, and a minute or so passed then it ended, and the loser quickly vacated. I put up five shillings, and this seemed to offend my opponent.

"That's old man change boy! Where's the rest of it huh? Did you spend it on that face?" asked the gambler.

"Take it or leave it, it's the best I can do for now."

"Fine, I'll take it you poor sod of a goat."

After the pleasantries, he started shuffling the cards.

"You had a rough week have you? Putting up piss poor wagers like that in Kingston."

"I start small but I win big, that's how I operate here."

The gambler smirked, then he prepared our card piles while a few bystanders came to watch. His shuffling was terrible, and unfortunately for him I received three of the four jacks in the game. He had a big pile after getting the last jack, but it didn't save him in the end.

"Blasted sod!"

He relinquished his shillings, then grumbled about his winning streak and left the table. It was funny to see his frustration get the better of him. His former opponent approached me, and he looked like he had the same attitude as his colleague.

"Five shillings then! You single minded willy," said the gambler.

Despite his taunts I only had to gamble half of my winnings from the previous game, so there was less to lose and everything to gain. He shuffled the deck and dealt out our respective cards piles, then we faced off. My opponent acquired three of the four jacks in the game, and all though I lasted longer than I expected, luck wasn't with me this time. I admitted defeat and surrendered my winnings, then I moved towards the blackjack table instead.

"Better luck next time Willy!" jeered the gambler.

Yeah, because next time we meet, I might just carve those words into your chest... piss face. I hurriedly walked towards the blackjack table, because if I didn't I might get real impulsive. A game had just ended for the three players at the table, and I put my wager in to reserve for the next one.

"I'll wager eight shillings."

"You have to wager ten boy, otherwise bugger off," said the dealer.

"Fine."

The dealer took my wager and dealt out everyone's hand. The dealer revealed a hand of twenty, while I came second with a hand of eighteen. The dealer took pity on me and returned half my wager, so I was able to play one more if I wanted. I hadn't lost too much yet, so I could risk one all or nothing game.

Once again the price was ten shillings, so I had to win this so I could get the other supplies.

Upon revealment I tied with another player, and we both had the same number of cards but neither of us had a natural blackjack.

"My hand has more value than my opponents."

'But you have the same number of cards as me, so what difference does that make?" Countered my opponent.

"Why don't we let the dealer decide? For fairness?"

"Very well, dealers favour then."

"I'll bend the rules just this once, I'll split your winnings equally so you'll both get twenty shillings," said the dealer.

Twenty shillings? I couldn't complain about that.

I collected my winnings then left the tavern, and I rushed towards the stores in order to buy my essential supplies. I went to the blacksmith as well, but he tried swindling me on a deal so when he was distracted I pinched one of his daggers. I purchased my sail and rope after, then headed towards the ship while trying to not get noticed. A while passed then I boarded, and I dumped the rope and the sails inside the cabin. I drank some water and rested, then with the supplies sorted it was now time to head to the manor. I grabbed my grappling hook and departed, then I scurried towards the streets. The quiet and peaceful atmosphere returned while I walked the streets, and I took the path towards the manor, while the night turned friendly around me. A while later I bypassed the buildings and the manor gates appeared once more, along with its fence and nearby sentries. I didn't intend to cross blades with them tonight, but if I wasn't careful I just might.

I moved towards the west side of the fence, and searched for a spot where I could grapple to. The guard's attention was firmly fixed upon the gate, so I should be fine while I tried to grapple and climb over there fence. I began spinning the grappling hook, then I threw it towards the top of the fence. It didn't lodge properly, so I was forced to try again. I threw it again and this time the hook connected, and when I was sure it was secure I started my climb.

The fence was large and climbing it was tiresome, but I made it to the top and quickly pushed myself over the bars. I safely reached the other side, then I fiddled with the grappling hook until it dislodged. A few attempts later I got it loose, then I jumped down and moved the hook over the fence. The drop was gentle but it was noisier than I expected, and the impact rattled my knees. With the fence clear I was safe for now, but I still had to find where the commodore was located. Moments passed and a sentry appeared on the roof, and I quickly raced towards the enclosed deck.

The sentry was probably a gunner, so instead of one line of defence I now had to worry about two. I approached the manor cautiously, and tried searching for a spot on the roof to grapple to. I had to make sure that I didn't alert the gunner, otherwise it wouldn't matter if I found a spot or not. A light was on in every window of the manor, yet I couldn't hear anything from within it. I located a spot where I could grapple to, then started spinning the hook once more.

I threw it towards the roof though I failed to secure it, and I dislodged the hook and spun it again. I threw it and this time it connected, the only downside would be getting back down again, but I'd rather be up there then getting shot down here.

I started climbing and took a steadily approach, and I pulled myself closer and closer towards the manors roof. I reached it, then slowly pulled myself onto its surface. I left the grappling hook behind and traversed the planks beneath me, then I scoped out the area and another sentry revealed themselves. I crept towards the first one and cupped his mouth, then I stabbed him in the throat and carefully dragged his body out of sight. I then waited for gunner number two to appear. Gunner number two scoped out the garden behind the manor, and while he did I quickly removed the blade from gunner number one's musket.

I moved towards him and gunner number two turned around and saw me, and I reacted through desperation. Upon seeing me I immediately hurled the musket blade towards him, and it punctured his throat perfectly, though he fell off the roof instantly.

CHAPTER 34

Manor Assault

I grew nervous as the body hit the ground, and I waited for something to happen, but no one came. With the sentries gone I became calmer, and with that calmness I could now plan my way into getting inside. I could use the guard's corpse as a distraction, and it would attract attention if anyone saw it, but I'd have to get down first. I returned to where my grappling hook was located, and I hoped that it would be good for climbing back down again. I had to try, so I grabbed on and began descending. The line held while I wrapped my legs around the rope, then I lowered myself down one hand at a time. This climbing had worn me out, but slacking off now wasn't an option. I reached the bottom and rested, and I became thirsty but I had no water to drink from.

Minutes later I moved towards the dead guard's location, and I picked up his body and moved it in front of me. I moved him towards the closest door, and knocked on it using his hand. I moved to the left and waited, and moments passed and nothing happened. I tried again, knocking a little louder with the guard's hand. No response, so I'd have to find another entrance. A balcony above seemed to be the only alternative, but I had no way to reach it. Moments passed then another idea came to mind, but I would have to charge at the door with the corpse in hand. Hesitation ate away at me, but I prepared to charge and placed the corpse in front of me. Suddenly the door opened and an elderly woman emerged, she looked very confused though and I approached her with the guard in tow. She noticed him and immediately relaxed, then I revealed myself and she panicked. She rushed back inside and reached the door, then she started closing it and I forced it open.

"HELP! Please guards help, there's an intruder," screamed the woman.

I unsheathed my dagger and placed it next to her stomach, then she tried screaming again and I pressed it into her.

"Don't do that again, otherwise it'll go deeper."

"What do you want commoner? Are you here to kill us like that guard? You won't get away with it you know."

"I'm only here to kill the commodore, tell me where she is and you'll live."

"She isn't here, she hasn't been for days."

"What do you mean!? Her fleets still here, so she has to be around."

"She isn't the commodore anymore, after she captured the insurrectionists she relinquished her fleet and title: you've wasted your time you fool."

I pushed my dagger into her and she squirmed frivolously.

"If she's not here then where is she? Someone has to know."

"The governor would know, or maybe her former crewmen, but I don't expect you to reach them alive."

"We'll see about that."

I let her go and she screamed, then I backhanded her. She fell into the ground unconscious, and I left her a nice little bump to remember me by when she awoke. The old hag was a nuisance anyway, so knocking her out was no skin off my bone. Pianos and violin's played in the background, and I hoped that the woman's screams had fallen on deaf ears. It seems my new mission tonight was to find the governor, since the commodore was apparently lost to me.

I walked down the hallway and kept a lookout for colonials nearby, and I overheard a couple of slugs while they walked down the nearby stairs. I moved towards them and two rich blobs appeared instead, and I moved past them while they gave me unflattering looks. I walked up the stairs and two colonial sentries appeared, and they immediately spotted me.

"Governor Manson is up ahead, so move along stranger, this area is off limits," said the first guard.

I complied with his instruction, but at least now I know where he is, which is fine by me. It looks like I'll be dealing with the crewmen instead, which was wonderful since I had a bone to pick with them. I walked back down the stairs and prepared myself for the chaos to come, and the crewmen came into view, and I hid behind a cabinet while they dawdled. The piano and violin conversed into a kind of orchestra while they talked, and I approached and the opera continued.

I unsheathed my sword and they quickly recognised me, and they smirked and did the same.

"Where is the commodore!? One of you clots is gonna tell me whether you like it or not."

"Your demands mean nothing to us, and the commodore isn't here to shield you this time: you'll be dead meat long before you can find her!" said the first crewman.

He slashed towards me with his cutlass, and I sidestepped his assault and quickly slashed his underarm with my dagger. He groaned painfully, and swiftly retreated while holding his injured arm. The second crewman advanced and thrusted his sword towards my rib, and I parried his blade away then quickly grabbed his arm. I redirected him into a wall and he crumpled into the ground after colliding with it, then I turned to confront the third crewman. The third crewman reached for his sword then changed his mind and reached for his pistol. He grabbed it and I kicked it out of his hand, then I slashed it and he yelped in pain. The three crewmen were down, and I went back to confront the first.

"I've heard that the commodore is no longer here, and that she's no longer the commodore, so where is she!? One of you must know."

"Maybe we do, but what's in it for us princess?" taunted the first crewman.

I grabbed his arm and squeezed it until he cursed, then I cut his arm again and he cried while I moved on to crewman number two.

"You won't reach her Casper! even if you best us the colonials will you kill you afterwards," said the second crewman.

He appeared to be recovered from his head clash, and he thrusted towards me again and I swept him off his legs.

"Make this easier on yourselves boys, at least if you tell me where she is I might fail, but if you refuse then you'll continue to suffer."

I moved towards the third crewman who looked terrified while he tried covering up his blood ridden arm.

"Tell me what I want to know and I won't cut the other one, where has she gone!? Tell me and this stops."

"She's gone to Greenlit Island, not that that matters to you after tonight," said a man's voice.

I turned around and Governor Manson stood nearby, and four colonial guards escorted him.

"Governor Manson, a displeasure to see you again."

"You're the man from her ship, the prisoner or servant, I couldn't tell at the time: but it seems obvious what you are now."

"He's a survivor from the Revenant sir, its last survivor," said the first crewman.

"Impossible, the commodore herself declared the Revenant crew dead months ago."

"It's true sir! I swear it by England! She left him alive after it sank, there was a second survivor as well," said the second crewman.

"Then she betrayed us! She betrayed us and none of you wretches felt brave enough to tell me sooner, fools! Fiends!"

"You can't prove that though, you have nothing to tie me to the black with, no flag, no brand, nothing."

"Perhaps not, but your still an intruder in my manor, and after attacking these men here, that still makes you guilty."

"Those men forced me to fight in unsanctioned battles, this was just payback, and as for the trespassing, well, I'll be leaving now so don't worry."

"Oh you will be leaving, but not as a free man, take him men!"

The guards pointed there muskets towards me, and I grabbed the nearest crewman and hurled them towards the guards. While they were distracted I engaged them in swords, and all of them hesitated, like the pathetic bunch they were. I pushed the first colonial into the governor, then kicked the second away as soon as they approached me. A third colonial thrusted towards me with their musket, and I sliced off their blade then ripped the weapon out of there hand and whacked them with it.

A forth colonial charged and missed me, and the idiot pierced the wall instead. With his blade stuck I stabbed him in the back with my dagger, then I turned my attention to the frightened governor. The first guard suddenly recovered and swung his musket towards me, and I grabbed another nearby musket and thumped him in the face with it.

The governor fled towards the stairs and I pursued him, and we both pushed past people while I chased him down. He climbed the stairs and reached for a door to a nearby room, and I lunged towards him and grabbed the door before he could shut it. We wrestled for control and I held the door open while we pushed against each other.

"Where is Greenlit Island governor? Tell me and I'll spare you."

"Never! Pirate or not you'll never see her again, you've lost fiend, and you're better off dead and forgotten."

"If you won't tell me where then tell me why, why did she go there? What's so special about this island? Give me something while you still can."

"I don't have to give you anything, more guards will be here soon, and once there here you'll be finished."

On cue more colonials suddenly showed up, and I was running out of strength to fight them. They approached me and I quickly slashed the governor then fled into the next room.

I hoped that they would tend to their pitiful master first, and if they did then I'd look for an escape route. The gates would still be guarded so I'd have to use the fence, and I'd have to grapple over it again but before that I needed to climb out of here. A balcony was in the next room, and I moved towards it and climbed down. I dropped and slightly injured my knees, but I couldn't worry about it right now. I ran towards the grappling hooks location and a few crewmen suddenly ambushed me. I couldn't avoid this fight, so I unsheathed my weapons once more.

"Finally... piracy will be ended for good," said the first crewman.

He flurried his axe eagerly and advanced on me alongside his crewmates.

The first crewman swung wildly towards me, and I dodged it and caught his axe head with my blade, then I kicked him in the chest after. The second crewman advanced and wielded a much larger axe, and he swung it towards my head and I narrowly avoided it while it whooshed past me. He hacked at me again and I rolled underneath his weapon, then I quickly stabbed him in the belly. He dropped his weapon and grabbed me after, then I twisted the dagger inside of him and he let go.

The third crewman fired his pistol at me and I used his comrade to absorb the shot, then he panicked and the first crewman reengaged me. I dropped my weapons and retrieved the other crewman's axe, and the massive weapon was heavy, but the first crewman backed away while I tried wielding it.

I gritted my teeth and moved towards him, then I swung the axe towards his shoulder and the crewman froze while he contemplated whether he could avoid it. He held up his axe to block and the block failed while the bigger axe sliced deep into his chest. A massive cut formed and a thick trail of blood oozed out of him, then he died while the third crewman helplessly fled.

I chased after him and a short while later I tackled him into the ground. I banged his head into the surface, leaving him dazed and confused; then I mercilessly beat him while he struggled.

"STOP! Please stop!! I'll tell you anything, just leave me be."

"Tell me how to get to Greenlit Island!! If you do that I'll spare you."

"I don't know I swear! Please don't kill me."

"Why is it so important then!? Why has she gone there!? TELL ME!"

My patience was gone, but so was my energy, I was wasting time with this worm. Frustrated I stabbed him in the throat, then I willed myself to my feet. I kicked his corpse angrily and cursed, then the second crewman moaned something at me. I moved towards him and ripped the dagger out of his belly, and blood drizzled out instantly, yet he still moaned.

"What will you do now huh? You have nothing for your foolish crusade against the commodore, how will you find an island that no one here knows about? You'll never kill her, you'll just kill yourself."

I plunged the dagger back into his belly, and witnessed the life quickly fade from his eyes. He was right though, how was I going to find her? Tonight had been a waste, and I still had to leave here alive. A few minutes passed while I walked back to where the grappling hook was located, and I quickly dislodged it from the roof. I didn't want to fight anymore, so I prepared myself to depart.

I spun the grappling hook again and threw it towards the fence, and it connected and held then I grabbed on while I climbed it. My arms were exhausted, as was most of my body, and I gritted myself while I climbed bit by bit towards the top. I reached the fence and crossed over, then I lowered myself down and dropped to the ground harmlessly. I left the grappling hook behind and raced towards the streets and docks, pitch black awaited me and I struggled to visualize what was in front of me. The ship appeared and came into view, and I sprinted towards it with haste. Upon arrival several colonials appeared nearby, and they all appeared to be former recruits of mine.

"Hey Casper, out for a nightly prowl are you? Good to see," said Michael.

"Not now recruit, I need to rest."

'Hey hold on, can't we just have a nice chat since we're all here now?"

Without thought I suddenly snapped, and I drew my sword and slashed the mouth breather across the chest.

The other recruits recoiled away in horror, and they backed away fearfully while I preyed upon them. I pushed the first recruit into the sea then quickly disarmed and booted the second off the pier. The third one fired his musket at me, and he missed because of his nerves. He thrusted his bayonet towards me and I grabbed it and wrenched it out of his hands, then I smacked him in the face with it.

The fifth recruit thrusted towards me and I broke off his blade then slashed his throat. The recruits in the water fled, and I pounced towards the first one and ruthlessly stabbed him in the shoulder. I pursued the second one who whimpered while he ran, and a short while passed and I chased him down and plunged my dagger into his mouth. I quickly yanked it out and wiped it on some nearby sand, then I cleaned it in the shallows and backtracked towards Michael. He quivered in fear while I approached him, and his chest gushed with blood.

"What's happened to you Casper? What made you into this… thing! I admired you, but now…I'm terrified for you."

I slashed his neck and a rush of blood oozed out of it.

"So am I recruit, but this is all I am now."

Exhaustion hit me and I wasn't sure if I could make it back to the sloop. I needed to leave, and I couldn't rest yet, not until I was safely out of Kingston.

I returned and stumbled towards the sloop, and I prepared to disembark and while I did I kept an eye on the fort. I got underway and rested by the rail, and I waited and wondered if the fort would kill me. I sailed out of range and breathed a sigh of relief, and I imagined the chaos that would brew within this city after tonight. Kingston's mainland faded from view, and I headed towards the cabin for rest. All I could think about was sleep, and I arrived at the bunk and collapsed into it while letting it envelop me.

I awoke the next morning and struggled to move, my body was drained and my mind was like an encumbered anchor. A few minutes passed while I debated with it, then I forced myself out of my bunk. I needed food and water, and I feasted on the fruit since it was closer to spoiling than the bread. I finished breakfast and gazed at the map, and a few minutes passed while I got lost in it. Several unmarked islands were on it, and I wondered if any of them were the one I was searching for. It was a risky voyage, and it would take weeks for me to investigate them all. But there was nowhere else to go, so if I didn't do this then I'd be lost. I'd have to resupply after a few visits, and I didn't have the wealth to spend on those necessities. I brooded on alternatives, but there was none, I had to find her; I couldn't let it end this way.

I still didn't have an answer for what I would do if I succeeded, because life after that was like a dream; or an afterlife whether I lived or died. I skimmed over the unmarked islands and figured out my position, and when I did I estimated that I wasn't far from the first one. I left the cabin and adjusted my course, then I set it towards the first island. The wind blew comfortably and a pod of dolphins appeared nearby, and they happily swam and followed. This was the first time in ages that I'd been able to sail freely, and finally I had control, but would it be enough to get what I wanted? Hopefully… I would soon find out.

CHAPTER 35

Lost Times

Several hours passed until I reached the first of the unmarked islands, a small sand island with only a few rocks and trees inhabiting it. It wasn't what I was hoping for, but it was worth a short visit while I was here. No wildlife inhabited the island, and no ships were docked at it. Being stranded here would be a death sentence, and I was thankful that I wasn't stuck in a place like this. I docked at the islands shore and departed immediately, and several minutes passed while I explored it. The island was completely baron, and several more minutes passed until I surmised that there was nothing helpful here. Disappointed I headed back to the sloop, and while I prepared to depart a glint in the shallows caught my eye. I took a closer look and the glint became clearer underneath the sand. I exited the ship and started digging, and a minute or so passed and a peculiar item revealed itself. A gold hilted dagger lay buried in the sand, and it had a silver curved blade which made it foreign but also fancy.

An image of a young woman appeared in my mind, a blonde woman with blue eyes and this glistening gold dagger.

I'd seen this weapon before, but I couldn't remember the name of who wielded it. Motivated I dug up more sand, and a short while passed then I uncovered a hand. It was skeletal, and it appeared to be old. I continued digging and a few moments passed until a skull revealed itself. I continued digging and I unveiled a corpse, and I wondered why it was buried here. Why was this person buried in the shallows? I didn't know, but I wanted to learn who this corpse was. I searched the nearby sand and nothing appeared, then I searched the corpse itself and a pendant lay inside it. I opened the pendant and a note was inside, and I unfolded the note and skimmed over it. Captain Ash; that was the name I was looking for, this was her corpse.

Captain Leigh Ash

Dated October 1727- date unknown

I've been stranded here after my defeat at the hands of England, everyone is gone, Neagan, Maroo, Weiss, I feel so alone. There's no one on this island to keep me company, except for one who'll probably not live to see another sunrise. All I can do now is wait, and record my final confessions. My first regret is that I didn't see through the deception of our second captain, Thornton was always questionable, but I should've known he was a fake. Casper was right it seemed, as were the others, and for that I'm truly sorry.

I'm also sorry to my crew, who are mostly dead... but I feel better about putting that to paper. I tried my best to fight off the colonials, but there too powerful, and I don't know how to cope with it.

Yours truly

Ash

Captain Ash was the first woman to become a pirate captain under Alva Maroo's resurgence, and Maroo fought hard to keep it that way. She was kind and commanding, and she always asked for a lot but always made it worth it in the end. I met her after I left Kingston a month later, it was a brief relationship, since Maroo and I had to keep running.

In another life I might've fallen in love with her and joined her crew instead of Maroo's; but I think things would've ended up the same either way. Her angelic blonde hair and blue eyes always attracted me, and if her personality was a little more compatible with mine; then perhaps I would've pursued her affections. I put her dagger and pendant back with her body, then I said some final prayers and reburied her. I reflected on her passing after burying her, then wondered if I should try and find her companion. It was better if I left, so I headed back to the sloop and boarded it. I moved towards my cabin and surveyed the map inside. The second island wasn't far according to my positioning, but after I'd visited it I would need to restock at a nearby port.

I disembarked and remained at the helm, then when I was clear of the island I rested in my cabin.

A few hours passed and the second island came into view, and this one seemed more promising than the last. Tropical palms and a colourful reef greeted me, and while I moved closer no ships appeared nearby. I docked in its shallows and departed the ship, then I scoured the sands for signs of life. A mysterious figure lurked in the distance, a man I think, but not a normal one. There might not be ships here, but that didn't mean that there weren't any people either. A few minutes passed and a trio of skeletons appeared, and one of them carried a map in their hands. I approached them and carefully removed the map from its hand, then I gently unfolded it. A treasure map! My heart suddenly skipped on the inside, but until I returned to the sloop I had to keep my excitement in check. I pocketed my prize and turned to skeleton number two, and they had a pistol in one hand, and a bottle of water in the other.

The pistol appeared to be unloaded, and the skeletons skull explained why. I turned to the third skeleton who also had a pistol in hand. The weapon was loaded and a nearby musket was with them as well, but it was out of reach. I examined the musket and it looked to be loaded, but if it was loaded then why was it out of reach? I couldn't figure out a theory. What was the story between these three corpses? Feud? Map? Weapons? I didn't have an answer.

I wanted to explore further but I needed to take my findings back to the ship, then return to the cabin to try and locate where this treasure is. I headed back towards the sloop and upon arrival raced on board towards the cabin. A few minutes passed while I measured and scanned the map, and I learned that the treasure was far away from me. It would take a month to reach from my current position, but it was located on the forth island, so it wasn't totally out of the way. Treasure didn't matter to me anymore, but since I was practically broke it would be wise to try and uncover it. I unsheathed my dagger and swapped it out for the pistol, and its bark brown complexion was a nice change from the light brown I was usually more accustomed too. I placed it in my belt opposite my sword, then I headed back to the island.

I headed further inland and movement rustled nearby, my nerves suddenly spiked, and I searched around for its source. Up ahead I walked towards a thicket of palm trees, and strange animalistic noises churned out.

I treaded carefully, then moved on while they continued. Something suddenly hit me in the back of the neck, and I pulled it out and a dart resided in my hand. Noises continued emanating then a figure emerged, a half-starved, half-crazed looking man.

"Weiss! You are Weiss! The captain's Weiss!!"

Brown hair flaked from his scalp, and his slim malnourished body reeked of barf or even boogers. He moved towards me carrying a blowpipe and a dagger, and I drew my sword in response. I moved towards him and all of a sudden fatigue and light headedness washed over me. He's poisoned me! His damn dart was draining me and I couldn't do anything about it. I swung my sword towards him and the effects got worse, and the man dodged and moved away. I fired my pistol at him and he fell to the ground, then I collapsed as well, plummeting head first into the ground.

I awoke later and became drowsy and sore, and my head throbbed as well. The corpse of the man laid nearby, and I observed it while nursing my injured head. A feeling washed over me that I was being watched, and I suspected that there was more than one mad man on this island. I walked over towards the man's corpse and a spear suddenly hurtled towards me. I ducked away from it then another man suddenly charged towards me.

A ravenous wild man approached, and he carried a club in one hand, which was partially comprised of bone. I reached for my sword and dropped the pistol that I was carrying, but I wasn't sure if I could fight him in my current state. He swung his club towards me and I blocked it, and the impact knocked me back and I fell over. He charged at me again and swung his club towards my gut, and I couldn't block it, and the blow struck me in the stomach. I keeled over and he pushed me into the ground violently, then he walked away.

"Weiss! Weiss! You are Weiss! Alva's Weiss!"

He walked over to the corpse and investigated it, and I tried recovering while the air left my lungs. He appeared very interested in the body, and he dragged it across the sand with him after investigating it.

"Weiss will be pleased, yes! Weiss will be very pleased."

Messy brown hair stranded down his eyes, and malnourished white skin stretched over his withered and unfit body. I guess I just met the natives of the island, or were they just a couple of mad men? Who knew, but either way, I had to leave quickly. I observed closer and bloodied teeth came into view, and they looked like a beaver's teeth rather than a human's. His brown eyes grew moist, and his mad rasps suddenly returned to me.

"This is you isn't it... Thornton? The former captain of the Sickle."

I should be angry, this is the man that sabotaged and conspired with Weiss, at least that's how it seemed, yet all I could do was pity him.

I was disappointed that I had to use the pistol already, but I couldn't risk the guy killing me then dragging my body away instead. I wasn't sure if coming here was a waste of time or not, but I guess that depended on the treasure, and if I managed to find or reach it. I stumbled back towards the ship, clutching my injured stomach along the way. A while later I returned, and I moved towards my cabin upon arrival. I groaned and painfully stumbled towards my bunk, and I grunted and lied upon it. With this island searched I'd now have to make for port, but I couldn't remember which one was the closest.

I rested and got up however long after, then I walked towards my map and scanned for where the closest port was. Port Royal was the closest, and going there would cost me the rest of my wealth. There was no choice however, since not going there would cost me much more. I prepared to depart and adjusted my course, then I set it towards Port Royal.

Thornton emerged on the shores of the island, and I reached for my spyglass and observed him. The wild and ravenous thing that I'd seen before seemed unrecognisable, and he stood on the shore motionless, tears spilling from his eyes. He must know who I am, there's no other reason for why he would be here.

His words returned to me, along with my answer.

I left the ship and stumbled towards him, and he dropped his club and waited. A few moments passed and I stumbled over with my sword in hand, and he mourned and crept towards me. I held out my sword while he approached, and blood, sweat and tears dripped off him.

"You know who I am? Don't you?" I asked.

"Nait, you're Nait."

"That's right, you betrayed me: you betrayed me to Weiss."

"Weiss!! Weiss is here!?"

"No, she's not, but she was wasn't she? Weiss was here."

"Weiss was here, Weiss brought me here, left me here, along with others."

"Your friend said Maroo's Weiss, did you know? Did you know about Maroo and Weiss?"

"Weiss and Maroo? Yes, Weiss and Maroo close, close but not close enough."

"Do you know what happened to Maroo? Do you know what Weiss did to him?"

"Weiss kill Maroo, Weiss chase Maroo across sea to kill him, Weiss loved Maroo but Maroo no love Weiss."

My hand tightened on my sword, then I remembered that he was unarmed.

"Weiss killed Maroo, and Weiss almost killed Nait as well, Weiss burned Nait in the attack, and Weiss killed Fletch afterwards."

"Fletch? Fletch not survive? Fletch die alongside Maroo?"

"Yes, and now Nait all alone just like Thornton."

"Thorn...ton? Thornton me? Thornton not been spoken for long time."

I didn't know how to respond, the man couldn't even remember his name.

"You stay with Thorn...ton? You stay and I stay? Together?"

"No... I have to find Weiss, I have to kill her for what she's done."

"Find Weiss? Weiss not be happy if you find her, Weiss be very unhappy."

"I know, that's what I'm counting on."

"Thorn...ton sorry about Fletch, Thorn...ton sorry that he not live to stay with you."

I breathed deeply and looked away, I wanted to hurt him, to slice his neck, to stab his throat, to cut off his flesh, but what would that solve? The man was already dead the way he was.

I turned away and headed back towards my ship, and Thornton cried almost immediately.

"Nait not stay with Thorn…ton!? Nait can't leave Thorn…ton behind! Not like Weiss!!"

I sighed and stopped walking, it would be wrong to leave him, and it would be pointless to kill him, I laughed, it seemed there was only one option left.

I turned my head and groaned.

"Thorn…ton stay with Nait, on ship? Thorn…ton travel with Nait? Together?"

Thornton nodded and sobbed, then he grabbed his club and pointed towards it.

"Yes you can bring that, but don't hit Nait again."

"Thorn…ton not hit Nait, Thorn…ton promise."

I returned to the ship and stumbled towards the helm, then Thornton boarded and sat down on the deck. I finished my departure and set sail towards Port Royal, then while we sailed I sat down near the rail. My stomach pain eased and became easier to handle, and an idea formed while Thornton crawled along the vacant deck.

Sunset beckoned and I arrived at Port Royals dock. Pain continued emanating from my stomach, but it had become easier to manage over time. As usual Port Royal bustled with activity, and fishermen were scattered all across its pier. Some of them pissed instead of fished, like the scoundrels they were, and civilians swarmed the area, making it a crowded, noisy, and convoluted place of bustle. Port royal was never a place I liked much, too much people, too much distractions, and yeah it looked nice, but it always seemed to be working itself to death. I docked and headed towards its pier, and some frigates appeared nearby, along with a single Man of War further along the shore. It was an impressive sight, but very daunting as well; I'd only ever seen one Man of War in action before, and its destructive power was nightmarish.

CHAPTER 36

Family Treasure

Five days passed and I stocked up at Port Royal, visited island number three, and now approached island number four. A beautiful reef awaited me, and all though I'd swam in many so far, this one stood out; bright luminous colours glistened from it, and diverse bustles of life flowed through it. The third island I visited was much like the second, skeletons resided there along with more weapons to salvage. I never learned the identities of these skeletons, so I kept wondering if I was corpse robbing from former pirates. I was also frustrated with my lack of progress, but I still had one more island left to visit. If she wasn't there then I'd give up, but if I located the treasure then maybe I could sustain the search for a little longer. If I found it then I'd have the chance to create an alternative life, but that was only if it was worth something.

I retrieved my spyglass and observed the island, and a single house came into view. No other enclosures were in sight, but perhaps there was life on this island. Minutes passed and a young boy emerged from the house, incredible, simply incredible! Perhaps he could help me with my search for Greenlit

Island. If he couldn't it didn't matter, as long as he had food and water then perhaps I could stay a while. I docked and departed the sloop, then I moved towards the single house. A sand hill appeared and I climbed over it, and I reached the sandy green patches above it. A small canal of water partially split the island in two, and a passage of sand appeared after you crossed it. I crossed over the canal and the passage, and I approached and waited for the boy.

A few moments passed and he spotted me, and he was older than I expected. He had snow white skin and thin brown hair which stranded down to his eyes, and he was neither skinny nor fat, and he reminded me of someone, someone I'd just met. The boy looked eleven or twelve, and what was he doing all on his own? It was strange. His brown eyes remained fixed upon me as he approached, and they were constantly serious, and they made him look older than I suspected.

"You're the first stranger that I've seen in a long time, what brings you out here?" asked the boy.

"I'm looking for a place called Greenlit Island, I've been island hopping trying to find it; and I was hoping you could help me with this? After that I can leave."

"I'm afraid I'm not familiar with your island, but there's still plenty out there so don't lose hope, what's your name?"

"Casper, I'm a former naval man turned sailor, all though that's behind me now."

"You don't look like a naval man, you look more like a pirate."

His words struck like knives, how could he know that?

"Pirates are gone kid, how can I be something that's considered dead?"

"I don't consider them dead, but your face makes you look like one, only pirates have scars like that, from what I've read anyway."

I was curious as to what he may've read, but I also had work to do.

"Is your family home? Perhaps they could help me with finding my island?"

"My mother's out at Port Royal and my father's dead, so no, it's just me, as usual."

"And you are?"

'Not inclined to tell you, and if you ask again I'll shoot you."

The boy unveiled a flintlock from the back of his shirt, and he pointed it towards me.

"I'm not here to hurt you, but with your permission I'd like to explore, the pistol won't be necessary."

"Maybe, but while my mother's out I'll keep it regardless."

"I understand, I'm sorry about your father."

"He was a pirate, so don't be."

The boy walked away and headed back towards his home, keeping the pistol in hand.

He was a pirate? Could it be? Could there resemblance be what I was suspecting, it's unlikely that I'll ever find out, considering the boys frostiness. What could've happened to him? Whatever it was I didn't want to ask, I came here for treasure, not to get shot and killed by an urchin. Finding the treasure might be more difficult with him around, but as long as he didn't see me with it then I should be ok.

I pulled out the map and unfolded it, then I scanned it for the treasure's location. The treasure seemed to be buried away from the house, and the spot seemed to be located near a trio of tree's;

opposite a small rock island. I headed back towards my ship to retrieve my shovel, one which I'd purchased in Port Royal. Upon returning I ate some food and retrieved it, then I quickly left to retrieve my prize. I backtracked and wandered, and a few minutes passed and I stopped at the supposed location. I started digging and heaving, but I held my excitement at bay, since the search could be long and tiresome. A few minutes passed and I struck what I hoped was the treasure, and I quickly uncovered it after. A brown and silver chest revealed itself, and I bashed its lock repeatedly until it opened. I pushed the lid back and revealed its contents, and the chest glowed slightly, as countless shillings glistened inside of it.

Transporting this back would be hard, but at least it was uncovered, and there was still the task of counting it, which I'd do once it was safely on board.

I left the shovel where it was and lifted the chest up, then I steadied it and walked back. I walked slowly as a precaution, then kept an eye on my surroundings.

I reached the shallows and rested, and I placed the chest on the sand and breathed. Moments later I pressed on, then I moved towards the ship and heaved the chest onto its deck. I covered it with my extra sail then turned around and rested. The boy suddenly reappeared, and his expression told me that he'd seen everything.

"You are a pirate! I knew it! Why else would you be carrying a chest onto your ship?"

I turned to him and he bolted, leaving me alone before I could reply. I really needed this haul, and yet treasure always complicated things, damn it! I was stuck in a hard place again.

An hour or so passed while I rested on my bunk, and the afternoon arrived and it grew hotter then I was used to. The reef was nearby, but I wasn't thinking of swimming in it just yet. I got up off my bunk and departed my cabin, then I surveyed the reef and a small boat appeared. The boat was of a similar size to my sloop, but it was decorated and more weathered. The boy appeared on its deck, and he had a wooden cage in his hand. He dived into the water with the cage in hand, and he had a small knife sheathed on his hip. A few minutes passed and he resurfaced, then two or three creatures wriggled inside his cage. I retrieved my spyglass and observed him, and two black eels were trapped inside. Eel hunting? I'd never heard or seen that before, and the boy seemed adept at it. He placed the cage on top of a barrel and opened it, and the eels wiggled out. I didn't see what happened next, but the boy bent down and drew his knife, then moments later an unmoving eel resided in his hands. He repeated the process with the other eel, then set them aside and spotted me watching him. He turned away and grabbed the cage once more, then dived back into the sea.

A while passed then he returned to shore, and three black eels resided in his cage. He departed his boat and walked past mine, and his eyes glanced towards me.

"These are for dinner so you should check out the reef if you want some, there's only one safe species to hunt, as the other two are more dangerous and aggressive."

"Is it tricky? Hunting eels."

"Yes, but there not hard to find if you look in the right spots, capturing them just takes practice."

"You seem like you've had a lot of practice."

"My mom and dad taught me when I was seven, so I've been practising ever since."

"You're lucky then, lucky to have such a simple and exotic life."

He grunted and walked off, leaving me annoyed but determined.

I had what I wanted, yet I couldn't leave yet, this boys identity was pestering me, I had to learn it, I had to be sure if he was what I thought he was.

I moved towards the reef and stripped off my clothes, then I entered into the water and it was everything that I'd hoped for. A while passed and the sky grew darker, and the reef started to glow. While I swam some of the fish glowed as well, and a glowing jelly fish suddenly spooked me further outside the reef. The jellyfish remained stationary and its slow movements mesmerized me, I glanced under the surface and everything below was like an underwater painting. Lime like corals glistened, blood like fish glowed, and pink like jelly fish radiated, it was a world that I'd never experienced before.

I continued swimming and a group of red squids passed me by, they were about the size of a tadpole, and it was hard to identify them without directly looking at them. I swam out deeper and luminous white sting rays resided below me, they were easy on the eyes, as long as they stayed where they were. I remained afloat and spied on them, and moments passed while they remained still. I guess they were dormant or disinterested. I gazed at the sky and no stars were in it, but the moon was out, and it was full tonight.

Minutes later I exited the reef and lay on the grass nearby, and a minute or so passed while I rested, then I dried myself off after. I retrieved my clothes and headed towards the house, and smoke drifted into the air, and I assumed that the boy was cooking his eels.

I reached the house and the boy had a fire sizzling nearby, two eels were skewered across it, and he appeared cold as he waved his hands over it.

"What are you going to do with that treasure? It was buried on my island, maybe you should offer a portion of it to me?" Suggested the boy.

"That's called taxing someone, that's what creates pirates, that's why they do what they do."

"They do what they do because there greedy, greedy and evil, just like my father."

"I'm sure that's what you've read, but it isn't always true."

"Your quite young to be a pirate, younger than my dad, when did you join them?"

"In 1726."

"HA! You confirmed it, finally."

"You weren't going to drop it so I might as well."

"What happened to your face? Did pirates do that to you? Did you kill or steal from one of them?"

"No, it was just an incident at sea, pirate hunters, all though there usually former pirates."

"And you survived them? You survived them burning your face?"

"For now, but it's never going to heal."

"It looks painful, but it's also cool, despite being a pirate I have to admit that."

I smiled and looked down, this kid sure was strange.

"Aren't you scared? Why didn't your mother take you with her? It seems irresponsible to leave your own son here by himself."

"No one really comes here so there's not much to worry about, besides I can look after myself, and I don't like shopping."

I laughed and the boy joined in, and I sat down next to the fire. The boy's pistol was beside him as well as his knife, he could take care of himself all right: if I was anyone else I'd probably hesitate in sitting near him. He removed the skewer off the fire and scraped his eels off into a bowl, then he cut into them with his knife and chopped them up piece by piece.

"If you give me a portion of the treasure you can have the third eel."

"I don't want it, eels look gross."

"Not if there cooked, but I suppose you're more of a crab person."

"Not by choice, but I will eat them."

"I've got one in the house, mom likes them but I don't, you can have that for dinner if you like?"

"Thank you, do I have to pay for it?"

"No, but if you spoil it then yes."

The boy got up and headed towards his home, then he opened the door and disappeared inside. A minute or so later he returned with the crab, and he skewered it onto the fire.

"May I ask about your father? I have a question that's eating away at me?"

"I don't like talking about him, at least not in detail. What do you want to know?"

"Does he look like you? I knew a man once that you remind me of, you seem different to each other but the resemblance is... striking?"

"You're saying that you may have knew him? You knew him but I didn't?"

"What's his name?"

The boy sighed, and he paused and grabbed a piece of eel.

"Thornton, his name is Thornton."

"Thornton, Thornton Mel!? He's dead? How?"

"Piracy, it doesn't matter how, he's dead and he left his family to go and die! He left me and my mum when we needed him most! All because a little treasure was more important to him."

I paused, I didn't want to risk upsetting him.

"You knew him? You knew my father?"

"Only a little, I understand why you hate him, but I don't know him well enough to judge. I just know what he did to me and my family."

"What did he do?"

"He betrayed us, he conspired with another and betrayed us, he didn't bring about the end but he sure as hell contributed to it."

"You consider pirates as your family? Why? There a greedy and vicious bunch."

"We're not all the same, some of them are, but not the pirates that I was with, they were better men then the ones I used to serve with in the navy."

"Not my father though."

"No, not your father, but I don't know why he did what he did."

"I told you why!! Treasure was more important to him than people, position and power was more indulgent then living with a mom and his son on an island. He was greedy and evil, and I'm glad that he's dead."

"You can't mean that, a bad father is still a father."

The boy cried and started gorging on his eel, and a minute or so passed while he finished it.

"Your crab will be cooked soon, once you've eaten it we should go to sleep."

"Thanks, I'm sorry if I upset you."

The boy remained quiet, and he got up and carried his bowl with him.

I sat by the fire and removed the crab with my sword, then I cut it up and rested it in another bowl. I crunched down on it and stuffed myself silly, then when I'd finished, I dozed off by the fire.

I awoke the next morning and a large chest appeared in the area, a brown and silver one. The chest was open but no one was around, and I got up and my sword was missing. The boy, Thornton's boy, perhaps he was more like his father than he let on to be. I touched my left boot and my dagger was still there, and I unsheathed it and brandished it cautiously.

"This treasure is family treasure, and if you want to use it then you're going to give me a share," said the boy.

Thornton's son appeared nearby, and his pistol and dagger were pointed towards me.

"You stole it from me! This was your plan all along!! To extort me while I slept."

"That's my father's treasure, I'm not gonna let you walk away with it, not without getting my share."

"Your father's treasure? How can that be? You said he was dead'? You said he abandoned you."

"I lied, my mother is dead but my father is alive, and he'll be back soon, and he can take what's left after he's killed you."

"I had the map for it and I dug it up myself, I don't owe you anything, and if you kill me over it then you're no better than him."

"Come on Casper! Be reasonable."

"You can have ten shillings, that's all I'm willing to offer."

"That's not enough."

"The rest is staying with me, it shouldn't even be out here in the first place."

"How about a hundred? Ten shillings isn't enough!"

"NO."

"There's enough here to make us all happy Casper, just do the right thing and give me what I'm owed, then you can leave."

"I need that treasure for my voyage, and I haven't even counted it yet, so I don't know how valuable it is."

"Does it matter? It's a chest full of coins! It's valuable either way."

"Give me my share!!"

"No."

Thornton's son eyed me angrily, and his arm wavered while holding the pistol.

"Your father isn't coming kid."

"You don't know that! You don't even know if he's alive or dead."

"Actually I do, you're not the only one who lies."

"What do you mean?"

"Your father's in Port Royal, he is alive, but he's not himself."

"You're lying! You said you barely knew him, your just trying to trick me."

"If you shoot me then you'll never know, but I met him before I came here, and I brought him to Port Royal to be looked after. The man is gone but he's not lost, and despite everything that he's done he still needs care."

"I don't... I don't believe you! He's alive, and he's coming, you'll see."

"Do you want to let your mother decide? Or do you want to shoot me and never find out? Maybe he abandoned you but right now you could go and see him, he won't be himself, but you could help him find himself."

"He's a pirate! I don't want to help him find anything."

"He's not a pirate anymore, he's just a man, a broken and lost man, who needs his son now more than anything."

Thornton's son froze and lowered his pistol, and I quickly moved towards him.

He raised it again and I smacked it aside, and he released it and it fell to the ground.

Thornton's son thrusted towards me and I grabbed his arm, then I twisted it and pushed him into the ground.

"I wanted that treasure for myself!! I wanted a portion of it for my family! Please, please just give it to me."

"I thought your family was dead, your mother, your father, or vice versa, you seem pretty desperate to plead for the dead."

"Shut up!! You don't know anything, you're just a greedy evil man who lies."

He slashed towards me and I weaved away, then I moved towards the chest and lingered near it. He slashed again and I avoided him.

"You can take my offer now or I'll cut you down and walk away, make your decision, while I'm still sensible enough to allow you to."

"Do it! kill me and watch my dad come and kill you! or watch some of my friends come track you down and blow your eyes out."

The boy slashed towards my rib and I parried, then he slashed towards my chest and I weaved, then he slashed towards my knee and I moved away. I moved behind him and slashed his knee, and he fell to the ground crying.

"My KNEE! You sliced my knee! You curse ridden, vile faced, blood butcher."

"Where's my sword?"

The boy continued crying and I grabbed him by the scruff of his shirt.

"WHERE is my sword?"

The boy pointed a few paces away, and I released him and he continued crying and nursing his knee.

"You cut me? You hurt me over treasure!?"

I ignored him and searched the sands for my sword, and I padded down the area and minutes passed until I touched it.

I placed it back in its sheath and moved towards the chest, then I collected the boy's weapons and looked at him.

I fired the pistol and Thornton's boy flinched as it struck next to him, then I threw his dagger away.

"What's your name? You're not shooting me now so you might as well tell me."

"…David, my name is David."

"David Mel."

The boy nodded and turned away out of fear.

I grabbed a handful of shillings from the chest, then I tossed them towards him and he glanced at them. I closed it and lifted it up, then I steadied and carried it back.

I walked towards the ship and my mind presented me with a weak but possible choice. With the treasure in hand I could go anywhere that I wanted now, maybe even live anywhere; but there was still one more island to search, and therefore one more chance to find the commodore. Fletch always warned me that this vendetta would be the death of me, that I'd lose whether it was through sheer numbers or from a lack of experience against her. She was much older and wiser than me, and Fletch said that if I fought her one on one then she'd kill me. But I had to try anyway, this was my only shot at her, and I was the only one left who could defeat her. I returned to the Sloop and headed into the cabin and placed the chest inside. I moved towards the map and scanned it for the fifth islands position, then I headed towards the helm and set and adjusted my course. I returned to the cabin to begin counting my haul; along with the days it would take to arrive at my final destination.

CHAPTER 37

Identity

I sailed from morning till evening, then dropped anchor miles away from island number four. I counted the treasure haul during that time, and at least a thousand shillings were recorded. I suspected more, but my brain grew too weak to continue. Rain lightly drizzled outside, covering the horizon with a thin blanket of non-visibility. It was a good opportunity for sleep, and sailing had taken much out of me. I lied on my bunk and my thoughts trotted along inside me, many of them were about the coming conflict, but some were also about the past. Neagan, Maroo, Ash and Weiss, these were the pirates that were connected, along with Thornton if you counted him. I never saw Thornton as an individual though, he was just a tag along that Maroo clung too for unknown reasons. With Bonnet gone this confirmed that I was the last, but I couldn't help but hope that maybe his crew was still out there. My thoughts turned to Fletch and Maroo, wondering what they would think of me now. I've defied them both, and with my actions I've jeopardised the future of piracy for good.

Later I fell asleep, and I was transported into another dream. The dream was darkness, and the world itself was like a void of shadows. I stood in a corridor, alone and unaware. My weapons weren't with me, and this made me naked on the inside.

"Casper!" shouted a male voice.

I turned and there was no one around, and the voice was familiar.

"Casper!" shouted another male voice.

This one was familiar also, but for some reason I had trouble distinguishing them.

"You've provoked the wrong powers Casper, you've endangered everything! You've corrupted everything," accused a man's voice.

I turned and the face of Fletch collided with me, and he was older, much older than he should've been.

"I could've had peace Casper, we could've had peace!! If you'd just let go, let go of everything," said Fletch.

"I...I can't, I'm sorry but I can't."

"YOU CAN! But you're too stubborn to do so, your resentment and rage has consumed you, perverted you beyond belief."

I couldn't respond, and Fletch disappeared in front of me, and a new figure strode towards me. A gruff middle-aged man approached, with blue eyes and a short brown beard, he wore a scarlet coloured coat, along with naval blue pants.

"Casper... you've lost my maps, you've failed to keep Fletch alive, and you've committed yourself to die at Weiss's hands. You've lost yourself! And you've lost everyone around you, it's insulting that your still alive," said the man.

"Captain… I'm not lost! I know what I'm doing, please! Just… believe that I know what I'm doing!! Why doesn't anyone understand? Why?"

"The better question is, why don't you understand?"

"I… I'm only following my heart, I can't escape that, I can't ignore that; I won't survive otherwise."

Maroo paced back and forth restlessly, and Fletch suddenly returned, assuming his usual form.

"Weiss killed both of you and you're trying to stop me from avenging that, is she really above us? Is she really not worth a second skirmish?"

"She's won Casper! it doesn't matter if she's worth it or not, she's won, and she's backed by the powers that be," said Captain Maroo.

"We were the powers that be once, or more accurately you were, Alva Maroo, the fearsome captain of the Revenant, how can you say any of this? how can you give up and say enough?"

"Because without her… there isn't enough."

"You don't mean that, if you did you never would've recruited me."

Maroo paused and Fletch quickly chimed in.

"You've learned the fates of Ash and Bonnet, haven't enough people died yet? How many more until you say enough?"

"Just one, me…or her, it's too late to turn back now, after Kaleen, after Kingston, it's too late to do anything else."

"What about Zaria? Would she respect you after what's happened? Would she side with you?"

"I don't know, but I'm prepared to live with the outcome."

Maroo and Fletch vanished, leaving me alone in the void once more. I walked further and further along the corridor until

I reached an invisible wall. I pushed against it and it prevented me from advancing.

"Casper," echoed a girl's voice.

A dark skinned woman emerged from the shadows, with black hair and brown eyes, and she wore a rose coloured shirt along with royal blue pants.

"Zaria?"

"Yes."

Blood dripped from her body, and she stumbled towards me, then a figure formed behind her. A faceless shadowy man appeared nearby, and he was dressed in red and white and carried a musket which was black and dripping with red. He was formless, all though his weapon wasn't.

"What have you done!!?"

He didn't reply.

I rushed towards him and grabbed him, and he didn't resist, in fact he didn't even move. I rammed him into the wall, then punched and kneed him in the stomach. He fell down after, but I wasn't sure if it was from pain or not. I returned to Zaria's side, and her blood stained the floor beneath her.

"You said you'd fight for me."

"I tried, I really did, I'm sorry! I'm sorry!!"

Zaria vanished leaving me alone to face the wall.

My mouth suddenly bled and dripped, and my face darkened, and moments later I faded from the void.

I was quickly transported into another void, and the commodore and her son were with me. Commodore Weiss was on her knees motionless, and her boy was sitting there, faceless and silent. I approached him and the commodore moved towards me, then my weapons suddenly returned, giving me a chance for revenge.

"Casper!! Leave him alone, please! Leave him alone," pleaded the commodore.

Blood dripped from my mouth, and my face reeked and rotted: but I didn't care, because I was close to achieving peace. I grabbed her son by the throat and the dagger hovered over him: inches away from cutting into his flesh.

"NOOOO!!"

I suddenly awoke... and my face oozed with sweat and stress.

"What am I doing?"

"What are you doing?"

Dying, that's what you're doing.

CHAPTER 38

All I Have

Four days passed until I arrived at the fifth island, at long last. There was so much ocean and so very little land between those days; but this was the biggest island so far. Huge rocks emerged from underneath the sea as I approached it, and thick jungle and cliff faces covered the islands landscape, making it seem difficult to dock at. Only one apparent entrance awaited into the island, and I grabbed my spyglass and observed it. A small pier appeared, along with a single ship docked at it. I steered the ship a smidge closer then peered through the spyglass again. A large smoky grey ship floated up ahead, and its sails were covered in black spots, this was it, this was her! I peered around to learn more. I skimmed upon the ships name, the Risen, fitting I suppose, considering her past. There was no way that I could sail into the pier now, but the ship was found, at last! The ship was found. I continued surveying and the pier filled with multiple crewmen, along with the island. At least twenty of them were there, and the commodore's crew was much larger than that.

Perhaps Fletch was right, maybe this was suicide: most of her crew were still here. I continued watching them, and a few minutes later, I put the spyglass away. I returned to the helm and moved on from my current position, and while I sailed I struggled to find a convenient location. I lapped the island and learned of only two options, and both of them involved navigating through the jungle, which would be dangerous but unavoidable. I'd have to rest before I departed, and I'd need preparations since I had none. I grabbed the musket that I'd salvaged from the second island, and I armed myself with the two pistols that I'd collected from the third. Stealth would be essential if I hoped to survive what was ahead, but if I lost that advantage then at least I'd have some firearms to resort too. I'd place the musket in a special location in case I needed it, but I hoped I wouldn't, and I hoped that I wouldn't need the pistols either.

I grabbed the two knives that I'd salvaged from the third island as well, and they were both small enough for me to conceal inside my boots. With the weapon preparations made I ate some fruit and sculled some water. All I needed now was rest, and I moved towards my bunk and lied on it.

I awoke from my nap however long after, and quickly departed the ship with everything that I'd prepared. I moved towards the jungle and drew my sword, then I cut through the canopy and continued.

It was a beautiful sight, but I remained vigilant since the canopy could hide numerous unseen threats. The leaves varied between emerald or basil like colours, darkened green or natural green, either way, it was bewildering to be around. Birds sung in the background and I cut through more thick branches of life, and when I'd cleared it a rock face suddenly appeared. I started climbing it and a short while later I reached the top, then the green engulfed me once more. Many minutes passed while I cut, trekked, and climbed through the canopy, then I rested and observed the green nearby. I drank from my bottle of water which I'd brought as a precaution, but I had no food on me, so if I became hungry then I'd be finished.

An hour or so passed then several voices came from the west, and I adjusted my course and moved towards them. A while later a path appeared which seemed to lead towards the mainland, and I followed it until I reached its end. I arrived and numerous buildings lay in front of me, and numerous crewmen lingered near them, but none of them noticed me.

I surveyed the surroundings and past the buildings was a wall and an archway, but getting there would be a challenge, at least getting there undetected. Tree's, bushes and rocks inhabited the space, but the area was mostly open, giving me very little to sneak or hide behind. The bush seemed like the best option for me to place a firearm in, but I headed towards a tree instead. I climbed it steadily and upon reaching the top I surveyed the area ahead. From this height at least forty people were present on this island, but I was only interested in one of them. I continued to spy and I became increasingly concerned that stealth wasn't an option, there was too much openness, and far too much civilization. I climbed down the tree and waited while the locals frolicked, then they moved on and I leapt towards the bush. The locals weren't paying attention, and fortunately my presence wasn't drawing any so far. I resisted the idea of hiding the musket in the bush, and I rushed towards the archway instead.

Two sentries quickly came into view and I stopped, then I dived behind a rock and waited while wondering if they'd seen me. The sentries heard the strange sounds, but they dismissed them and went back to talking amongst themselves.

I peered at the wall ahead, and it was surprisingly small. It was about six or seven feet high, but if I could get a boost then I could probably scale it, and then the two sentries wouldn't be a problem for me. I removed the musket and left it behind, the jump would be much easier if I did. This rock suited a hidden firearm anyway, I'd just have to remember to retrieve it afterwards. I breathed deeply and moved away from the rock, and I continued until I was far from it. I ran towards it and jumped just before I reached it, then I pushed myself off it and reached for the wall. The landing injured my hands, and a minor cut formed but it was nothing to worry about currently. For my first attempt I was actually impressed with myself, and I quickly climbed up and over afterwards.

I dropped down safely to the other side and a courtyard suddenly lay in front of me, along with a vegetable field and a large pile of logs and sticks. I continued moving and residents appeared close by, and I kept low. The residents were dressed like maids, so this had to be a manor of some sort, the commodore's manor. The oldest looked after a young boy, and I smirked because it must've been of him, this was the commodore's child; the one who could die today.

The boy was no older than ten, and he had shaggy brown hair which crept down to his eyes. He was skinny or daresay athletic, and he wore a bright yellow tunic and dark blue pants which stopped at his knees. His shoes were brown, and his skin was fair like his mothers.

The commodore's son ran around and the poor caretaker struggled to keep up with him. The boy continued running until he was far away from the care taker, and she gave up and returned to her other duties. I continued moving and the commodore's son suddenly spotted me, his eyes locked with mine, but his mouth paused. He said nothing and continued running, and he ran towards the manor's entrance. The residents disappeared and I moved towards the window, and I peered inside and the commodore was there, and she was alone.

"Who are you and what are you doing?" asked a female voice.

I froze then turned around, and a maid approached me while I remained still. I reached into my boot while she walked towards me, and the maid noticed.

"Hey, what are you,"

I retrieved the knife and plunged it into her throat before she finished, then I hurriedly dragged her body away. I moved her towards the log pile and she fell limp in my arms, then I laid her down upon arrival.

There were still two other women in the area, so I had to look out for them before I advanced. I hoped that I didn't have to kill them as well, since it's not their fault that this is happening on their doorstep. The question that still bugged me was how do I lure the commodore outside? Or do I just go in after her? I wasn't sure which approach to take. I concealed the maid's body inside the pile of logs, then I headed further in to the courtyard. A dining porch and a small stream appeared, adding to the pleasantness that this manor already had. I surveyed the area and approached the commodore's window, and she was writing at her desk. Her coat was off and she wore black garments underneath, and her hair was untied, free flowing in its natural state. Her glasses were off as well, and seeing her brown eyes was odd. The door to the manor was nearby, yet I hesitated on using it. I spied on the commodore then surveyed the courtyard again, trying to find another way into the manor. Two women suddenly came towards me, and I rushed towards the garden and hid.

"Ethan! Where are you dear? Where have you gone," said the first maid.

The second maid called out for Ethan's caretaker, and they moved dangerously close to where I was hiding. A few minutes passed while they searched the area, then they moved away but still lingered. My patience was thinning.

"Ethan!" shouted the first maid.

Both women continued calling out for their missing people, and I waited patiently nearby.

A few minutes passed then my patience ran thin, I was sick of this, I was sick of these two howlers.

I pulled out my knives and aimed at them, and I threw the first knife at the first maid's jawline. It struck and killed her instantly, and the second maid screamed while the knife pierced through her friend's mouth. I threw the second knife at the second maid's throat, quickly silencing her as well. The scream probably attracted attention from inside, and I returned into hiding immediately. A minute or so later the commodore arrived at the scene, and she froze upon seeing the bodies. She grieved instead of calling for help, and she cradled the bodies and mourned. This was my chance, my chance to end this. I pulled out my dagger and threw it towards her, and the blade pierced into her breast. She cried in pain but the blade only shallowly pierced her, and she removed it without fear of death. I emerged from hiding and drew my sword, then I charged towards her.

I slashed towards her and the commodore desperately dodged, then she unsheathed her sword and I thrusted and slashed towards her. She blocked each attack and waited, then I thrusted and slashed again and she blocked each assault.

"You fool!! Why are you here!? You could've been free but instead you've journeyed here just to die."

I didn't respond, I slashed at her again and she blocked it, then I slashed overhead and she blocked but lowered her guard. I pushed her blade down then kicked her, and she stumbled but then quickly rolled away afterwards.

"This is all I have now! I tried living within the law and I got betrayed, I tried living outside the law and I got defeated; I have nothing to return to anymore... so all I have is you; and that'll have to be enough."

"You could've lived here alongside me! You wouldn't be free but you'd be free from England, but no you had to resist me; and because of that I can't help you anymore."

"I never wanted your help!"

"No but you needed it, and I was the only one who could, all you had to do was trust in me."

"Trust you!? the woman who killed everyone I cherished and then left me to die, your insane! And you're also wrong."

"I left you to die because you were supposed to!! You and Maroo were supposed to go away! But you didn't, and when I learned of your survival I thought that I could save you; piracy was gone so there was no need for me to kill you, I didn't want too, I'd already killed enough."

"No life that you could offer would ever replace the one that you took, or the one that you took from him."

"Maybe not, but what you had was a fading life: trust me I know, but the problem was that Maroo refused to see it."

"So you betrayed and killed him for it!? Yet you still think that you were doing him a favour! You were only doing yourself one."

"I was doing us both one! At least if I killed him Maroo would die on my terms instead of England's; then I could move on and create a new life without him."

"Not if I destroy it first."

I slashed towards the commodore and she fled, and I pursued her towards the manor's entrance. A few minutes later she suddenly stopped in front of me, and her son Ethan was nearby, looking terrified at what was happening.

"Ethan! Run and call for help, tell everyone to come to the manor immediately, go now!"

Ethan ran and I chased after him, then the commodore threw sand in my face and knocked me into the ground. My vision returned and the commodore stood defiantly in my way.

"You won't hurt my son, and you won't leave this place alive; and even if you kill me the others will finish you off."

"Once you're dead I won't care about the others, all that matters is that you suffer and die."

"Revenge won't help you, and you won't live long enough to savour it: but even if you do, you'll still be alone."

"Maybe, but at least I'll have peace, peace within a soul that you viciously tore apart."

The commodore slashed towards me and I blocked and locked with her blade, then I pushed myself away from her.

I ran towards her son and she quickly followed, then while she pursued I ran towards the rock with the musket behind it. I quickly retrieved it while Ethan ran nearby, then I sprinted towards him and prepared my shot.

"No!! Leave him alone, please Casper."

Moments passed while I considered her plea, and I suppose it didn't matter anymore, since my anonymity was about to end. I held fire and sprinted towards him, and upon reaching him I tackled Ethan into the ground. A few locals witnessed what I'd done, and I engaged them with musket in hand. I smashed the handle into the first locals face, then I smashed the barrel into the others, injuring them before they became hostile. They were subdued but it didn't matter, Ethan's message was already delivered, it was too late.

A large number of crewmen ran towards me, and from behind the commodore also approached, and I grabbed Ethan before he could get away.

"Mom! Mom get him off me! Please."

He wriggled and I tightened my grip, then I retreated while the boy struggled in my arms.

"Surrender Casper, you've got nowhere to go and nowhere to hide, let's just end this," said the commodore.

I backed towards the jungle and discarded the musket, then I quickly drew my pistol instead. I pressed it firmly against Ethan's mouth and the boy stopped squirming, then everybody paused.

"If I can't kill you then I guess I'll just settle for him."

"Stand down comrades," ordered the commodore.

Tears quickly formed in her eyes as she spoke.

"Is this your legacy Casper!!? Is this how you want to be remembered!? As a pirate who killed a boy over a vendetta; is this who you are now!? Or are you something more?"

Tears formed inside of me, this wasn't how it was supposed to end; I thought I deserved better, I thought I deserved peace!! I dwindled more and more on these thoughts, and sadly she was right, this was too much, if I did this I was dead...if I did this... I was dead.

My fingers twitched over the trigger, and I cried, and everyone moved. I shoved Ethan towards the commodore, and immediately shot her nearest crewman.

The comrade fell dead instantly beside them, and the commodore and her crew recoiled in horror while I fled into the jungle.

Ethan was mortified as well, and he probably realised that his life had been traded away for theirs. I'd failed to kill Shanata Weiss, but maybe I didn't have to, because maybe someday... England would do it for me.

"KILL HIM! Find him and bring him back, piracy must not return," shouted Shanata.

I assumed I was being pursued afterwards, which meant that I had to leave now, I HAD to, no matter what. Many minutes passed while I ran and walked, and the sounds of the pursuit party quickly followed. I didn't know where they were coming from, and I didn't have any water left to drink from. I readied my last pistol in case I was attacked, and I continued moving as fast as I could.

More minutes passed then I reached my ship, and I was tired and stressed, and the pursuit party quickly gained on me.

I rushed towards the ship and boarded it, and a shot grazed my foot upon boarding. I groaned terribly as the injury stung like a salted wound, and I moved further onto the ship while trying to manage it. Moments later I turned to confront my attackers, and Shanata's two enforcers moved towards me. They were both armed with lone pistols, along with their monstrous axes as well.

"You won't leave here alive, not after what you've just done," said the blonde enforcer.

"Casper won't, but somebody else will."

The two women unsheathed there axes in response.

"Drop the pistol Casper! You'll die by the blade instead of the barrel," ordered the blonde enforcer.

"Drop it now so that we can fight blade to blade," added the redhead enforcer.

I didn't have much choice, I only had one shot between them. I discarded my pistol and drew my sword.

CHAPTER 39

Those We Fight Against

The enforcers fought together and I quickly learned that I was no match for them. Too many close calls piled up while they hacked and slashed at me, and they controlled the deck with ease, moving about my ship as if it were their own. They were too strong for me, and I had to try and get away from them. I ran towards the path that we'd all come from, and I could easily outrun them, so long as I kept moving then I'd lose them. No other crewmen were nearby, but I'm sure more will come looking for me soon enough. I ran for several minutes and made it back to where I was before, neither of the enforcers were behind me, so all I had to do now was decide where to go next.

The pistol shot on my leg continued bothering me, and it had been draining me ever since I received it. I needed to treat it when I could, otherwise I'd be too weak to treat it later.

I moved towards the second path which led further into the jungle, and it was the only option I had until I figured out a more permanent way to escape. While I travelled more of Shanata's crew suddenly appeared, and I hid from them upon sight. Unfortunately they saw me anyway, and I ran again and they relentlessly pursued. A while passed and a tree appeared with a platform above it, and I moved towards it to try and lose my pursuers. I reached it and prepared myself for the climb, and I struggled to move while I tried climbing it. I stopped trying and turned around, and instead of climbing to safety I'd have to fight them off after all.

The first crewman thrusted towards me and I scarcely blocked it, then he thrust again and I smiled at him. I intercepted his blade and swept him of his feet, then I moved in to finish him and his companion intercepted me. The second crewman wielded two axes, and he swung them towards me and I retreated away from his friend. I only had my sword, so I'd have to be patient and wait him out. He swung again and I dodged, then he slashed overhead and I weaved out of the way. He slashed once and missed, then he slashed twice and missed again, then he slashed a third time and an opening revealed itself. I avoided his axe blades and slashed both his legs; he fell to the ground painfully, then struggled to get up. The third crewman slashed towards my neck, then slashed again towards my rib, then slashed a third time towards my chest. I blocked each slash instinctively, then waited while planning for my own.

The third crewman slashed towards my leg and I parried him, then I sliced his chest and pushed him into the ground. He cupped his wound but it was no use, blood drizzled through his hands while he lay on the ground. The first crewman heaved himself to his feet then stumbled, and I stomped on his face to prevent a retry.

With the three crewmen defeated I moved on, and I continued moving until a large rock attracted me. I rested behind it and a few minutes passed while I tended to my foot. I cleaned it with nearby leaves, then tore off some unneeded clothing to bandage it. A few minutes later I rested, and I fell asleep as well.

I suddenly awoke to the sounds of nearby footsteps, and voices muttered as well, and I got up and left. I continued moving and another wooden platform appeared up ahead, but I wasn't sure how I could reach it. I kept my eyes on it and a bent over tree suddenly appeared, providing me with what I'd need to climb towards it. I'd just have to jump afterwards, and if I timed everything right then I'd be ok… and if I didn't then I'd be finished.

I reached the bent over tree and a few moments passed while I tried getting my balance on it, then another few moments passed while I tried calming my nerves as well. When I was secure I ran towards the platform and jumped, and I held on, and pulled myself to safety. I reached the top and stayed low, then I searched for any pursuit parties. A while passed while I kept watch, and there were no signs of activity. I climbed back down and when I was low enough I dropped instead of climbing, my foot hurt slightly as a result, but I hoped it would pass. My wound continued weakening me even though I'd bandaged it, and I would have to keep resting in order to keep that weakness at bay.

I walked back the way that I'd came and the voices returned, and I quickly crouched and hid in the shrubs. I continued moving and a nearby patrol appeared, and three men searched the area around them. I observed them and eyed the shrubbery ahead, if I waited then they'd pass me, then I could reach it and continue. A few minutes passed and I remained still, then they walked on and I crept towards the shrubbery. I hid inside it and their attention suddenly turned towards it.

"Hunters! Return to the commodore, you've been summoned to the Risen," called a man's voice.

The patrol left and dismissed whatever strangeness had occurred inside the shrubbery. After they were gone I emerged from the green, then headed back towards the ship. A while passed while I traversed the path that I'd taken earlier, and I made it back to the ship and a horrific sight awaited me. The redhead enforcer blocked my path, she sat on a stump nearby, waiting. She gazed at her axe then returned her eyes to the scenery around her, her friend wasn't around, but either way I'd have to fight her to leave. I drew the pistol that I'd recovered before fleeing from them, but the only problem was that if I used it then I'd alert everyone. I had to do it, and I emerged from the path and fired at her.

The shot grazed the side of her neck, and my nerves destabilised my aim. Blood streamed from its side, and she appeared weakened, and she tried stemming the flow with her hands. Her allies would've heard the shot, so I didn't have long before they all arrived to come and help her. I had to beat this behemoth quickly, but I wasn't sure if that was remotely possible, considering the time and odds that I was facing. I discarded my pistol and drew my sword, and I charged towards her and she stopped nursing her wound. She engaged me for a second bout, and swung her axe towards my vicinity. I quickly stopped and weaved to avoid it, and her swing appeared to drain her, giving me hope. I slashed towards her ribs and she deflected it, then she kicked me backwards. I stumbled heavily into the ground, and the impact was like getting smacked by a tree trunk.

While I was down she bandaged her neck with some cloth, probably hoping that it would lessen the bleeding and keep her focused on the fight ahead; she finished treating it and seemed less concerned, all though I doubted that it would help her in the long run. I got up and reengaged her, and I thrusted towards her belly. She blocked my thrust and I thrusted again, then she blocked it once more and I feinted another thrust. She flinched and blocked air, then I thrusted towards her thigh and pierced her. The thrust wasn't very powerful, but it was enough to annoy her and her thigh dripped with red. Her face contorted angrily, and I almost regretted my decisions.

"You should've accepted the commodore's offer! She could've given you another life: where as everyone else would've just killed you."

"A life without freedom is not worth pursuing, it's those kind of lives that create people like me."

"People like you always lose."

"True, but people like me are always remembered: where as those we fight against aren't."

The redhead powered through her injuries and swung her axe towards my skull. I avoided it and she swung again, and I barely weaved away. She swung a third time and I blocked it, and I struggled with the impact.

Her axe crashed into my sword and the blade inched closer and closer towards my face. She was stronger than me, and if I didn't act soon then I'd be overpowered. I gritted and pushed myself away from her, then I stomped on her thigh before she could react. She grunted in pain and I desperately grabbed at her neck as well, and I squeezed it to ensure that she had more than one area of pain to worry about.

She recoiled ferociously and quickly ripped my hand away from her neck, then she smacked me in the mouth with the base of her axe. The blow bloodied my nose and two teeth instantly dislodged from my mouth. I desperately shook off the pain, then I spat the two teeth out. I slashed towards her neck and she slowly reacted and weakly blocked, then moments later I slashed again and broke through. I sliced the other side of her neck and she roared and screamed in pain, she stumbled on her feet, then she flopped to the ground helplessly. She reached for me while she bled out, as if she was looking for a reprieve that she would never get. I gazed at her while she reached and bled, and a short while passed then she collapsed into the ground.

I'd survived, but I was badly hurt as a result. Several minutes passed while I recovered, then I went and retrieved my lost teeth. My pains died down a little, and I moved towards the ship and boarded it. I prepared to disembark and a rustling sound occurred, then I turned to see the blonde enforcer nearby.

She leapt towards the ship while I departed, and she landed on it while it cleared the land. Other crewmen arrived as we sailed away, and they saw the enforcer on board and smiled to themselves.

They didn't care that they'd missed me, the enforcer was on board so I was in deep, deep trouble.

"Your tale ends here Casper, you'll never hurt anyone ever again."

"Your friend probably thought the same thing, and yet here I am."

The blonde enforcer roared in response and swung her axe towards me. The blade speared towards my gut and I moved out of the way, and the axe struck the railing instead. She pulled it out instantly and I retreated towards the bowsprit.

She slashed again and the blade zoomed towards my shoulder, I avoided it and the axe pierced the deck instead. A sizeable hole appeared afterwards, and I slashed towards her arm. She avoided it and pulled the weapon out effortlessly. I couldn't continue with this pattern for much longer, as she'd already done considerable damage to the ship as it is. I had to engage before she did more, even if it killed me as a result. She slashed again and I slashed, then we locked blades and I struggled with our lock. She was just as strong if not stronger than her redhead counterpart, and she overpowered and pushed me into the mast. My head banged against it and she swung towards my face, and I avoided it and the blade cut into the mast instead. I turned around and recovered, and a huge gaping mark resided where my head could've been. She pulled her weapon and it remained stuck, and I quickly slashed her thigh and retreated. Instead of weakening her the blonde enforcer grew infuriated, and she ripped the axe out and marched towards me with furious intensity. I'd never seen an angrier woman in my life, and hatred festered within her.

Upon reaching me she slashed horizontally towards me, and I narrowly blocked then she slashed diagonally, and I blocked again and the blow rattled my arms. She swiftly slashed overhead and I blocked, and the blow wore me out and I stumbled backwards. My exhausted defences lowered, and with nothing left the blonde enforcer rammed the base of her axe into my face. I tumbled into the ground upon impact, blood oozing from my teeth and mouth.

She bashed the blunt side of her axe into my stomach, then sadistically skimmed it across my chest. I groaned and whimpered from the pain, and she didn't seem finished yet, just like her and her friend weren't finished with Bellamy after they'd defeated her. She smacked me in the mouth with the base of her axe, bloodying it further while its ooze stained the deck below.

She dragged her axe across my stomach, then stomped my face furiously as I looked at her.

"You were a fool to fight us Casper, did you really think that you could take on the world and win? Well look at you now! You're at its mercy, and there's no one left to help you survive it."

She slashed towards the ships mast, and if she succeeded in cutting it down then I'd be dead. I gritted my teeth and slowly rose to my knees, and images of Fletch and the others burned within me.

'Casper Nait might not survive, but maybe somebody else will,' echoed Fletch.

'Have you woken up lad? Have you seen what kind of hell you've dug yourself into,' echoed Maroo.

'Why are you here Casper?' Echoed Zaria.

'Because of colonial rule.'

Zaria giggled.

'Why are you here?'

I roared in pain and forced myself to my feet, then moments passed while I rose.

The blonde enforcer noticed my rise, and she stopped chopping at the mast instantly. Much of its surface was missing. I needed to get her off my ship, I didn't have to beat her, I just had to get her off, but how? My eyes quickly turned to the ropes, and an idea suddenly formed inside of me. I dropped my sword and immediately rushed towards the ropes, and I quickly climbed and leapt off them before she could respond.

I landed on top of the blonde enforcer and wrestled with her, then a few moments passed while I grabbed her around the neck.

I pulled her towards the ships railing and she struggled against me, she was difficult to hold onto, but I squeezed and squeezed while she squirmed and attempted to escape. She desperately elbowed me, and I tightened my grip while grimacing through the pain.

She pulled herself forward and decreased the pressure, but she was fading quickly, so all I had to do was hold on. I wrapped my legs around her body and squeezed her like a squid, then I hung from her, and several moments passed and she went limp. She flopped onto the deck unconscious, and I released her after. I lifted her towards the railing and dropped her instantly, she was too heavy, and I was too weak to throw her overboard.

I lifted her again and dropped her once more, then I pushed her closer towards it, and heaved and heaved. I cried from the effort while raising her, then I lifted her onto the railing and pushed her into the sea. I threw her axe off after, then sighed in relief and stumbled back onto the deck.

I wasn't finished yet, I needed to plot a new course and leave immediately, and I moved towards my cabin and quickly searched for the map in order to assess my options. I examined it and suddenly grew weak, and all of a sudden my exhaustion overpowered me. I struggled to stay awake, and I struggled to stay standing. A few options were open to me but I had no time to decide on one. I moved towards the helm and steered the wheel west, and I silently prayed that I'd made the right choice. A few minutes passed then I collapsed, and it didn't matter afterwards.

I awoke however long after and a different ship greeted me, it wasn't Shanata's, so I had no idea whose it was. I rose up slowly and immediately cursed and groaned with pain, I lied down again and I was half-naked and covered in bandages. My clothes had been replaced with new ones, and I moved to try and reach them. I fell to the ground instantly, and painfully landed next to my bunk, then I stumbled towards the door and opened it. A Spanish schooner awaited me, but we'd been boarded and Shanata's crew were nearby.

"Where is the pirate!? Bring him to me and I won't sink you, I don't care if you have family on board," said Shanata.

I didn't have much time, I needed to leave now before they found me. I went back inside and dressed myself as quickly as possible, then I reclaimed my sword. I quietly exited and slowly snuck off while both crews were distracted.

CHAPTER 40

Exile

A towing line connected to my ship, and I was afraid that I was too weak to climb across it. I grabbed it and climbed anyway, and just as I feared I struggled to move across it. I stopped and one of Shanata's crew spotted me, and I dropped into the sea immediately. I landed awkwardly upon impact, but it was a short swim that I hoped I could manage. I was very weak and I struggled to swim, and I struggled to move forward as well. A short while passed then I reached the ship, and it took longer than it should've but I pulled myself aboard. I quickly severed the towing line and the sloop slowly drifted away.

"Open fire!" shouted Shanata.

Shanata's crew fired muskets towards me, and I braced for the shots after hearing them. I reached towards the wheel and steered the sloop away, and a shot whooshed past my arm afterwards. The firing stopped and the crew reloaded, and I quickly took control of the helm.

I looked behind me while I sailed away, and Shanata's ship didn't pursue: instead, it immediately fired upon the Spanish schooner. I didn't know if the attack was out of rage or necessity, but the poor vessel stood little chance against her invincible frigate. I guess she still wanted to ensure that my existence was secret, that it would just be her and I until the end; but that wouldn't be the case, and she'd soon learn that. A minute or two passed while her sudden attack on the Spanish continued, and a gap formed between us, and I turned to observe the damage. Massive holes plagued the schooners hull, and splintered wood sunk into the sea, while sickening screams cried from its wreckage.

"MOM! Mom where are you!!? Help!! Please!!"

"DAVID"!! NOOO!!" please no!!"

There was nothing left, nothing left of the ship that had saved my life. I headed towards my cabin to check if everything was still there. The map was still on the table, the supplies were still in order, and the chest of shillings still remained. The Mel's had left it all untouched.

An hour or so passed and I led the Risen comfortably, all though I hoped that its pursuit would end soon.

I needed to plot a course to somewhere more permanent, and sunset arrived, and I had to use it wisely. While there was daylight I inspected my wounds. My mouth hurt the most, and the wound to my chest was also bad.

The gunshot wound to my foot also stung, and I had deep bruising on my stomach and face. My gums ached ever since I'd lost my two teeth, and my mouth was just sore, and blood continued to inhabit it.

The toll was severe, and I'd be feeling it for weeks to come. I returned to my cabin and ate and drank some sustenance, then I returned to the helm, and gazed at the Risen once more.

Another hour or so passed, and all of a sudden the Risen turned away; perhaps it was because of the darkness, or perhaps it was because she wasn't getting any closer; either way the chase was over, and her ship slowly faded from view. Several minutes passed and the Risen faded away like shadows, and when it was gone I sailed towards a small sand island nearby. I stopped and quickly returned to my cabin, then I surveyed the map and assessed my next move.

A realization suddenly came to me, this isn't what I wanted anymore; I had no desire to return to civilization, and piracy was gone so there was nothing left for me anymore. I'd lost my way because of all this violence and hatred, and it was all that was left of me, all that was keeping me alive.

What does a man like that do? One who has become so hollow and so numb on the inside, because of all the choices that he chose to live or die by? It was an interesting question, and it was one that I needed an answer for by nightfall. I drank some more water and moved towards my bunk, then I hoped that sleep would give me the answer that I seek.

I awoke and immediately set sail, and an inhabited island came into view. Despite the rest I still had no idea what I was doing, but sleep had told me one thing; that the life of a pirate was no longer what I wanted. I sailed towards the island and retrieved my spyglass to observe it.

A small populace resided on it, and large grey rocks formed in the centre of it, like a formation or henge. This would suit me fine, and I sailed towards its shores. I dropped anchor upon reaching it, then headed towards the cabin. I unloaded the food and water from within it, and I took whatever rope and cloth that I had left.

I carried them onto the shore, and when the essentials were unloaded I grabbed the playing cards as well. I grabbed a handful of shillings from the chest, then departed the ship with the cards and the shillings.

With everything in hand or on the sand, I moved towards the bow and slowly pushed it towards the shore. I pushed and pushed and the sloop moved a few paces, then I stopped, and I grew too tired or sore to push it any further. Ragged locals looked at me strangely, and I ignored them and began the long haul of moving my cargo towards a more suitable spot. A while passed and a large rock crevice appeared nearby, the more private setting appealed to me, and I carried the cargo there then left to go and look for tinder. Several minutes passed while I gathered up sticks and branches until I had what I needed, then a few more minutes passed, and I got my fire going as well. I warmed myself by it then checked through my supplies, and I wanted to see how much I had left.

I finished and estimated that I had about two weeks left of food and water, and after that I'd have to purchase more. I didn't want to use the treasure for that though, I only wanted to use it for materials or equipment. If I bought them I could hunt again, and the rest would be saved for later. I used the rope and cloth to make a bed for the night, it wasn't comfortable, but it was better than nothing. There was enough cloth for a blanket and a screen to cover the crevice with, but I lacked the skills or the means to create that screen. After finishing the bed I fiddled with the cards, and they reminded me of how far I'd gone in recent times. I didn't know why I'd kept them, especially since they meant so little to me, but maybe Shanata was right; maybe we do need a relic to remind of us of what we're fighting for. I wanted to sleep but my mind wouldn't let me, and I constantly fretted on what tomorrow was going to look like.

I'd been focused on one or two lives for so many days, and because of that I didn't know what a third or fourth could look like. It was like a dream world, except all I could imagine was darkness. I stopped trying to think about it, and instead focused on what I'd need come tomorrow.

A shelter would be nice, but after being a castaway for so long it seemed unnatural for me to start living in one. I'd need hunting tools, and perhaps crafting ones if someone could help me with them.

Since I was a pirate I was essentially a hunter, and this is what I should be, or should become. Hunters earned their own keep, and they kept every ounce of it no matter what; nobody could take that from me, because that was at the very core of what it meant to be free. Whether it was within the law or outside of it, either way, piracy had taught me how to live free; forever.

I awoke the next morning and gathered my handful of shillings to take to the islands markets. I walked towards them and an old decrepit man greeted me.

"Where can I buy hunting supplies?"

"There isn't much here I'm afraid, but I have a fishing spear that I can offer you," said the man.

I tipped him twelve shillings and the man's face instantly lit up.

"Thank you stranger! Are you sure you're happy to pay that much for it?"

"I'm sure, as long as it works that is."

The spear was made of stone and it comprised of wood at its base, basic, but still far better than what Fletch and I had on Twin-Reef Island. After buying the spear I examined the islands populace, and they all looked the same, which concerned me. The men were ragged and poor, and there clothes were dirty or torn. A few women were here as well, and they all had frizzled hair and black soot covering their faces. Everyone was thin and frail, and they all appeared half-starved and unhealthy. The island was like a populace of societies rejects, rejects, and unwanted.

I walked towards another market and lingered nearby, and while I did an English ship suddenly pulled into shore.

The locals immediately flocked towards it, and the ship docked and English soldiers emerged. They swatted and pushed the locals aside, mistreating them like slaves even though they appeared to be regular people. I wished that I could intervene, but that would end badly for me if I did.

They carried shipment crates onto the shore and several papers were smuggled onto them. I approached and the locals blocked my way, then I turned back and dismissed them.

"The cargo is smaller than last time! What's going on officers?" asked a female voice.

"The cargo is not smaller, and you're lucky to be getting any at all after what's happened," grunted an English officer.

"What's happened?"

"Read the parchment."

I turned away and walked towards another market, and with no other hunting gear to acquire I spent whatever was left on restoring my sword. A scrawny man restored it to its optimal best, then I finished and headed back to camp.

Upon returning I washed myself in the shallows nearby, my wounds quickly flared up, but I continued despite the pain flowing through them. The good news was that I was cleaner than I'd been in weeks, and I finished and headed over to camp for some food and water. I attempted a memory game with the deck of cards afterwards, then with some help from the old man from the market, I created my screen from the left over cloth. Later on I walked around the island to pass the time, and I tried working out a schedule for my time here.

A young couple emerged while I walked, and they appeared to be on the verge of making love. They saw me and quickly scurried off, then I continued pondering with my thoughts. There wasn't much to hunt on this island, and it seemed that I'd chosen my exile poorly. There were birds, fish and crabs, but there was nothing to forage, and two of those animals were difficult to catch. There seemed to be no work options here, and with my resources it seemed that I'd condemned myself to death.

I'm not sure how long the wealth will last, and I'm not sure how well the hunting will go, but so far; I'd survived far longer than I could've imagined.

A storm closed in on the island's position, and I headed back while wandering the shores. I returned and an elderly woman lingered nearby, and she saw me approach and looked at me expectantly. Black soot covered her face, and her dark hair was knotted and untidy, just like the rest of her. I ignored her and she heckled me.

"Hungry, so hungry, young man have food?"

I walked past her and entered the camp, then she lunged for my rations. She was hungry, hungry and desperate it seemed.

I allowed her to eat and she calmed down, then she gorged through two days' worth of rations.

"The colonials have been starving us, each month the shipments have been getting smaller. In a few weeks everyone will be like me, hungry and alone," said the elderly woman.

In a few weeks I'd be in a similar situation, maybe I shouldn't have let her eat so much.

"Beware the populace of Salt Shore Henge stranger, few faces here are friendly, and no one ever stays here long."

She left leaving an ominous linger behind her.

Many minutes passed then the storm hit, and an uncomfortable cold wind seeped through my screen. I was protected from the rain, but not the wind it seemed. While the storm raged I feasted on half a day's rations, and when I'd finished I reflected on what I'd learned. From my walks on the island it seemed that my ship was the only one here, so it must be dependent on England. But why was that? Why was my ship the only one here? Even if the woman did warn me about its unfriendliness.

I wasn't so sure if I should stay here or not, perhaps I was too hasty in unloading everything. The storm continued and I pondered on what the colonials were up too, and I wondered what I was supposed to do about them. Moments later I dozed off, then I awoke to the sounds of voices outside my camp.

My screen suddenly cut open and a white bearded man emerged. My eyes turned to my sword, and I froze as more voices revealed themselves. They surrounded me and armed themselves with various makeshift weapons, and I grabbed my sword and immediately fled. More of them spotted me instantly, and I ran from them desperately. Minutes passed and

I ran while trying to find a place to hide, and I couldn't, so my only option was to run to the ship.

I ran until I located it, then I vigorously sprinted towards it. I groaned heavily as I remembered that I'd have to push it back into the shallows, and I was afraid that I didn't have the time.

I reached the sloop and pushed against it, and I pushed and pushed and it remained still, it was no good, and the mob was quickly closing in. I had to confront them, even if they outnumbered me I had to stand against them.

The mob approached and desperation filled their eyes, desperation, and maybe something else. The bearded man carried a parchment in his hand, and a guilty feeling washed over me.

"Casper Nait, sole survivor of the Revenant and wanted fugitive of Kingston, this bounty belongs to you, and we've come to collect it," said the bearded man.

The man was bald as well as bearded, and his brown eyes pierced into mine, all though there was no malice within them, just... loss.

"I didn't come here to be collected, I came to live in exile."

"I'm sure you did, but being a pirate has its price, ask anyone here and they'll tell you the same."

"You're pirates? But that can't be, they were all killed months ago."

"Not all, this crew here are all that remains, the crew of Neagan Bonnet, captain of the Arisen; and the final hope for the pirate world."

"I'm afraid Captain Bonnet is dead, I don't know when but he was killed by maroons."

"Then I guess it's over, once we're gone that'll be it, same as you."

"Not if you tear up that bounty, not if you refuse to submit to England's rules; you know that they can't be trusted, you have to know that right!? You have to."

"Aye we do, but they run the seas now, and they control everyone and everything; and those that opposed them were sent here, so that they could kill us without anyone ever knowing."

"Those that weren't sent here died, or they were captured or exiled by the new commodore in Kingston," added the bearded man.

"They don't control me, not yet, so maybe I could help you? All of you, so that one day we can strive towards a life without control."

"I'd say your naïve, but I'd also say how?"

"We've depended on them our whole lives, all of us, but together we could start again; so that maybe not now, not next week, but one day, we could be free again; and one day, we could be strong again, strong enough to hunt, strong enough to do whatever we wanted!! Just like we used to be. I have a ship, I have wealth, and for now that's all we'd need; because the rest we will take back, day by day, inch by inch, we will live again, as pirates, and as free men."

"But the colonials will find us if we leave! They always do," said the bearded man.

"Not this time, because I know of a place where they will never find us, and it's a place that no civilization will ever expect anyone to survive in; but we will, because we're better than them."

"But what about when they return? And what about your exile?" asked the bearded man.

"When they return... well that's weeks away, and when they return, they'll know that it was I that defeated them; and they'll be unable to stop it, because they will have already lost."

"And what's to stop us from doing this ourselves? Just taking your ship and leaving you to your exile?" asked a scrawny man.

"You're all men who haven't sailed for months, and your also half-starved and not in good health; if you maroon me here to die then you'll end up joining me, and then England wins because of you."

The scrawny man fell silent and disappeared from view, and the other members of the mob started conversing amongst themselves. Moments passed and the muttering quieted, then the bearded man silenced them.

"This all sounds like a mad man's fantasy, but... I suppose it's better than your bounty, Mr Nait," said the bearded man.

I smiled and shook hands with him, and the mob seemed to be in agreement.

"I can't take all of you at once, my ship can't sustain that; but I have enough food and water for two trips, so if you're ready, we can start today."

"One of our folks ate some of your rations recently, are you sure you'll be able to sustain this?" asked the bearded man.

"No, but I'm willing to try, and I'm not saying that it will be easy, but I am saying that it will be better, someday and somehow, we will do better."

I moved towards the ship and pushed it towards the shallows, and the locals helped me and we eased it back into the sea.

We smiled and celebrated after, then we rested while the others lifted and carried various supplies on board. It was estimated that the colonials cargo shipment could sustain the crew or the survivors for twelve days, and during the two time voyage here and back, those that remained would have to survive off that for the duration. This was achievable, as long as we were disciplined. I had no idea how long the journey would take, and it would be arduous no matter where we went, but I believed it would work out, given time. After resting I helped everyone pack up there remaining supplies, then I helped carry any other personal belongings that they may have had with them. Once everything was on board Bonnets crew had the difficult choice of selecting which of them would travel first, and I took no part in the process.

I sought out the bearded man while the rest of them conversed.

"I never knew Bonnet, and frankly I don't think I ever knew Maroo either, I went against what he wanted, and I went against what the crew wanted as well; what does that make me?"

"It makes you Casper Nait, the pirate outlaw," said the bearded man.

"And Bonnet?"

"Bonnet was Maroo's first mate and original crewman, in fact the story of their ships tells the story of them," said the bearded man.

"What do you mean?"

"The Revenant is Alva Maroo, from Alva Maroo arose Neagan Bonnet, from Neagan Bonnet rose Shanata Weiss; and to tie them all together... was Governor Lee Manson, the man who created them all," said the bearded man.

"I never thought of it like that, so the ships were… human?"

"Yes, so all that remains now is you, who is Casper Nait?" asked the bearded man.

"I don't know."

"You won't have to, England will decide that for you," joked the bearded man.

After the crew was selected we readied ourselves to depart, and we waved goodbye to those that remained on shore.

Five days passed and we arrived at our destination, and the crew was shaken, and admittedly so was I. Massive white rock protrusions emerged from the sea below, as if to ward off any intruders that came to close to them. Another rock grazed above the sea, a tooth shaped rock, a hooked tooth, or perhaps even a beak. On the wall outside the cove were marked rocks that looked like scales, and on its other side there was a shell like construct attached to it.

"You brought us to Riptide Cove!? Are you mad Casper?" asked a nearby crewman.

"This location was on Alva Maroo's maps, and it's on the map that belonged to the original owner of this ship, if it's good enough for him then it's good enough for us."

"The place is cursed, its tide is unholy, and its rips are even unholier; and the place itself looks like a creature," said another crewman.

"Then it will keep others away from us, but we can't go back to Salt Shore Henge, and I'm not sure if we have an alternative."

"Getting in there won't be easy, even for a sloop there's plenty to be wary of," said an elderly man.

"I'll worry about that, but there's others to go back for so we have to dock here."

I steered the sloop towards the cove, and upon entering it the crews concerns revealed themselves. Yellowish rocks protruded from the water within, and a spike shaped stone dug deep into the depths below. A triangular shaped basin awaited at the cove's end, and it looked like an opened mouth.

"You want us to dock at that? What if it swallows us?" asked a male crewman.

"Then I'll feel sorry for you after."

"I don't like this place, it gives me the willies," grumbled another crewman.

"It's not forever, try and remember that."

I steered the ship towards the basin, and the crew reluctantly departed.

"I'll return alone, and I'll purchase supplies for the journey back: I'll bribe someone if I have to."

"Be careful Casper, your bounty is quite large and plenty of men will want a piece of you," warned an elderly woman.

"I know, that's why it's best that I go alone."

A day passed and I docked near Port Royal on the way back. Port Royal was close to Kingston but it still had its fair share of scoundrels here; and all I had to do was find one, and then bribe them into staying quiet.

Red and orange, every roof in this town was red and orange, white and grey buildings complemented them, but EVERY roof was red and orange; why? I couldn't tell you why.

My bounty was posted nearby, and they'd given me a new name to go along with my features. Mr Bloodrush Nait, AKA Casper, tall, facially burnt, bloodied mouth, with white skin and brown hair and eyes; if seen please let the English know right away. A weak man would bow to that opportunity, but a weak man would also give in to personal greed; that was the duality of England, opportunity, and the means of how you strived towards it.

A Spanish boy approached me after, and he had short brown hair and tattered clothes all around. His brown eyes seemed hopeful or curious, and he looked at the bounty then gazed back at me.

"You're him?" He asked.

"Maybe, what do you want?"

"You're looking for anonymity, that's why you have a bag of coins in your pocket."

"You're very observant, does Port Royal still have these services?"

"It does, but it's pricey, and the consequences may affect another."

"Who?"

"Don't know, but in this new world anything can happen."

I sighed, and pondered on where to go from here.

"Can you buy me supplies? Then ask around for a woman named Kaleen."

"You know her? You know the infamous easterner?"

"I do, we've had brief encounters."

"I'll see what I can do, but I suggest you stay out of sight."

A while later the Spaniard brought two weeks' worth of rations to the docks, and two helpers were alongside him. I spied on him from off shore, using my spyglass to observe the surrounding bustle. I sailed back then docked, and he and his friends immediately loaded the goods onto the deck. After they were done, I handed him the bag of shillings.

"These soldiers could come after you at any moment, are you sure you don't want the anonymity?"

"I don't want to hurt anyone that I don't have to, I've already done that."

"Suit yourself."

"What about Kaleen? Any news on her?"

"She's in the wind but she's alive, and the word is that she's just as troublesome for England as you."

"Well she's got plenty to hate them for."

I departed the docks and the boy and his friends quickly left, and a colonial patrol swept the area after.

Four days passed and I returned to Salt Shore Henge, and the remaining crewmen were alive. An English vessel headed towards the island, and I quickly docked and rushed to get everyone on board. Everyone raced on deck with supplies in hand, and when everyone was accounted for, I quickly departed and pulled out my spyglass. I sailed further off shore and observed the vessel from afar, and my amusement kicked in. Governor Manson appeared on deck, and Shanata Weiss was alongside him. Weiss was distraught and distressed, while the governor appeared furious, furious that the island was abandoned.

I may not have killed them but I'd survived them, and while they looked on at what I'd done to them, they would soon learn that truth for themselves.